Library of
Davidson College

PAGODA, SKULL, & SAMURAI

PAGODA
*
SKULL &
*
SAMURAI

五重塔　対髑髏　ひげ男

3 Stories by Rohan Koda

translated by
CHIEKO IRIE MULHERN

CHARLES E. TUTTLE COMPANY
Rutland, Vermont & Tokyo, Japan

REPRESENTATIVES

For Continental Europe:
BOXERBOOKS, INC., *Zurich*

For the British Isles:
PRENTICE-HALL INTERNATIONAL, INC., *London*

For Australasia:
BOOK WISE (AUSTRALIA) PTY. LTD.
1 Jeanes Street, Beverly, 5009, South Australia

The stories in this book were originally published in 1982 in typescript form by the Cornell China-Japan Program as one of its East Asia Papers.

Published by the Charles E. Tuttle Company, Inc.
of Rutland, Vermont & Tokyo, Japan
with editorial offices at
Suido 1-chome, 2-6, Bunkyo-ku, Tokyo

Copyright in Japan, 1985
by Charles E. Tuttle Co., Inc.

All rights reserved

Library of Congress Catalog Card No. 84-052723
International Standard Book No. 0-8048 1499-6

First printing, 1985

Printed in Japan

TABLE OF CONTENTS

page 7   Introduction

    21   The Five-Storied Pagoda *(Gojū no Tō)*
          Selected Allusions   *109*

  111   Encounter with a Skull *(Tai Dokuro)*
          Selected Allusions   *146*

  149   The Bearded Samurai *(Higeotoko)*
          Selected Allusions   *257*

  261   Afterword

  275   Historical Notes on "The Bearded Samurai" (with map)

Note: Throughout the text, Japanese name order (surname followed by given name) has been followed. Macrons, signifying long vowels, have been retained except in very well-known place names. For Chinese names, the Wade-Giles system of romanization has been used.

INTRODUCTION

Kōda Rohan was born Kōda Shigeyuki in Edo (present-day Tokyo) in 1867, the last year of the feudal Edo period. Both his grandfather and father served the Tokugawa shogunate as direct samurai retainers in a hereditary position in charge of protocol, ceremonies, and shogunal audience appointment. Their official stipend of sixteen *koku* (roughly forty bushels) of rice a year was quite modest by any standard, but they also had an annual cash income of three hundred *ryō* from other sources. (In the late Edo period, a household servant's yearly pay was two to four *ryō;* one *ryō* bought one *koku* of rice, equivalent to a full adult ration for a year.) Thus, the Kōda family was relatively well-off until a cataclysmic event shook the entire nation.

After a complex and protracted series of political assassinations and insurrections subtly involving the advent of Western intervention, the shogun surrendered political power and the shogunate estates, worth seven million *koku*, in favor of Emperor Meiji in 1868. The abdicated shogun's heir soon moved to the original Tokugawa fief, which amounted to seven hundred thousand *koku* and was comprised of Enshū, Mikawa, and Suruga provinces (parts of present-day Shizuoka and Aichi prefectures). This marked the end of the feudal Tokugawa regime and the beginning of the modern monarchy in Japan. Rohan's father decided to remain in Tokyo, thereby forfeiting his hereditary employment and stipend, and eventually secured a minor post in the Ministry of Finance of the new national government.

Rohan had three brothers and two sisters, all of whom distinguished themselves. The eldest brother climbed to the presidency of a large cotton-spinning company. The second, a naval lieutenant, attained national fame as the heroic explorer of Japan's northern territorial waters and as organizer of the settlements on the Kurile Islands (taken over by the Soviet Union in 1945). Rohan's younger brother published scholarly works, making invaluable contributions as professor of international commerce. Both his sisters were nationally prominent: a brilliant concert pianist and a violinist, and tutors to the Crown Princess and the Empress. One sister shared with Rohan the honor of being among the inaugural members of the Imperial Academy of Arts established in 1937. This impressive family tradition has continued into the next generation: Rohan's nephew Andō Hiroshi has been twice nominated for the prestigious Akutagawa Literary Prize under the pen name Takagi Taku; and Rohan's only surviving daughter, Kōda Aya (b. 1903), is a highly acclaimed novelist.

Rohan was raised under austere discipline and received the standard education for sons of the samurai class. He was taught the usual reading, writing, and the recitation of Chinese classics at a private school before he entered and completed compulsory elementary school. Thereafter, his education was erratic in terms of formal schooling, but nonetheless effective in retrospect. Largely due to financial hardship following his father's loss of employment during governmental reorganization, Rohan was forced to withdraw from Tokyo First Middle School after one year in 1880, and from Tokyo English School in 1882, also within a year after his entrance. He eventually graduated from the government-subsidized telegraphers' school. Notwithstanding his lack of higher education, Rohan would become widely acknowledged as a leading scholar and intellectual writer from the early stages of his career, while contemporary novelists boasting Imperial University degrees were often accused of decadent trivialism.

The most significant factors formative to his character and scholarly expertise were the Tokyo Library (the former Shogunate Academy library, now the National Diet Library) and a private academy of Chinese learning called Geigijuku, both of which occupied his time from 1880 to 1883. Rohan ravenously read books of all kinds at the library; throughout his life he would maintain this habit of avid reading, which resulted in encyclopedic knowledge in intellectual as well as practical fields. The master of Geigijuku, Kikuchi Shōken (1806–86), was a Confucian scholar of considerable repute who provided Rohan with thorough training in the Neo-Confucianism of the Ch'eng-Chu school and the practical philosophy of Wang Yang-ming (1472–1528) based on the doctrine of the Unity of Knowledge and Action. Rohan soon developed sufficient insight and analytical ability to explore on his own Taoist mysticism, older commentaries on Confucian canons, and Buddhist sutras. For mental concentration, physical exercise, and relaxation, Rohan continued to practice swordsmanship in his adult years, often using a real blade as well as a wooden or bamboo sword.

Rohan began working as a telegrapher in 1884; this was

to be his sole experience of practical employment. When he was stationed in an office in remote Hokkaidō, the Japanese literary world was bustling with new talents possessed by a vision of literary renaissance. In 1885, Tsubouchi Shōyō (1859–1935) published the *Essence of the Novel,* in which he renounced the moralistic didactic approaches inherited from late-Tokugawa literature and advocated the adoption of modern realistic techniques from the West. In the same year, the eighteen-year-old student Ozaki Kōyō (1867–1903) organized what was probably the first Japanese literary coterie, Ken'yūsha, which dominated the Meiji literary scene for over a decade.

As an equally ambitious eighteen year old, Rohan was increasingly frustrated in his mundane job. In August 1887 he abandoned his post and headed for Tokyo. His pen name, Rohan, "companion of the dew," derives from his haiku describing this journey, during which he was forced to walk through the night to catch his train:

Sato tōshi	Far from towns,
Iza tsuyu to nemu	I'll share with the dew
Kusamakura	A pillow of grass.

Back in Tokyo, he found that his family had coverted from their hereditary faith of Nichiren Buddhism to Christianity. Rohan did not consent to be baptized, but attended church lectures and Bible-reading classes. (Not surprisingly for a future writer of mystic stories, he seems to have taken particular interest in the Apocalypse.) At the same time, he participated in group studies of Buddhism viewed as metaphysics and philosophy. Then a friend from his Tokyo Library days introduced him to the works of Ihara Saikaku (1642–93) and other writers of the Genroku period

(1688–1704). The newly rediscovered realistic and objective techniques of the Genroku literature soon inspired Rohan to launch into a literary career which was to span six decades and make him one of the pillars of Meiji literature.

Rohan's career is often discussed in five phases. The first may be called the Idealistic Phase (1889–93), during which he produced the bulk of his best fiction, brilliantly embodying his idealistic themes in ideal heroes. "Taidokuro" (Encounter with a skull, 1890) and "Gojū no Tō" (The five-storied pagoda, 1891) are the twin summits of this period and of Rohan's career as a whole. The second, Mature Phase (1893–96), is represented by his unfinished but most expansive novel, *Fūryū Mijinzō* (Storehouse of infinitesimal life, 1893–95), which revolves around two central characters and unfolds by means of a complex narrative technique called the chain-link structure. Here Rohan viewed life as it is, rather than as it ought to be (as he did in the works of the Idealistic Phase). Through keen observation and realistic description, he endeavored to delineate the existence of Absolute Truth as manifested in human life. He was no longer concerned with individual characters but rather with the grand dynamics of fate and the correlation between an individual's personality and fate. But it was also during this period that he began to turn away from fiction as his faith in its intrinsic value waned.

During the Stagnant Phase (1896–1903), Rohan was uncomfortable in his attempt to adopt realistic techniques and the *gembun itchi* style (the unity of written and spoken languages) in writing a series of minor modern stories. Yet he found success, ironically, in reverting to his masterful *gazoku setchū* style (a mixture of poetic diction and vernacular). One example is "Higeotoko" (The bearded samurai/The bearded man, 1896), a historical tale set more than three hundred years in the past. The fourth, Syncretic Phase (1903–19), yielded his last long novel, *Sora Utsu Nami* (Waves dashing against the sky, 1903–5). In this contemporary narrative, Rohan synthesized realism and idealism, the *gazoku setchū* and *gembun itchi* styles, poetic imagination and scholarly learning, Oriental tradition and Western philosophy, and more fundamentally, fiction and academic treatise. The Russo-Japanese War (1904–5) and influenza prematurely terminated this work. Thereafter, Rohan began to publish more and more scholarly treatises on Chinese and Japanese classics. These recondite theses eventually earned him an appointment as lecturer of Japanese literature at the prestigious Kyoto Imperial University in 1908 (from which he resigned after one semester to devote his time to writing) and the Doctor of Literature degree in 1911.

Rohan made his literary comeback with the celebrated story "Ummei" (Destiny, 1911), based on the power struggle between the Chien-wen Emperor (r. 1399–1402) and the Yung-lo Emperor (r. 1403–23) of China's Ming dynasty. During this Last Phase (1911–47), Rohan produced a series of serenely reflective short stories beloved by his fellow writers and scholars. Shortly after completing a voluminous commentary on *Rokubushū* (Six collections of linked verse) by the haiku master Matsuo Bashō (1644–94), Rohan died from pneumonia at age eighty in July 1947.

Rohan's standing in Japan's literary history is illustrated by the term "Kō-Ro jidai," the age of Kōyō and Rohan, applied to the period between Rohan's debut in 1889 and 1903, the year of Kōyō's death and Rohan's last novel. Two of the first modern Japanese writers to make a living by the pen, Ozaki Kōyō and Rohan were responsible for the bloom of neoclassical literature. By revitalizing indigenous literary traditions, they fully answered in their own way Tsubouchi Shōyō's urgent call for a new literature of intrinsic value and realistic techniques. At the time, theirs was a more popular alternative to the tired old Edo fiction than the epoch-making innovation by Futabatei Shimei (1864–1909). A specialist in Russian language and literature, Shimei signaled the birth of modern Japanese novel with *Ukigumo* (Drifting clouds) in 1887, but his primary model and inspiration, Russian realism, was not immediately accessible to the majority of aspiring Japanese writers. It is no small wonder that the neoclassical Kō-Ro school reigned supreme in the Japanese literary world for nearly two decades, until supplanted by *shizenshugi*, a Japanese brand of naturalism.

Kōyō's superior genre novels in Genroku style somehow jaded with age and faded out of fashion as the mainstream of Japanese literature has become more and more oriented toward the West. In contrast, Rohan's stories, charged with poetic passion, philosophical insight, and mystic vision, still remain high on the list of favorite works among today's intellectual readers. The influential academic journal *Kokubungaku Kaishaku to Kanshō* (Interpretation and appreciation of Japanese literature) reported in its January 1969 issue the result of a poll ranking the most admired Meiji writers. Rohan placed third after Natsume Sōseki (1867–1916) and Mori Ōgai (1862–1922), considerably ahead of Shimazaki Tōson (1872–1943), Futabatei Shimei, and Kōyō.

Japanese literary history usually classifies Rohan as an idealist writer (the only other Japanese writer so labeled is Mori Ōgai) because his idealistic early fiction is the best known and the most significant of his diverse works in terms of their impact on Japanese mind and literature. All three stories in this book belong to the idealistic type by theme, impulse, and genesis. Even "The Bearded Samurai," completed in 1896, was originally begun in 1890, during his first phase. Rohan's idealism is a synthesis of diverse ideas: philosophical (a Platonic belief in the Absolute); metaphysical (the universal salvation of Mahayana Buddhism and the Taoist unity with Nature); humanistic (Buddhist-Christian love and compassion); moral (Confucian ethics/Taoist detachment/Shinto cleanliness/the samurai code of honor); social (a sense of mission to lead progress in positive and lofty directions); and aesthetic (a faith in the power of art to humanize and enlighten mankind).

Rohan was one of the few writers who stood aloof from the subsequent tide of naturalism, which swept through the literary scene, quickly degenerated into trivial, sentimental slices of life and masochistic confessions, and soon exhausted itself. Today, long after the demise of the once overwhelming mainstream, Ōgai and Rohan remain a prominent pair of luminaries whose humanistic, positive, and idealistic visions cast bright beams of hope across the morbid, pessimistic clouds that all but smother the modern Japanese literary landscape.

Beneath his accomplished classical style and historical setting, Rohan is surprisingly modern and universal in his theme and perspective. Modern Western readers are in a better position to appreciate the aggressive individualism and glorification of creative minds that Rohan advocates in "The Five-Storied Pagoda." Ironically, it is the modern Japanese reader who must first struggle through Rohan's rich traditional diction and syntax. Japanese readers, moreover, must extricate themselves from their preconceptions about particular historical settings before they can fully enjoy Rohan's fertile imagination and poignant insight. Critic Masamune Hakuchō, Rohan's contemporary, marveled after reading Arthur Waley's translation (1925–33) of *The Tale of Genji:* "For the first time I feel I could understand this eleventh-century novel." Rohan may well prove another case in which an English translation is more accessible than the original, though, of course, no translator can ever hope to approximate, let alone recreate, Rohan's resonant, surging poetic prose, which has its own force and rhythm so inimitably Japanese.

"The Five-Storied Pagoda" was originally written as a serialized piece of fiction in the intellectual newspaper *Kokkai* (Diet, or Parliament), beginning in November 1891 and ending in March of the following year. As a consequence, chapter divisions in this story, and in the other two as well, do not necessarily coincide with the breaks in plot progression or narrative pauses. Any attempt to analyze its structure or its cadence in dramatic intensity must take into consideration the peculiar conventions of the newspaper serial novel, a popular but rather complex genre in Japan, where practically all newspapers (including sports and racing dailies) carry fiction serials by prominent or popular novelists.

As a rule, Rohan gives his major characters meaningful names that indicate their personality traits or symbolic functions. In "The Five-Storied Pagoda," the characters are commoners without family names: Jūbei (lit., "tenth man" or "heavy man"); Genta ("lumber" in carpenters' jargon); Seikichi (pure and lucky); Eiji (sharp second man); Rōen (radiant sphere); Okichi (good luck); and Onami (wave).

The protagonist, Jūbei, is often lauded as a champion of modern individualism for refusing all compromises, or is mistaken for a ruthless social climber. But the crucial keys to his character are the nature of a pagoda and the religious implications of pagoda construction. In Buddhist scriptures, especially the Lotus Sutra (virtually the sole devotional object in the Nichiren sect), the pagoda, or *stupa*, is identified with a variety of religious concepts: Buddha's body; testimony to the truth of the Lotus teachings; the universe itself, in which the ancient Buddha (the symbolic moon) and the present Buddha (the sun) dwell side by side; and the Western Pure Land (whence the ancient Buddha returns to save mankind and whither the present Buddha will lead it). The construction of a pagoda is deemed equal to the preaching of the Lotus gospel in its ultimate religious merit.

"Encounter with a Skull" appeared in the monthly journal *Nihon no Bunka* (Literary flower of Japan) in January 1890. Initially entitled *Engaien* (Karma outside of karma), it deals with a fortuitous encounter of two souls not necessarily ordained by karma, the cumulative effect of one's own actions through numerous reincarnations, according to the Buddhist theory of transmigration of souls. This allegorical story illustrates multiple processes of enlightenment. The humble traveler who offers prayers on behalf of the spirit of the skull at the end is no longer the brash young man who set out on an impulsive journey at the beginning. The beautiful lady of the mountain tells him of her own tortuous steps in attaining perfect enlightenment. In turn, the young man is presumably going to enlighten people by retelling the agonizing story of her life. Similarly, the readers of Rohan's "Encounter with a Skull" are supposed to be enlightened vicariously through the experience of this young man. The means to enlightenment in this particular tale are suffering, compassion, and transcendence of all distinctions to practice love of all things.

"The Bearded Samurai" is a historical tale set in the mid-sixteenth century, the last phase of a strife-torn period that has provided fertile ground for popular samurai yarns. Its initial conception dates back to 1890, when Rohan wrote five installments for the *Yomiuri* newspaper. Six years later, he rewrote them to completion with a totally revised plot. (The "glorious victories" mentioned at the beginning of the story refer to the Sino-Japanese War, 1895–96). The setting is the battle of Nagashino, fought in 1575 between the Takeda army and the combined Oda-Tokugawa forces. The central characters are creations of Rohan's imagination: the bearded hero Kasai Dairoku(rō) (great sixth son) Takahide (lofty and eminent); his aged uncle Takatoshi (lofty and sharp); the boy Kotarō (young first son) Muneharu (heir-spring); and his beautiful sister Yanagi (willow) Tamae (jeweled spray). Most of the other people who populate this story are historical figures, some of them with legendary fame for having shaped Japan's history. Rohan intends no suspense, since foreknowledge of the ultimate fate of each character enhances a sense of tragedy and of the inevitability of fate.

Unlikely as it may seem for a war tale, "The Bearded Samurai" delineates a human side of the warrior and a constructive view of the samurai ethos, both of which had been deliberately and officially stifled ever since the early seventeenth century. A distant and unwitting precursor of the historical novel that has proliferated in Japan for the past few decades, Rohan demonstrates one ideal approach to this genre. He unfolds a stirring fictional narrative, faithfully keeping to the historical facts and ingeniously using known idiosyncrasies of famous personalities; at the same time he manages to deal squarely with universal fundamental issues, such as life, death, love, honor, loyalty, ambition, aspiration, and compassion. Despite the recent staggering output of this genre in Japan, very few samurai stories have been rendered into English. This translation of "The Bearded Samurai," furthermore, makes available to readers the popular portraits of at least two of Japan's most important heroes—Oda Nobunaga (1534–82) and Tokugawa Ieyasu (1542–1616).

In "The Bearded Samurai," Rohan meticulously supplies full names of all historical personages, even the messengers and executed agents. In the translation, nonessential details in regard to personal and place names have been trimmed down to ensure a smooth flow of the narrative; some minor place names are rendered as literal translations, where possible, in an attempt to reflect the local color. Those in need of complete information should refer to the original text and historical sources. Wherever applicable, names of characters are given family name first; but well-known figures are referred to by their personal names, according to common usage.

Historical, literary, and religious allusions are found following each of the stories. An Afterword containing further explanatory material on religious and other aspects of the stories is included at the end of the book, as are additional Historical Notes on "The Bearded Samurai."

The translations of "The Five-Storied Pagoda" and "Encounter with a Skull" were originally part of my doctoral dissertation, "Kōda Rohan: A Study of Idealism" (Columbia University, 1973), completed under the guidance of Professor Donald Keene, to whom I am profoundly and

forever grateful. More extensive information on Kōda
Rohan, such as a biography, discussions of his central
themes, and a literary analysis of his major works including
the three stories contained herein, can be found in my book
Koda Rohan (Boston: G. K. Hall & Co., 1977).

—CHIEKO IRIE MULHERN

Champaign-Urbana, Illinois

THE FIVE-STORIED PAGODA

⟨1⟩

FACING A STURDY rectangular brazier of elegantly grained zelkova wood edged with red oak sat a woman about thirty years of age who looked rather lonesome in the absence of anyone to keep her company. Her handsome, almost staunch eyebrows were shaved off, an indication that she was married, leaving an appealing suggestion of bluish green, like the brilliant color of mountains after rain. Her nose was straight, and her sharply etched eyes tilted upwards. She was plainly made up, her freshly washed hair rolled up into a severe chignon held tightly in place by a large hairpin, a strip of paper its only trimming. But a lock or two of lustrous black hair falling loose around her temples in an almost provoking way gave such charm to her rather dark yet pleasing face that even a man who usually preferred younger women could scarcely have refrained from expressing his admiration.

No doubt each infatuated man had his own opinion on how he would dress her if she were his woman, and no doubt each gossiped behind her back, but she by no means invited such speculations. She was dressed as though she gave no thought to her appearance, but rather as if she took pride in her respectability. Her choice of pattern was not without taste, but her finery consisted of nothing better than a quilted kimono of double-strand fabric with a satin collar, quite devoid of any touch of brightness. The quilted coat of wide-striped silk draped over her shoulders might have been something of value years ago, but even that appeared to have gone through the wash many times.

Except for the distant sounds of the maid doing the dishes in the kitchen, the house was still. The woman bit off and spat out the tip of a toothpick with which her tongue had been idly toying. She raked the ashes in the brazier and neatly rearranged the hot charcoal in it. Taking out a small cloth from a basket, she polished the trivet, already as shiny as silver, wiped off the ash-pan, and even cleaned the lid of the copper water-pot. After carefully placing a large Nambu iron kettle over the fire, she pulled toward herself, using the tortoise-shell pipe in her right hand, a pretty inlaid-wood tobacco box, apparently a souvenir from someone who had stopped off at Hakone on a pilgrimage to Afuri Shrine. She puffed leisurely on the pipe and let the smoke out slowly, so that it seemed to be rising from an incense stick. Abruptly, she heaved an involuntary sigh.

"In the end, my husband will probably get the job," she was thinking, "but how annoying of that Nossori to set himself up against him! Forgetting his own lowly station as well as the gratitude he owes us for having employed him last year, he fawns on the Abbot unabashedly in his attempt to get his hands on this job. From what Seikichi tells me, even if the Abbot should be inclined to play favorites, the parishioners and donors are not likely to let such an important job go to an unknown. There is little doubt of our ultimate success, though—Nossori is so obviously doomed to fail. The likes of him could never handle a project of this magnitude, let alone find a crew willing to take orders from him. Nevertheless, I do wish my husband would come home soon, smiling and telling me that he has received the contract after all. He seems to have found an unusual challenge in this work. He was saying with so much enthusiasm, 'I'm dying to take on this precious project. Never mind material gains. I want to hear people say, "Genta of Kawagoe built the five-storied pagoda of Kannō Temple. Splendid! How well done!" ' If someone else should snatch this job from him now, he'd surely lose his temper and fly into a fine rage. He'd have more than enough reason for such an outburst; I couldn't possibly find any way to mollify him. Well, I hope he returns soon —in good spirits."

Out of wifely concern, she sat silently worrying about the man whom she had sent out this morning after helping him into a coat she had made with her own hands. Suddenly the latticed front door rattled open, and a young man entered.

"Ma'am, where's the Boss? . . . Oh, gone to the temple? Well, it can't be helped, then. I hate to trouble you, but I've got to ask a favor, Ma'am. You see . . . I didn't mean to get drunk last night but . . . you know how it is. . . ."

"What do you mean by 'It can't be helped'? You'd better settle down a bit, you know." Smiling with a mock frown, she got to her feet and handed him some money.

He returned after lengthy negotiations with someone out in the street. Pressing his fist against his forehead, he made an awkward bow. "I'm sorry for imposing upon you like this. Much obliged."

⟨2⟩

"You can share the brazier with me. Come right up."
Tactfully amiable even to a subordinate, the woman

laboriously picked up the heavy iron kettle and made a cup of cherry tea. Her silent hospitality was more winning than a mouthful of piddling lecture. Even after his shameless request, she seemed to spare none of her usual affability. All the more uneasy and embarrassed, though, as if his soul were itching deep inside, Seikichi could hardly stretch his nervous hand to accept the teacup. After more apologetic bows, he was about to moisten his parched tongue, when the woman began to speak:

"To come home at this time of morning, you must have made quite a conquest in certain quarters last night. Well, it's all right for you to have a good time, Seikichi, but it would hardly be manly of you to miss work and worry your mother. The other day when the work at the main residence of the Kōshūya of Nakachō was finished, you were assigned to the tearoom job in their Negishi Villa, weren't you? Your boss loves carousing just as much as you and treats you boys to frequent sprees, but he absolutely hates the work to be neglected. If he could see your face right now, the veins on his forehead would bulge out as they always do when he's upset. It's already a little late, but rush over to Negishi and plead some excuse—your mother's suddenly taken ill or some such thing. I know the foreman Goza to be an understanding man. Since you haven't wasted a whole day loafing, he'll surely cover up for you even if he sees through your excuse.

"By the way, you haven't had breakfast yet, have you? . . . San, set the table for Seikichi. . . . We have nothing nearly as fancy as steamed beancurd and clams, but you don't mind fresh pickles and sweet beans, do you? Have some rice and run along to work. If you get sleepy on the job, just remember what kept you awake last night. That ought to help you make it through the day. No need to worry about your lunch; I'll see that Matsu delivers it later."

Listening to her advice, far from cutting yet quite effective, the naïve Seikichi broke out in a cold sweat, remorseful of his transgression. "Well, then, Ma'am. I'll accept your kind advice and get to work right away."

Wiping his forehead with a towel, he went to the kitchen, quickly downed four or five bowls of rice with tea, and reappeared promptly. Inclining his head with a brisk "So long," he replaced his pipe in the tobacco case hanging from his sash. A spry Edoite, he was practically sliding into his sandals on his way out the door when the woman called out after him in a voice as fiery as the sparks from flint stones:

"Have you seen that slowpoke Nossori lately?"

"Yes, I did, I did," replied Seikichi, whirling around. "And just yesterday at that. I caught him walking as slow as you please along Goten Slope, drooping his limp head like a dead chicken. He's been getting too ambitious for a dimwit lately, setting himself up against the Boss like that. There's nothing for you to worry about, mind you, but knowing he was making some trouble for you and the Boss, I found it hard to bear his miserable face. So I told him off. 'Hey, you! Dimwit!' I said. But being what he is, he didn't even notice me. 'Hey, Nossori! Nossori!' I yelled right into his ear. That finally got to him. He stared at me with those owl-eyes of his and mumbled in a sleepy voice, 'Oh, it's you, Master Seikichi.' I said, 'Hey, you've become a big man lately, haven't you? Did you climb the dyer's drying roof or some such high place in your sleep to pick up your high-and-mighty attitude? You want to build something awfully tall, huh? I hear you've been busy playing up to the Abbot of Kannō Temple. Are you in your right mind, or are you sleepwalking?' I said this right to his face, but you know, Ma'am, a dimwit is honest, if nothing else. What do you suppose he said? 'I am trying terribly hard to play up to the Abbot, but with Master

Genta for a rival, I'm having a hard time of it. How I wish the Master would waive his claim this once and let me have a try at the job.' Such wishful thinking! It makes me laugh just to remember that face of his, so anxious and dead serious! It was downright comical. In fact, it almost made me forget how mad I was, so I just said, 'What the heck!' and left him."

"Is that all?"

"That's it, Ma'am."

"Well, then. It's getting late; time you got going."

"So long."

Seikichi went off to work, leaving the woman deep in thought. Outside the house, children were spinning their tops in a battle game, shouting belligerently.

"One killed."

"Two down."

"Serves you right."

"Got you back!"

Come to think of it, that is the way the world is: we are all rivals one to another.

⟨3⟩

"Those who are wealthy and prosperous have no worries even in the eleventh month, the time for changing into winter clothes. Unaware of the apprehension of the poor facing the cold season, they dress in their choice silk and make extravagant demands: 'Let's celebrate the hearth opening with a house-warming tea ceremony. By all means, complete the tearoom and repair the eaves of the waiting booth in time. Without a cup of properly prepared tea, we can hardly appreciate the sudden night shower pattering on the window.' They seem to consider winter a time to be enjoyed—the trying winter, when the frigid winds blow violently, and even the peals of temple bells seem to freeze. But a lowly workman must sharpen the blade of his plane and smooth the floor boards of their tearooms with his numb hands. He must work outside in the wind to nail down the shingles of their eaves, sometimes coming down with the grippe as a result. What evil karma from his former lives condemns him to a life of such torment and anguish, while others are allowed to enjoy the same season?

"Even among the workmen, my husband is exceptionally untutored in the ways of the world. He's such a skilled craftsman that he received commendation from Master Genta on the job that the master was kind enough to provide for us last year. But, he's much too large-hearted; more often than not, he fails to get a job, losing good orders to others. How wretched is our lot, forever condemned to such a dreary life! As a woman I'm ashamed to have him be seen with a pair of pants barely patched around the knees. But this dearth is caused by poverty quite beyond our control. Take this striped quilt I'm sewing. It's so worn out and full of repair stitches that no amount of mending would make it look good on our little boy. Even so, it was enough to delight my innocent Ino. Before running outside a while ago, he said, 'Whose kimono is that, Mama? It's small, so it must be mine. Whoopee!' Exhilarated by this uncommonly warm weather, he must be swinging his sticky pole to catch the red dragonflies flitting about in the sky. I wonder how far he has gone chasing after them.

"I'm beginning to hate sewing! If only my husband's wits were half as sharp as his trade skill, we would be spared such dire poverty. 'Wasting a treasure in hand' goes the saying. He's merely a journeyman for all his talent, a petty carpenter doomed to obscurity. How vexing that he should be given even a mortifying nickname—Nossori, Slowpoke —by his colleagues, to be made the butt of their ridicule. I can't help but fret, yet he's totally unperturbed by it all. It's frustrating to watch him.

"This time, however, something happened to him. As soon as he heard about the five-storied-pagoda project of Kannō Temple, a fever gripped him. Unmindful of his lowly station and the wishes of the Master, to whom we are so deeply indebted, he's trying to get the contract for himself. When even I, his own wife, can't help but feel that he's overstepping his bounds, what must others think of him? Worse yet, the Master must be outraged, cursing him as 'that damned Nossori,' and Madame Okichi must think he's an ingrate. He left home this morning expecting the Abbot to choose one or the other. Anxious as he is to get this job, I feel it's beyond his reach. It would be better all around if the Abbot gave the job to the Master—we owe so much to him. At the same time, I can't resist dreaming either. May he win, but if only the Master would be gracious enough not to be vexed too much by it! I don't think it could happen, but what if the job does fall into my husband's hands? I'm afraid to think how angry the Master and Madame would be!

"Oh, all this worrying gives me a headache! If he were here now, I would probably get the usual scolding, considerate enough but most unreasonable, for worrying myself sick over nothing. I ought to stop right this minute. Oh, my head!"

The woman, about twenty-five years of age, stopped sewing. With a grimace on her slightly pockmarked, pallid face, she rubbed patches of headache ointment on her temples. Although her features were not homely, her skin was pitifully dry and rough from malnutrition. Tattered clothes and disheveled hair added to her wretched appearance.

All at once, the broken kitchen door clattered open. "Mama, look what I've made!"

"Ino, how long have you been there?" exclaimed the startled mother. The next moment, however, she saw scraps of lumber piled high in imitation of a five-storied pagoda.

"That's a good boy!" With tears in her voice, she clasped Ino into her embrace.

⟨4⟩

Constructed by Genta of Kawagoe, a reknowned builder of the time, Kannō Temple was indubitably without a flaw. The fifty-mat main hall with its fretted ceiling, the long winding corridors, the numerous guest halls, the Abbot's chambers, the tea room, the dormitories for students and acolytes, the priests' quarters, the cookhouse, the bath, and the entrance hall—some structures were graceful, some were patinaed, some approached stately solemnity, and some had attained solid immutability. Each of them measured up to perfection in its own way, leaving nothing more to be desired.

Who was responsible for the transformation of an obscure old temple into one of such distinction? It was Abbot Rōen of Uda, a priest so esteemed that at the mere mention of his name even a three-year-old would fold his palms in veneration. In his youth he pursued rigorous training and religious studies at Mt. Minobu, the headquarters of Nichiren Buddhism, and in his middle years he traveled throughout sixty provinces as a mendicant practicing austerity and asceticism. He had sharpened the sword of tranquil wisdom through contemplation of Samsara, this world, and Dharma, the Law. He intoned the sacred gospel of salvation in four dialects of Sanskrit. Now a septuagenarian, the abbot was as lean as a crane, the result of abstinence from unclean food—meat, fish, and ill-smelling vegetables. His eyes were always half closed so that he might transcend the turmoil of the human sphere. Having learned the Principle of Emptiness, he no longer kindled the flames of desire in his heart. Having comprehended the truth of Nirvana, he was free from the taint of worldly attachment.

It was not that he had wished to erect a pretentious edifice. Rather, it all started when so many disciples and students were attracted to the temple by his personal charisma and spiritual virtue that the original buildings could no longer accommodate them all. One day he had muttered to himself, "I wish our halls were a little more spacious," and soon the rumor spread that the holy Abbot had declared his intention to rebuild the temple on a larger scale. Bright disciples traveled far and wide encouraging donations for this worthy cause, while parishioners extolled the eminent virtues of the Abbot, persuading wealthy men to contribute. The Abbot himself had already commanded worshipful adoration of innumerable followers, and such active efforts spurred on the fund drive even more. From the noble lords down to the townspeople, all competed in making donations; each wished to be the first to sow seeds in the field of good fortune in hopes of reaping peace and happiness in his next life. The rich offered gold and silver, while the poor gave copper coins in strands of a hundred or two, each according to his ability. Streams of money poured in to make an ocean in no time at all. Some men of practical wisdom volunteered to oversee the entire project as agents and managers. Thus did the magnificent temple come to be completed. It is a heart-warming story.

After the general manager, Tame'emon, had added up all the expenditures and settled the accounts without a single oversight, there still remained a large sum of surplus funds. He consulted with the administrative priest, Endō, the secular top-knot and the monastic shaven head cocked in concerted effort, but worthy ideas eluded them. They thought of buying a paddy field or dry farm land, but since more than enough fields had already been donated, there was no need to spend cash to buy more of the same. They knew very well that the Abbot would no doubt say in his hoarse voice, "How troublesome! Do as you think is best." Nonetheless, Endō in desperation found an occasion to inquire if the Abbot might have a particular wish. "Build a pagoda," said the Abbot without even glancing up. He continued to read the sutra or commentary or whatever it was in silence, but there lurked a faint gleam in the eyes behind the large tortoise-shell-framed spectacles.

It was about two months ago that Nossori had come to request an audience with the Abbot regarding the pagoda project, with or without the knowledge that Endō had already ordered Genta to submit his estimates.

⟨5⟩

The man was wearing patched old workman's pants under a half coat whose customary dark blue was faded nearly beyond recognition, having been weathered, sweat-stained, and washed numerous times until the collar markings were faint and illegible. His hair was white with dust, his face sunburnt and without refinement. This undignified figure apprehensively approached the main gate of Kannō Temple, only to be halted by the gatekeeper's sharp "Who are you?"

The startled man stared wide-eyed for a second, bowed his head deeply in excessive politeness, and replied falteringly, "I am a carpenter called Jūbei. I have come to make a request concerning the construction project."

Although the visitor appeared inordinately nervous, the gatekeeper disdainfully gave him permission to pass, assuming that he was one of Genta's apprentices sent over on an errand.

Encouraged by the permission, Jūbei proceeded, gawking about on the way until he reached the solemn entry hall. "Hello! Is anyone there?" he called a few times.

"Yes," answered a little acolyte who appeared through the sliding doors. An experienced receptionist, he quickly sized up the man and stood fast, neither bowing nor stepping down to the reception level. "If you have come here on an errand, go around to the cookhouse," he said frostily and closed the doors, leaving behind a hush unmitigated except by the faint singing of a lone thrush somewhere in the trees.

"As you say." Muttering to himself, Jūbei ambled over to the cookhouse and asked for admission again.

Tame'emon, the manager, emerged with a sanctimonious air. "Unfamiliar-looking master-carpenter, from where and with what business have you come?" He affected a deliberately stilted manner of speech and a condescending tone of voice, no doubt judging the visitor by his shabby attire.

Totally unperturbed by the man's attitude, Jūbei took a deep bow and said, "I am a carpenter called Jūbei. I have come to see the Abbot with a certain request. Please announce me to him."

Tame'emon looked searchingly at the visitor from his dirty head down to his sandals with their discolored thongs and replied with the all-knowing air of a shrewd manager, "No, I will not. The Abbot does not concern himself with worldly affairs. Just tell me what you want, and I might grant your request, depending on what it is."

"That is very kind of you, but I see no use in speaking to anyone but the Abbot in person. Please, I beg you to announce me to him," answered the tactless Jūbei, insensitive to the other.

"You didn't understand me at all, did you!" Tame'emon exclaimed angrily, nettled by Jūbei's distrust. "The Abbot has no ear for a lowly workman like you. Since there is no sense in announcing you anyway, I was only trying to help grant your request. Now that my kindness has been wasted on you, I will not listen to you another moment. Get out!" As can be expected of a small-minded man, his tone had quickly taken on harsh edges. He was already rising to go back inside.

"But . . . could you just . . . ," Jūbei began hastily.

"Shut up! Stop bothering me!" shouted Tame'emon, quickly disappearing into the rear room.

Jūbei stood on the dirt floor with a blank look of consternation, as if a firefly had just slipped away from his hands. Having no other recourse, he raised his voice again to ask for someone. Whether or not there was any living soul about, deep silence reigned in the huge, chilly temple —but for the echo of his own voice, not even the sound of a cough reached his ears. He trudged back to the front entry and asked again. The spiteful-looking little acolyte peeked through the door opening. "I already told him to go around to the cookhouse," he muttered to himself, shutting the door tight.

Jūbei shuffled back and forth between the cookhouse and the front entrance several times more until he lost his reserve and shouted in a voice loud enough to carry as far as the main hall. "I beg you! Please, I do beg you!"

"You damned fool!" bellowed Tame'emon in an even louder voice, reappearing promptly. "Men, throw this madman out of the gate. You all know how much the Abbot abhors noise. If this racket should reach his ears, we'll wind up with a lecture."

At his order, the servants, who had been loafing about in their quarters, came out and pounced upon Jūbei and tried to drag him out. Jūbei planted himself firmly on the dirt floor to resist their attempt. "Hold his arms!" "Pull his feet!" As the servants were cursing and shrieking, the Abbot happened along, clad in a magnolia-hued kimono, holding flowers in one hand and a pair of shears with red lacquer handles in the other. He had been taking a stroll in the garden, collecting a few blossoming sprays to display in his alcove.

⟨6⟩

"What is all this commotion?"

At the sound of the Abbot's authoritative voice, the lowly servants froze on the spot. Some were caught with their fists swung up midair, looking like monks petrified by an opponent's shout in the middle of a heated Zen dialogue. Others hastened to hide behind one another, tugging at their rolled-up sleeves in embarrassment. Tame'emon, who had been at the height of his haughty wrath, all but billowing flames out of flared nostrils, must have felt at least somewhat ashamed, but there was no escape for him, the ringleader. Drooping his head down and obsequiously rubbing his hands together, he began to explain the situation, coloring the story to his own advantage.

The Abbot slowly broke into a smile, etching the lines more deeply in his thin, wrinkled face. "There was no need to make such a disturbance," he said softly. "If only you, Tame'emon, had announced him to me with good grace, there would have been no problem at all. Jūbei-dono, I believe? Follow me this way. I am sorry that you met with such a regrettable reception."

Befitting one so admired and adored by all, the Abbot showed no disdain for the uneducated nor contempt for the lowly. With warm hospitality and serene grace, he led the way for Jūbei, who was unable to hold back tears of gratitude. His compassion had penetrated even the carpenter's simple mind. The two of them traced the winding path past a stretch of moist red soil, artistically laid stepping stones, a Chinese parasol tree offering deep shade, and a graceful bamboo grove. At last, through a modest folding door they entered a small tranquil garden rather conspicuous for its lack of colorful flowers. Pine needles were scattered over an Uraku stone lantern, and the green moss covering a star-shaped water basin carved in stone seemed bright enough to clear one's eyes.

The Abbot stepped out of his wooden clogs into a room. "Please come right up," he invited Jūbei, casually dropping his sprays into a hanging vase.

Not a man to be hesitant or sheepish, or careful enough to dust his feet with a towel, Jūbei doffed his sandals, lumbered into the small tea room, and sat very close to the Abbot. His silent bow was not in exact accordance with the proper rules of the tea ceremony, but it was clearly imbued with sincerity. After a few attempts to speak, he at last forced his heavy lips to falter out words:

"The five-storied pagoda. . . . I have come to make a request about the pagoda." Abruptly leaning forward, he barely managed to wring out his thought in an uneven voice. Cold perspiration moistened his forehead and armpits.

The Abbot smiled in spite of himself and replied affably, "I don't know what you have in mind, but don't be afraid of me. You can dispense with ceremony and just speak your mind. Judging from the way you anchored yourself on the kitchen floor, I can see that you are quite determined. Please consider me as good as your friend. Take your time and speak without reserve."

Jūbei was so moved that his round eyes, which could disparagingly be compared to an owl's, were already flooded with tears. "Thank you, Reverend. I did come with a desperate mind . . . that pagoda. . . . I am such a lowly fellow, as you can see, called by a degrading nickname, Nossori Jūbei. But honestly, Reverend, I am not unskilled in my trade. I know I am a fool and I am made a fool of. I am a guileless man who cannot lie, but, Reverend, I can do carpentry. I learned the Ōsumi style in my childhood, and I am also versed in the Gotō and Tatekawa styles. Please let me have . . . that is . . . I would like you to let me build the pagoda. This is what I have come to ask of you.

"Several days ago I heard that Master Genta of Kawagoe had submitted his estimates. Reverend, I haven't had a peaceful sleep ever since. A five-storied pagoda is a rare project that might come our way but once in a lifetime, or even in a hundred years. It is not my wish to take a job away from Master Genta, to whom goodness knows how greatly indebted I am. Yet, how I envy sharp-witted people! Master Genta gets to work on a once-in-a-lifetime job, a once-in-a-hundred-year project, and his name will survive to posterity. No builder can hope for a better reward than that. Oh, I envy him, how I envy him! As far as our trade skill is concerned I am confident that with an adz and a chisel I fall behind no one, be it Master Genta or anyone else, even if a one-in-a-million chance the carpenter's ink-string marker should fail to draw a straight line. But year in, year out, I get nothing but such meager jobs as repairing the siding of a tenement or building stables and gutter covers. I tell myself time and again to accept my lot, for Heaven has not granted me sharp wits. But in my heart I cry over my misfortune every time I see inept carpenters build shrines and temples. Why, a discerning person could not help but feel sorry for the patrons and parishioners who commissioned such frauds. Sometimes I feel resentful, Reverend, and hateful toward those who have no talent but worldly wisdom. Oh, how I envy Master Genta, Reverend, who is blessed with both the wisdom and the talent! He is going to undertake a work to be envied, isn't he? But I am so . . . ah, Master Genta is so . . . ah, what misery!

"One evening my envy grew so intense that I went to bed in tears without even speaking to my wife. During the night an awesome figure appeared and said to me, 'Build the pagoda. You must build it at once!' I started up in fright and reached into my toolbox. It was half dream and half real, Reverend. When I came fully awake, I found myself clutching at the toolbox. I had cut my fingertips on the chisel. How foolish to have crawled out of bed without even knowing it. I sat by the lamp feeling wretched and stupid. Can you, Reverend, understand how I felt then? Can you? If only someone could understand this much, I would not have to build the pagoda any more—this stupid Nossori Jūbei would gladly die then. I don't particularly care to live on like a broken saw anyway. To tell you the plain truth, Reverend, ever since that night, whether I turned to the clear sky or to the dark corner of a room, I kept seeing a five-storied pagoda of plain wood looming above me, until I felt I must build one myself. Though I knew that it would not come close to the one in my vision, I set out after work every day to make a fiftieth-size model. Last night I finished it. Please take a look at it, Reverend. How ironic that I've been able to complete the work no one ordered but am not allowed to take on the work I truly want! 'Oh, there's nothing more regrettable than karma,' I lamented. 'You'd be far better off without your skill, for then you wouldn't even be aware of your own misfortune,' my wife cried, shaking the model. Since what she said was true, it made me weep all the more. Have mercy, Reverend, and let me build this pagoda. I beg you, like this."

Folding his hands in prayer, Jūbei lowered his head to the floor, tears streaming from his eyes.

⟨7⟩

Silent as a wooden statue of an arhat, the Abbot listened to Jūbei's rambling, all the while fingering the linden-nut beads of his rosary. He gestured to stop Jūbei from bowing and made his reply:

"I do understand. I comprehend perfectly. You are possessed of a beautiful heart and an admirable aspiration, truly a fine exemplar for my student monks. I was moved to tears in spite of myself. By all means, I will go to see your model. However, even though I am extremely impressed with you, it is not up to me to promise on the spot that the pagoda contract will be granted to you. I want you to understand right here and now that the final decision will be handed out, not by me, but officially by Kannō Temple. I do have some free time today, and I would like very much to see your model. Could you take me to your house right now?"

Jūbei had been pumping his head up and down blindly as if he were pounding rice with it, beaming and muttering, "Yes, yes" between the Abbot's words. At last, he exclaimed excitedly, "You grant my request? Thank you, thank you! You will come to my house, you say? That would be more than I deserve. I will fetch the model immediately. If you will pardon me. . . ."

With an alacrity belying his nickname, he took a deep bow and dashed home, driven by joy, almost tripping over the stepping stones on the way. Without a word to his wife, he lifted the model with the aid of a helper and rushed back to the temple. He set the pagoda in front of the Abbot and took his leave.

The Abbot studied the model carefully. It was a splendid piece of work, not a flaw to be found anywhere—from the balance between each story, the slope of the roofs and the eaves, the height of dadoes, and the distribution of rafters down to the shape of the nine rings, the corolla basin, the dew drip, and the jewel cap atop the spire. It was so exquisite that one could hardly believe it had been created by an awkward-looking man like Jūbei.

In his mind the Abbot deplored the irony of life. "How can a man with that much talent be doomed to spend his life in obscurity? When his fate seems pitiable even to me, how resentful he himself must feel. Alas, if possible at all, I would like to help such a man achieve distinction and fulfill his heart's long-cherished dream. A man's life, as short as a plant's, is of course nothing but a temporary illusion woven by the working of causes and effects, useless to cherish and impossible to prolong. Yet, trifling as the way of something such as carpentry may be, a carpenter can achieve nobility immeasurable in gold or silver if he stakes his body and soul on his work, free from human greed and selfish motivations, thinking only of carving well when a chisel is in his hand, only of shaving well when he works with a plane. How exceedingly pitiful that this man is forced to bury his heart of gold in the cemetery ground for lack of an opportunity to express it. How regrettable were his talent to be taken to the other world like so much excess baggage. It is no different in essence from the grief of an excellent horse without a deserving rider, or the regret of a man of lofty character spurned by his lord. Well, then, karma must have ordained that I should discover the obscure glitter of the priceless jewel in Jūbei's heart. I shall grant him the contract for this project and reward his selfless aspiration even in a small way."

The Abbot, however, suddenly remembered that Genta had been exceptionally anxious to undertake this job himself. Genta, who had built the main hall, the cookhouse, and the guest halls, had already submitted his estimates four or five days earlier. Far from inferior to Jūbei in his skill, Genta outrivaled Jūbei in public confidence and esteem. Two masters for a single job. The Abbot wanted to grant it to one just as much as to the other. He was at a loss in deciding which one to choose.

⟨8⟩

"Present yourself at the temple by eight o'clock tomorrow morning. The Abbot will speak to you in person regarding the pagoda contract, for which you have expressed your desire. See to it that you appear properly attired," stated

Enchin, a comical monk-clerk with a red nose (infelicitous evidence of his overfondness for red pepper), ever boastful of his oratorical ability. Being on friendly terms with him, Genta usually teased Enchin, calling him by his nickname, Reverend Cayenne. They had seen each other every day during the construction of the main hall, but their familiarity had since faded somewhat. Standing on ceremony as befitted his role of the official messenger, Enchin laudably hid his hands, with which he had the habit of scratching the top of his helmet-shaped shaven pate, behind the sleeves of his robe. Genta, his head courteously lowered, replied to the effect that he would respectfully and humbly comply with the summons. Perhaps in an effort to make her husband popular even with such a common monk, the tactful Okichi wrapped some money together with the untouched cakes and forced them on Enchin—a rather improper way of offering alms. Enchin continued on to Jūbei's house to deliver the same message.

The next day, Genta went in the back entrance of Kannō Temple, clean-shaven and neatly dressed in formal attire. He sat erect in the waiting room, all but certain that the Abbot himself would award him the contract. Jūbei, unimpressive though he was in his appearance, waited alone with equally tense anticipation in a deserted, chilly room. He wondered, "Will the Abbot send for me any moment now? Will he decree that the entire pagoda job be entrusted to me? Or has he summoned me to say instead that he decided to grant it to Genta? If that should be the case, what am I to do? There will be no more hope for my talent to blossom. Now I can only pray that, out of pity for my foolish heart, the Abbot will grant me the job." Not even noticing the beautiful pictures of golden and silvery phoenixes aflight on the paper sliding doors, Jūbei let his thoughts float in space, blindly groping in the dark.

After some time had passed, the same clever-looking acolyte appeared and announced, "The Abbot summons you. Would you please come this way?"

Jūbei became agitated. "At last the time has come for me to learn whether my dream will come true!" he thought. No sooner did he follow the acolyte into a room than a pair of sharp angry eyes pierced him from the side. To his surprise, they belonged to Genta; not even a shadow of the Abbot was visible in the room. Taken aback, Jūbei stood fixed in one spot for a few seconds, wordlessly staring back at his master. Having no other choice, he sat down two mats away from the other, his head feebly sagging and his enervate, sorry eyes cast down at his knees. Genta, in contrast, showed the bearing of a wild eagle standing against the wind atop a thousand-foot rocky peak and gazing down upon a small puppy. His heart full of self-confidence, he kept a handsomely erect posture, neither sagging his back nor slouching his shoulders. Both in his mien and his looks, he was truly a man of masculine charm who would inspire anyone's admiration.

The Abbot, nevertheless, loved them both, judging with a clear mind, one unswayed by worldly opinions or misled by surface appearance. Until yesterday he had been unable to decide on his final choice. But some solution must have come to him, for he had summoned them today to wait in the same room. At last, his stately steps falling lightly on the mat, he issued from his chamber and entered the room through the door, which an acolyte was holding open. As he silently took his seat, the two men at once prostrated themselves in utmost reverence, unable to raise their heads for some time. When Jūbei finally managed to look up, his face was pitifully flushed, as bashful as a village child who finds himself in the presence of a noble personage for the first time in his life. Hot perspiration flooded the wrinkles on his forehead, formed beads on the tip of his nose, and soaked his armpits. His thick fingers clutching at his knees looked as sturdy as withered pine branches, but they were trembling one and all as he desperately waited for a single word from the Abbot, as though such were a matter of life and death. It was an almost comical sight, had it not been so pitiful. Genta also intently awaited the verdict, not uttering a sound. Fully aware of the equally intense feelings of the two men, the Abbot could hardly find a way to begin and so remained silent for a while.

"Genta and Jūbei. Now listen well, both of you," said the Abbot at last. "There is only one pagoda to be built and there are two of you who want to build it. Much as I would like to grant both your wishes, it is of course impossible to do so. Unfortunately, there are no definitive criteria by which one can judge who is more deserving. It is beyond the discretion of the managers and administrative monks, and even beyond my own. Therefore, I will leave it to be negotiated between the two of you. I will stay out of it and abide by the agreement reached between you. Talk it over at home and report the result to me. Keep in mind that this is all I am going to say on the matter. You may leave now, if you wish. However, I have nothing particular to occupy me today. Would you stay a while to keep me company over a cup of tea and tell me stories of the outside world? In return, I will tell you some funny old tales I found yesterday."

Smiling gently, the Abbot talked to the two men as if they were his friends—whatever it was he had in mind.

⟨9⟩

When the acolyte brought the tea service, the Abbot poured tea and offered it to the two of them. They received their cups awkwardly, overwhelmed by such an honor.

"If you remain so stiff and reserved," said the Abbot,

"we can hardly expect to enjoy a congenial talk. I will not pick out cakes for you, so please help yourselves." He pushed the stemmed cake dish toward them and moistened his own throat with a cup of tea. "Old recluses like us do not have many interesting stories to tell. But in the sutras I have read recently, there was one particular tale which impressed me deeply. Now please listen."

This is the tale that the Abbot told:

Once upon a time on a beautiful day in a certain country, a wealthy elder took a stroll with his two sons into a large field blooming with fragrant flowers and carpeted with soft, thick grass. They came upon a large stream. Since it was the beginning of summer, the level of the water was somewhat low, but the stream still ran clear along the banks. In midstream stood a beautiful sandbar made of jewel-like pebbles and silvery sand. Carried away by his merry mood, the elder leaped easily across to the sandbar —a distance of about two yards—to find himself in an isolated realm set apart by an equal distance from the opposite bank. It was a land of purity, uncontaminated by the depravities of the world. The elder rejoiced and danced about.

Feeling sorry for his two sons, who were calling to him in envy, desirous of coming across but unable to, the elder said, "This is a land of purity quite unattainable for you. But since you seem so anxious, I will help you across. Can you see these pebbles under my feet? They are rare and precious, all shaped like lotus petals. Before me lie peerless grains of sand, each with the hues of the five precious metals."

Eyeing all this from a distance, the two boys grew all the more impatient to cross the stream. The father halted them gently and made a bridge with a palm tree which looked like it might have been uprooted in a flood. The brothers scrambled to be the first to cross. In the end the elder brother flung the younger to the ground and won his way. He started to hurry across the bridge, bursting with haughty pride, but when he reached the middle, his brother, full of resentment, got to his feet and rocked the bridge with all his might. The elder son fell into the water and, after much struggling and gasping, finally reached the sandbar. As soon as he spied the younger, who was now crossing without difficulty, he in turn rolled and jerked the bridge. Unable to cling to the round trunk, the younger son fell into the water.

The soaking wet boy had barely crawled up to the father's feet when the father lamented, "Now how does it look? Since you stepped up here, this sandbar has changed entirely. The pebbles have turned an ugly black, and the sandbar is now made of ordinary yellow grains. Look for yourselves."

The two sons looked down, their eyes bulging in astonishment. Their father was right. There was now nothing but mere pebbles and sand. "Did I torment my beloved younger brother over such worthless things?" "Did I almost drown my esteemed elder brother for these?" The two were ashamed and saddened. The elder son wrung the younger's sleeves, while the younger squeezed his brother's hems. As the two tended to and consoled each other, the father lifted the bridge and placed it across the stream behind the sandbar.

"Now we have no more use for this sandbar. Let's stroll over yonder. You two cross the bridge first." This time the brothers tried to yield to each other. At last, in the order of their ages, the elder son started first, while the younger held the bridge firmly so that his brother would not slip off. When it was the younger brother's turn, the other secured the log. The father leaped across with ease. While the three were enjoying a leisurely walk, the elder son happened to pick up a stone. The younger noticed that it had the shape of a beautiful lotus flower. When the elder boy glanced at the sand that the younger scooped up, he saw in it the dazzling colors of the five precious metals. The brothers rejoiced together and shared their finds, marveling at the mutual happiness they had attained. Out of his pocket the father produced a lotus flower made of gems and offered it to the elder son. Then to the younger, he gave grains of gold that he had been keeping in his sleeves. And he told them to cherish the gifts.

"It may sound like a fairy tale," continued the Abbot, "but there is no falsehood in Buddha's words. It isn't merely a story made up to beguile children. Ponder on it awhile and you will see how meaningful it is. Did you not enjoy it? I find it immensely interesting."

The Abbot thus concluded the story. Though casually told, the gravity of the parable's truth penetrated deeply. Genta and Jūbei looked at each other in bewilderment.

⟨10⟩

Jūbei walked home from the temple in a daze, his arms folded across his chest.

"The Abbot's tale is a riddle to teach us that one should yield to the other willingly. Dimwitted as I may be, I can see that much. But . . . I don't want to yield. I've taken such painstaking care in building the model. Even when Onami, simply out of concern, says, 'You must be chilled through. Why not go to bed?' I tell her to shut up and stop nagging. I've devised one new design after another, hardly sleeping nights. I'd give up my life with no regrets if I were allowed to finish this one work to my satisfaction, once and for all. How sorry I am about the Abbot's admonition. Of course, reason tells me what I ought to do, but if I should yield this job, is there any prospect for another pagoda to be built? Am I destined to be buried in obscurity? How deplorable! What a shame! How I resent my fate! It's not that I fail to appreciate fully the holy Abbot's compassion, but I don't know what to think. My rival is Master Genta, to whom I owe so much. I can't very well resent him, can I? Anyway, is there no choice other than to yield willingly, submissively? No, none at all. Even so, how frustrating! Had I not come up with a foolish ambition, had I remained content with being the Dimwit, I wouldn't be suffering such wretched anguish now. It was my own fault that I forgot my place. Ah, I alone am to blame.

"Yet . . . yet . . . oh, well, I shouldn't think about it any more. Everything will be all right if Jūbei can remain Nossori, ridiculed by the clever people of the world. If I only live and die as if in a dream, deplored even by my own wife as a worthless husband, that will be that.

"Now that I've abandoned my ambition, I feel wretched and resentful toward life and the cruel world. . . . This is nothing but useless grumbling. . . . It may be useless grumbling, but all the same I feel wretched. If the Abbot's unspoken admonition had penetrated my heart, his infinite compassion should have permeated my entire body, leaving no room for dissatisfaction. Isn't that so? He handled our dispute in such a way that neither of us would be hurt. He elucidated the holy sutra and instructed us through the tale of the two brothers to help us remain friends forever. To liken my situation to the tale, I am of course the younger brother, who is expected to yield first. Oh, how painful to be a younger brother!"

Completely lost in thought, his careworn eyes clouded with tears, Jūbei tottered like a marionette toward his house, where no particular pleasure awaited.

"You idiot! You madman! What are you doing to my wash!"

Startled by the abusive scream, Jūbei inadvertently kicked over a drying board propped against a pail. The clumsy man fell backward in consternation.

"Confound you! Are you possessed by a fox or something?" thundered an enraged maid, a girl probably from the countryside, her plump face distorted in anger like a composite face in a children's game. With the blind strength of the famous Okane of Ōmi, she pommeled Jūbei and shoved him with her outstretched arms.

Unable to withstand her furious onslaught, he was flung to the dusty ground. "Yes, yes. A fox must have cast his spell on me. I'm sorry." He fled in pain as the maid continued to shout invectives after him.

When he reached home, his wife said, "Oh, you're back at last. I've been worried. My, you're coated with dust! What happened?"

"Leave me be!" he said in a half-hearted attempt to stop her fussing. But her concerned face unleashed an uncontrollable sorrow, so that tears began to well up in his eyes. "Damn it!" he exclaimed, as though scolding himself, and then tried to cover up by casually pinching tobacco into his pipe, unable to speak.

Already surmising the reason for his extraordinary condition, his wife could find no means of comforting him. Painfully troubled in her heart, she picked up some embers with an iron chopstick and a wooden one and warmed a pot of tea over the feeble heat.

Before long, Ino came home from playing. "Oh, Papa is home. Is Papa going to build it? Ino built one, too. Look!"

Quickly opening the door, the boy pointed to a miniature pagoda, smiling innocently in anticipation of praise. His mother burst into tears, biting on her kimono sleeve to stifle her sobs.

Jūbei stared at the little pagoda with his tear-filled but

unblinking eyes and said, "Well done! Well done! Now I must give you a reward." But his tear-muffled laughter merely echoed vacantly against the ceiling. Looking up toward the heavens, he moaned, "What agony it is to be a younger brother!"

⟨11⟩

The front door opened with the usual cheerful roll. "Okichi, I'm home."

Hearing her husband's spirited voice, Okichi tossed aside the pipe with which she had been blowing anxious rings of smoke and rose to welcome him. "It's taken awfully long, hasn't it?" she said, rushing behind him to help take off his coat. She folded it adroitly with the use of her chin and put it aside in a corner. Returning to the brazier, she made the iron kettle sing like a bell-ring cricket in no time at all. She eyed her husband, who had settled down to relax, and said solicitously, "It's warm today, but the wind is cold. You must have been chilled on your way home. Shall I warm a bottle of saké for you?" With the noiseless speed and efficiency of an expert, she prepared a snack. Pickles were flavored with citron juice, and roe was trimmed with grated radish—so simple yet in good taste.

Despite the bitter thoughts in his heart, Genta was comforted somewhat by the table set before him. He emptied the saké cup rapidly two or three times and nursed the next cupful. "Why don't you join me?" He offered his cup to Okichi.

She sipped a bit, put the cup down, and cut some sheets of crisply broiled kelp. "Sanko is supposed to come by any minute now. . . ." Mumbling to herself the name of the fish vendor, she returned the small cup to Genta and filled it again for him.

Convinced that everything had gone well, she began again smoothly, "Well, I had no doubt of your success today, but I can't stop my needless worrying until I hear it from you. What did the Abbot say? What happened to Nossori? It makes me terribly uneasy to see you so serious and sullen."

"No need for you to worry," laughed Genta rather loudly. "The compassionate Abbot will let me be a man of honor when all is said and done. You see, Okichi, being kind to a younger brother makes me a good elder brother, doesn't it? Sometimes one must share one's meal with a hungry man even if one finds it somewhat painful. I fear no one and nothing, but being brave is not the only masculine quality, is it? Such is also a true man who restrains himself and makes an effort to be meek. Yes, a commendable man. A five-storied pagoda is a glorious project. I would like to build, all by myself, a masterpiece that will survive for a thousand years to be admired by posterity. I would like to accomplish it solely by virtue of my own talent with no help from anyone else. Nevertheless, a true man is he who controls his temper, a laudable man indeed, just as the Abbot says. The Abbot never lies. I loathe to give up even a half of the job on which my heart is set; it pains me, but I must be the elder brother. Okichi, I intend to split the pagoda job with Nossori. A commendably meek man, aren't I? Commend me, Okichi. The entire matter is too disheartening, so at least let me hear you commend me." Without amusement, he laughed absurdly loudly.

Unable to fathom her husband's true feelings, Okichi said, "I don't know what the Abbot told you, but I can't make the slightest sense out of all this. What an unpleasant thing to say! What do you mean by giving half the job to that blockhead? It doesn't square with your usual temperament. If you're to give something up, you might as well give the whole thing up entirely. When it was yours by right from the start, why should you ask for unneeded help? You're not the kind of sly man who would use a helper in dispatching a single enemy. Everyone knows, and you yourself always claim, that your heart is clean, clear, and spotless. How did you come up with such a fuzzy decision? It sounds like awfully weak thinking, even to a woman. I will not commend you. No, no, I cannot commend you. Who is your opponent but Nossori?—who owes you a debt of gratitude to begin with. He has some nerve, trying to steal your job in such a sneaky manner. If you ask me, I'd say you should chastise him so severely that he can't make another sound. Why should you indulge him so much by taking him on as a partner? Is being indulgent the only commendable way? Is being meek the only sign of an honorable man? I won't accept that. If you like, I'll run over to Nossori's house to make him give up the job and prostrate himself on the floor in apology."

Okichi was a clever woman driven by love of her husband, but Genta merely sneered at her now. "How could you possibly understand? All I ask is that you accept my decision, no matter what."

⟨12⟩

Brusquely silenced in effect, Okichi arched her eyebrows and appeared anxious to retort. But experience had taught her the futility of contradicting an irascible Genta, who was twice as headstrong as she. Though she felt resentful toward her husband for not confiding his thoughts to her, she sensibly made a quick decision to retreat for the moment.

"Well, I didn't mean to meddle in your business affairs. I was just so concerned about the pagoda job," she said, lightly dismissing her earlier words, which she had actually meant seriously, and so pretended to accept her husband's wishes, mostly out of a desire to soothe his troubled heart.

Relaxing his stiff expression, Genta said, "Everything is

ordained by the turn of fortune's wheel. So long as I remain amenable and cooperative, my good turn will come again. Looking at it that way, I rather enjoy the idea of giving up half the job to Nossori. Life can be miserable or pleasant depending on your own frame of mind, so I'll be content to live a simple clean one, untainted by the sordid rust of egotism."

He tossed down a cup of saké and then began to drink more moderately over harmless small talk—gossip of the theater, reports of his apprentices' performance, and so forth. They finished lunch sharing the same tray rather intimately, if a little inelegantly. Then Genta settled down to wait for Jūbei.

Time drifted steadily on; the shafts of sunlight pouring through the paper doors shifted a foot. But Jūbei failed to appear. Another foot later, there was still no sign of him.

"He ought to come to me with his head hung low and shoulders narrowed to negotiate. He ought to beg me to give him even half the work if only by grace of the Abbot's considerate advice. Why is he so late? Has he given up? Is he sulking alone at home, seeing no use in further negotiation? Or is he waiting for me to come to him? If so, he's too audacious for his own good. But I hardly think he'd be so arrogant. Slow-witted as he is, he's probably just taking his own leisurely time as usual. Even so, there's a limit to everything."

Genta smoked irritably. The short autumn day seemed interminable to the waiting man. It drew to an end at last, and flocks of crows returned to their nests. Genta was barely able to control his temper, which was threatening to flare up at any moment. When dinner was placed before him, he ate a bit for the sake of eating something, not even lingering over his cup of tea. "Okichi, I'm going to pay Jūbei a visit. If he shows up here, make him wait for me," he said, leaving the house.

Concerned but unable to help, Okichi saw him off and heaved a series of deep sighs.

⟨13⟩

His temper inflamed all the more by the uncooperative wooden doors, Genta forced them open and entered the house. "Is Jūbei home?"

Onami, immediately recognizing the voice, found it painful to face Genta, knowing that her husband had turned against his own benefactor. Her sensitive female heart was already pounding. "Oh, Master . . . ," she said almost instinctively, unable to utter a word of greeting in her panic. In the meantime, Genta's eyes caught sight of the lone figure sitting by a lamp full of needle holes and oil stains. Not waiting to be asked up, Genta marched into the room. Only then did Onami hastily invite him to sit by the brazier, betraying her inexperience in social manners.

Jūbei bowed awkwardly and said, "I was planning to call on you in the morning."

With a dark scowl, Genta assumed a deliberately calm tone. "Oh, were you? Short-tempered as I am, I've been waiting for you at home all this while. What a fool I was to come here tonight not realizing when you intended to come to me. Anyway, Jūbei, how did you take the Abbot's tale today? After advising us to go home and negotiate the matter, he told us the story about the two sons of an elder. I'm here to learn your decision. I'm a headstrong man, but I realize that quarreling does no good to either of us, just as the parable teaches. We are not exactly enemies, and I for my part mean to be fair. Curbing my own desires, I did a great deal of thinking in the hope of arriving at an equitable settlement. But first I'd like to hear your candid opinion. I'm a man who refuses to play unfair tricks, believe me."

Genta stopped speaking for a moment to observe Jūbei,

who hung his face low, mumbling, "Yes, yes." His disheveled hair flashed several gray streaks in the flickering lamplight. At the head of the bedding in which Ino had fallen asleep, Onami sat silent and immobile as if bating her breath. It was so quiet that even the noodle vendor's distant calls came faintly drifting into the house.

Genta composed himself and continued gently. "I'll try to be frank. It must be your lifelong ambition to demonstrate your hidden talent by producing a magnificent piece of work and succeed in attaining the artisan's supreme goal. It's no mercenary greed if you aspire to immortalize your own designs and craftsmanship for posterity. I can well understand that, for I feel exactly the same way. This sort of construction project will not easily come our way again. If we miss it now, our chances of finding another such job in our lifetime will be very slim indeed. I, too, am most anxious to leave my own designs and craftsmanship for posterity. Furthermore, Kannō Temple has practically kept me on retainers for some time, while you have had no such past connection. I was asked to submit estimates, but you were not. Others would say that I deserve this contract, while charging that you are not quite up to the scale of this job yet. But I don't take advantage of such arguments, nor do I rely on the opinions of others.

"I'm well aware of the plight you suffer despite your fine skill, and I also know you are crying in your heart without ever complaining of your misfortune in words. Yours is a life so sorrowful that I could not possibly endure it if I were in your place. That's why I've done all I can to help you for the past two years, little as it may have seemed to you. But please don't think I'm demanding gratitude now. It was only because the Abbot saw your pure heart and felt sorry for your misfortune that he admonished us as he did today. As for myself, if you were the kind of man who would turn against me out of greed or for some similar reason, I wouldn't let you escape before smashing your head with an axe, saying, 'You insolent good-for-nothing, getting in the way of my work!' But as I wholeheartedly sympathize with you, I even feel like giving the job up for you. But I can't cast aside my own ambition just like that, for I truly want this job at all costs.

"Now, Jūbei, this request is difficult to make and not easy to accept, but here it is. Please accept my offer to build the pagoda together, with me as the chief and you as my assistant. I'll plead with you—no, I *am* pleading. . . . Why don't you say something? Do you mean to turn me down?" Genta even turned to Onami, who was already moved to tears, and said, "If you understand what I've been saying, Onami, please persuade him to accept."

"Oh, Master, I thank you with all my heart. Who else in the world would be generous enough to make such an offer." Her left sleeve heavy with tears, Onami stretched her right hand to entreat with Jūbei, who had turned into a silent statue. "Why don't you express your gratitude to the Master?" She repeated her plea twice and three times but to no avail.

At long last Jūbei raised his face and replied curtly, "I can't accept that."

Onami gasped in disbelief.

"What?" exploded Genta, thrusting his head forward to glower straight down at Nossori, his eyes burning with rage.

⟨14⟩

"The Master made his generous offer solely out of kindness, complying with the dictate of social obligations, yet not losing the flower of human sentiments," Onami cried out inwardly. "I know my husband is not affable by nature, but how dare he say, 'I can't accept that?' Even a clay doll devoid of sensibility would not make such a reply.

How deplorably thoughtless, how mortifyingly reckless! How could he be so irrational?" Shocked and dismayed, Onami felt as if her own body were being tortured on the rack. Impulsively she edged closer to her husband.

"What on earth do you mean by that?" she implored. "The Master has been doing everything to help you. He could easily kick someone like you out of his way if he but wished. Yet he has made an exceedingly generous offer, letting you share a job which he would be more than happy to keep entirely for himself. Besides that, did he summon you to his house? No, he took the trouble to come to our wretched place, where we have not even a decent cushion to offer him. How could you be so ungrateful? It's nothing if not impertinent and willful to say, 'I can't accept that.' There's a limit to greed and arrogance.

"Can't you see this kimono I'm wearing? Madame Okichi gave this to me early last winter when she found me shivering without a coat. It's bad enough that you should compete with the Master, to whom we are so deeply indebted, but you even reject his offer altogether, refusing to trust in him when he is doing all he can to befriend his inferior, never calling you ungrateful or impertinent. Even if you hate to accept his offer, are those the words that could be uttered by a man with a memory? Please think of your obligation to the Master and of Madame Okichi's feelings. After this, how could I ever face her again? The broadminded Master may simply dismiss us as hopeless fools, but what will others say? Without a doubt you'll be ostracized as an ingrate, a social deviate, a beast without a heart, a dog, a crow. . . . What glory would you find in a job if you have to turn into a dog or a crow to obtain it?

"You yourself always lecture me not to be greedy or overeager. Aren't you ashamed now? Please go along with the Master's idea. People will admire the towering pagoda, knowing it was built jointly by two men—your name recorded side by side with the Master's. Your labor will be well rewarded, and the Master's kindness will become widely known, as it should be. How happy and proud I will be! Try to find a cause for complaint then. You must be possessed by the devil to reject such a proposal. Oh, how miserable I feel! Have you forgotten your place, which you must know very well without my reminding you?"

Her speech trailed off into tearful sobs. Even the thread through the sewing needle stuck in her chignon was swaying unsteadily, revealing her painfully shattered state of mind. It was a pitiful sight.

Jūbei, who had been sitting with his eyes closed, said gruffly, "Hold your tongue, Onami. How can I speak when you're babbling away like that? Master, please listen to my side of the story."

⟨15⟩

Bracing his hands over both knees to keep from trembling, Jūbei stiffened his back.

"It's heartless, Master. It is heartless of you to suggest a joint venture. Giving me half the job seems charitable, but it's actually heartless. I won't accept it. I can't. As much as I want to build the pagoda, I've already given up the idea. On my way home after the Abbot's admonishment, I gave it up altogether. It was my mistake to have conceived such an ambition in the first place. What a fool indeed to overstep my bounds! Everything will be all right so long as Nossori remains a dimwitted fool. I'll spend the rest of my life fixing gutter covers and tenement houses. Please forgive me, Master. It's all my fault. Never again will I even dream of building a pagoda. I'll look forward to seeing you, Master, not a stranger, but my own benefactor, build a magnificent pagoda all by yourself."

As Jūbei feebly mouthed his words, Genta pressed his knees forward impatiently.

"What a ridiculous thing to say!" he cried. "How unreasonable can you get? The Abbot didn't tell the tale just for you to hear. Don't you realize that he meant it for my ears also? If you heard it with your head, I heard it with my heart. How could I call myself a man if you carry all the burden and play the martyr at my expense? Are you foolish enough to think that everything will be all right as long as you yield and remain a loser? Do you think I'd jump at the chance to take over the whole job? I'd be ashamed to face the Abbot if I did! Furthermore, I couldn't fling my sense of honor to the wind after living by it for so long. And would you gain anything by yielding? No! Wouldn't that be the height of stupidity! What good would it do either of us? Now do you see why I propose an amicable joint venture? If you find that somewhat unpleasant, I assure you the feeling is mutual. But there is no reason why we can't compete in tolerance. There's no need for you to go out of your way to play the fool and waste your fine skill, as well as your endeavor of the last few days. If you can see the sense in what I've said, Jūbei, change your mind. I don't think I'm being unreasonable. . . . Why don't you speak up? Will you give in? Or do you still suspect my intentions? Jūbei, aren't you being a little heartless yourself? . . . Say something! Don't you agree? Well, don't you? It's impossible to understand you if you remain silent. Am I wrong? Or are you angry because my suggestion is not good enough for you?"

An Edoite scrupulous in performing his social obligations yet susceptible to sentiment, Genta was as unbending in his principles as he was unsparing in his kindness. Gratefulness overcame Onami, who had continued to listen attentively. She looked anxiously toward her taciturn husband, her eyes brimming with tears that betrayed her gratitude toward Genta more eloquently than words. Still motionless and wordless, Jūbei was immersed in thought, his head sagging low. Only the teardrops falling on his knees seemed to speak for him. Genta also fell silent, deliberating for some moments.

"Jūbei, don't you understand yet?" said Genta at last. "You must hate the idea of having to share the work you wanted so much for yourself. You must be resentful, moreover, that I should be the chief and you the assistant. Well then, let's settle it this way. I'm willing to take the position of assistant and acknowledge you as the chief. So take it with good grace and agree to build the pagoda with me," Genta concluded resolutely, forcing himself to compromise his own wish.

"Heavens no, Master! Even a madman could not do such a thing! It's a sacrilege," exclaimed Jūbei hastily.

"Well, then, would you agree to my original suggestion?"

"Well, I just . . . ," faltered Jūbei.

"Shall we make you the chief? Or is it still not to your liking?" Genta pressed.

As Jūbei groped for words, his wife was nearly driven out of her mind. "Why don't you accept?" she urged breathlessly, a note of reproach in her voice.

Trapped in a desperate impasse, Jūbei slowly raised his head. With his eyes enlarged in determination, he blurted out, "I don't want to share a job with anyone, whether I'm the chief or the assistant. I could never do it. Please build it yourself, Master. I shall remain a fool——"

"In spite of all my effort to be fair?" Genta angrily demanded, not waiting for Jūbei to finish.

"That's right. I am grateful, but I can't lie. I can't do it. I don't want to."

"How can you say that to me! Then you refuse to go along with my idea? Is that it?"

"I have no other choice."

"You shall pay for this, you Nossori! You ingrate. You're entirely devoid of human sentiments! Are you in any position to talk that way to me? Well, I shall never speak to you again. Spend the rest of your life fixing gutter boxes! I'm sorry, but I won't let a single finger of yours touch my pagoda. I shall build it splendidly by myself. Gloat over flaws in it, if you can find any."

⟨16⟩

"Oh, thank you very much. I feel awfully tipsy. I couldn't swallow another drop."

Though his words declined, Seikichi's hand holding out the saké cup would not withdraw—a curious habit of all drinkers. Already inebriated with the free drinks, he settled down sanctimoniously, his faculties still functioning enough for him to assume proper reserve.

"I'm sorry I've gotten so drunk while the Boss is away. Drinking with you alone, Ma'am, I should be careful not to wind up dancing to the tune of 'Twilight,' you know. Ha, ha, ha! I'm beginning to feel awfully happy. I'd better leave now. If I get too drunk, the Boss will take me to task for sure. But I'm always grateful to him, Ma'am, even for his scolding. I'm not currying favor or anything, mind you, but I really do appreciate the Boss more than the Tea Bag. On the Ryōun-in job some time ago, I got into a fight with Tetsu and Kei over a trivial matter and seriously injured Tetsu on the shoulder. His family then came crying to me. I was terribly sorry about what I'd done, but there was nothing a poor fellow like me could do for him. I was nearly driven to fleeing from Edo, when the Boss paid for Tetsu's treatment and care without reproaching me one bit. He only advised me, 'A fight is unavoidable under certain circumstances, Sei, but if you feel sorry for Tetsu, apologize just to make his parents feel better, and you'll be able to sleep in peace too.' How considerate of him! I was so thankful that I actually cried. I owed Tetsu no apology, but I swallowed my pride and took the Boss's advice. Strangely enough, since then Tetsu and I somehow became such fast friends that we're pledging to be the executor of each other's funeral. And we have the Boss to thank for our friendship.

"On the other hand, the Tea Bag does nothing but scold me and tediously grumble into my ear, 'Don't get into fights. Don't go to the pleasure quarters,' and such nonsense. Ha, ha, ha! She's utterly absurd. . . . What? . . . Oh, the Tea Bag is my ma. . . . It's not terrible at all. 'Tea Bag' is good enough for her—a tanned old cheap tea bag at that. Well, thanks for the treat; I must be going now. . . . What? You say, 'Have one more,' where the Tea Bag would have said, 'You've had enough.' Oh, I feel so good. I feel like singing. . . . Can I sing? That's a heartless question. My 'All the Pines' impressed even my woman," the guileless Seikichi rambled on.

"How dreadful! Must we hear about your amorous exploits next?" said Okichi, laughing. While she was teasing Seikichi, Genta returned.

"Oh, you're here, Seikichi. Very good. Let's drink. Okichi, prepare a feast. Seikichi, you may drink yourself to sleep tonight. I'll even listen to your gruff singing of 'All the Pines.' "

"What! You must have been eavesdropping, Boss."

⟨17⟩

The drunker one gets, the more careless one becomes. Seikichi forgot his manners and grew too comfortable with Genta's affable mood and Okichi's hospitality. He emptied the saké cup as often as it was filled until his ruddy face took on the color of ripe cherry. He laughed loudly, put on pompous airs, gossiped about his colleagues, and boasted about how his impersonation act had been applauded here and there. He told how his friend Sen had bungled an attempt to steal a brazier from a brothel over a wager, and how at another time he himself beat up a local hoodlum just outside the pleasure quarters. While he talked on, one story leading into another, he happened to touch on a bit of gossip about Nossori. All at once he popped open his sleepy eyes, pulled his slouching shoulders together, and sipped some cold leftover saké, comically pouting his lips.

"I can't understand, Boss, why you should be so kind to such a fool. His work is thorough to a fault and slow to an extreme. He's the kind who would sharpen his plane blade three times while he's shaving a single pole or rail. No matter what he's told to make, he never finishes on time. No wonder Sen sneers that a man like him would take three days to make one red-pine hearth-frame! You patronized him so much that for a while there that Kin, Sen, Roku, and I—all of us—felt quite neglected. Among ourselves we complained that you might have been too generous in giving that unworthy fellow so much credit. We even said that if thoroughness was what you liked, we ought to shave even a clapboard slowly and reverently, until it was as smooth as a game table.

"What's more, that Nossori's an unsociable character who never goes to the brothel with us or shares a pot of chicken stew. Once when we were planning to visit the temple of the Daishi, our guardian deity, I went out of my way to kindly invite him to join us; I thought we shouldn't leave out even one of the men who worked for you. The only response I got for my pains was, 'I'm too poor to go.' What an unsociable ingrate! One is expected to keep one's social obligation with friends even if one has to pawn the wife's only kimono, you know.

"He's such an imbecile, ignorant of even the simplest rule. But he's enjoyed your favor, Boss, until he's now treated as a full-fledged workman just like Kin and me. And, if you'll pardon my saying so, Sen and I have been with you since we were little kids delivering lunchboxes and staggering under loads of woodchips. But what is Nossori but a drifter? All the more reason why he should doubly appreciate your kindness. Boss, Ma'am, I'm beginning to feel sad. I'm ready to rush into fire and smoke for the two of you if necessary. But that dog! That miserable ingrate! Nossori the Dimwit! Would he brave into fire if he carried his debt of gratitude for cover? No, he couldn't possibly have a shred of decency in him. What an insensitive beast!"

Affected by his own unleashed grievances, Seikichi, by now very drunk, broke into tearful whimper. Okichi looked to her husband and pretended to be annoyed by Seikichi's familiar habit. With hatred of Nossori pulsating in her own heart, however, she was inclined to agree somewhat with Seikichi's remarks.

Genta, too discreet to reveal his true feelings, offered a saké cup to Seikichi and laughed loudly. "What are you mumbling about, Seikichi? Don't sleep-talk in front of me. And leave the pathetic last scene to Kabuki actors. If you make a pass with that technique, no woman will be able to resist you. But this isn't the chamber of the Mistress Kochō you've been bragging about. Ha, ha, ha!"

As Genta made a joke of it all, Seikichi, sobbing, tried to brush off teardrops as large as beads and ended up plunging his hand into a dish of raw fish. "How unfeeling of you, Boss! You treat me like a drunkard. I'm not tipsy at all; I didn't drink any saké called Kochō. As I think of it, even *her* face somehow reminds me of Nossori, and I can't bear her anymore. That dimwit Nossori, I hate him! He's obnoxious, competing against you and presuming to build, of all things, a pagoda! Of all the nerve! He's a traitor who's gotten spoiled because you were too kind to him. Even among traitors, Hakuryū the storyteller excuses those like Akechi Mitsuhide, who suffered enough provocation. But Nossori has got to be the most heinous of them all. When did you club him with an iron fan, as Oda Nobunaga did Mitsuhide? When did you threaten to take away his fief and give it to Mori Rammaru? If by chance Nossori should take advantage of your generosity and build the pagoda with his name next to yours, I won't let him get away with it. I'll beat him to death and feed his carcass to the dogs. Like this!"

Seikichi proceeded to knock off an empty saké bottle sideways, sending broken pieces clattering noisily against dishes and bowls.

"You fool!" Genta shouted. Seikichi slumped down, suddenly limp and quiet. Soon his face fell into the scattered sheets of seaweed, and he began snoring. "Get a cover for this amusing fool," said Genta, laughing. For some time he continued to drink by himself, all the while reflecting soberly upon his own conduct at Jūbei's house. Let anger get the best of me, and I'll be no better than Seikichi. I must be more prudent, Genta warned himself.

⟨18⟩

After Genta stormed out of the house, Onami turned to her husband, who seemed lost in thought, his arms folded across his chest. She heaved a deep sign and lamented, "You've made the Master angry, and you won't get the job after all. All those sleepless nights you spent building the model have come to naught. Not only that, you hurt the Master's feelings, and you'll end up being denounced as a heartless ingrate by others. What a shame! You may dismiss what I say as female meddling, but you can carry honesty and integrity too far, you know. Would it be so shameful to accept the Master's suggestion to work with him? Why are you so senseless and stubborn? Who will commend you for that? If you accept the Master's offer, you'll please your benefactor and have a chance to make a name for yourself besides. Your labor and anguish will be well rewarded, and everything will be fine. Why don't you like the idea? I can't understand your reasoning at all. Won't you change your mind? As soon as you decide to accept his offer, I'll run over to his house and convey your apologies in any way I can. If I refuse to budge no matter if I get beaten or kicked and just keep apologizing, the Master won't remain angry forever. He might overlook your temporary transgression. Please think it over carefully and try to go along with him. Don't be so stubborn. Please!" Onami, out of love for her husband, thus appealed to him with reason and logic.

But Jūbei did not even bat an eye. "Don't say another word. Don't mention the pagoda, either. I conceived such a useless ambition only to be called an ingrate and a beast. I have my own stupidity to blame for all this. What can I do about it? I'll never change my mind. I may employ helpers, but I refuse to get any advice about my work, just as I would not presume to offer advice while employed to help someone else. If I alone am responsible for a job, I can arrange the bracing of square supports or the balancing of the beams just the way I want. I'll be damned if I'll accept anyone's instruction on the smallest feature of my work. I want to be wholly responsible for both the merits and the flaws. When employed by someone else, I am just an honest helper performing the task assigned, never even dreaming of giving unsought, knowing advice. I can't tolerate a parasite who proudly shows off his particular style when he is not the principal builder. I don't want to be a parasite in another's work, any more than I want to have one involved in my own work. I just can't help it. I appreciate the Master's kindness in trying to persuade me in proper accordance with the dictates of social obligations and human sentiments. But I'm sorry he tried to meet me halfway, offering me a parasitic position. I don't mind being a fool and a dimwit, but the thought of prospering as a parasite is insufferable. I would much rather be a small bush, willing to become fertilizer for the large tree that protects me. In my heart, I've always despised those who are proud of being parasites. I'd be too ashamed to degenerate into one myself now by taking advantage of the Master's generosity. Go ahead and reproach me for being so obstinate, but please forgive me, for I just can't help myself. My very obstinacy makes me what I am: Nossori the Dimwit, a fool, an idiot. I deserve to be called names. Oh, the fire is dying out, and it's getting cold. Let's go to bed."

As he confided his feelings to Onami, she fell silent, unable to find a word to contradict him. The lamplight illuminating the bleak room had dimmed down to the end of the wick.

⟨19⟩

The same night Genta lay in bed unable to fall asleep. Hearing the first and the second roosters announce the dawn, he arose earlier than usual. After washing off the fatigue of undreamt dreams, he drank a cup of hot tea to dispel the saké odor of the night before. Seikichi awoke with a start, rubbing his sleepy eyes with a confused look on his face. Genta and Okichi broke into laughter together.

"What happened to you last night, Seikichi?" Genta teased.

Seikichi hurriedly straightened himself up and began to pump his head madly in apology. "I enjoyed your hospitality too much and fell asleep in spite of myself. Ma'am, did I do something naughty last night?" he asked apprehensively.

"Well, it's all right," said Okichi, amused. "Just have some breakfast and go to work."

All the more embarrassed with her amiable reply, he

appeared desperate trying to remember what happened, his arms folded across his chest in concentration. His simple-minded sincerity was rather engaging.

After Seikichi left, Genta again sank into thought. Unlike his usual cheerful self, he hardly spoke, even to Okichi. He pondered, reflected, and brooded. "Oh, I see now!" he would say to himself. "That poor fellow," he would sigh. Or he would ask, "Shall I wash my hands of it?" But the next moment he would angrily growl, "How can I pay him back for this?"

It pained Okichi to watch him. When she inquired to try to console him, she was told to mind her own business. She grieved helplessly, not knowing what to do.

Mindless of her concern, Genta deliberated into the evening alone. He apparently arrived at some decision, for he changed into formal attire and went to the temple to request an audience with the Abbot. He then reported everything that had transpired the night before, holding back no detail. He concluded, "Although I was infuriated at first with Jūbei's stubborn attitude, I gave it careful thought when I got home. I am perfectly capable of building the pagoda by myself, but I am not about to turn a deaf ear to your kind admonition. I refuse, moreover, to behave like a man too self-centered and honorless. On the other hand, Jūbei is not the least likely to change his mind. Our code of conduct dictates that if he suppresses his desire and yields to me, I must suppress my own and yield the job to him. Even though I had racked my meager brain to come up with an idea, it was useless—Jūbei would not go along with it. It would be senseless for me to blame or hate him, and I am not able to suggest any other solution. At this point, I only request that you, Reverend, kindly assign the project either to Jūbei or to me alone, or jointly to both of us. Even if you choose Jūbei alone, I will abide by your decision. Both Jūbei and I are ready to accept your final word. So there will be no more problem." Genta's sincerity was reflected in his earnest expression.

Softly smiling, the Abbot replied, "I know, I know. You are a praiseworthy man, just as they say. Fine, fine! That attitude in itself is already more meritorious than the building of a splendid pagoda. Jūbei came a little while ago with the same request. A dear fellow, isn't he? Genta, take him under your wing. Be kind to him."

"Of course, I certainly will," replied Genta without hesitation, immediately comprehending the Abbot's command.

"Fine. You are indeed a remarkable man," said the Abbot, his face crinkling into a delighted smile.

Deeply awed and reverent as Genta was, he raised his face involuntarily to pour out an unfathomable feeling in a few words, weeping. "With your help, I have made a man of myself at last, haven't I?" A noble resolution to back up Jūbei's work must have formed in his heart at that instant.

⟨20⟩

After Jūbei returned from Kannō Temple, where he had also seen the Abbot Rōen and tearfully withdrawn his request, he was disconsolate for the rest of the day. He could not even bestir himself to smoke. The more his mind rambled over his misfortune and hardships of life, the more depressed he became. Not that the foods changed their natural flavor, but at dinnertime even his hand seemed reluctant to hold the chopsticks, and somehow his palate refused to taste anything. Instead of the six or seven hearty helpings he was accustomed to enjoying, he stopped after two or three bowlfuls of rice. But he drank an inordinate amount of tea—a sure sign of a person with a troubled mind.

With the master of the house in such a gloomy mood, the wife and even the impish young Ino were also rueful, deepening the desolation in the impoverished home. They passed the day without hope or merriment and spent the night in chilly dreams.

Onami awoke with the dawn bell and slipped out of the bed that she shared with Ino. She wanted to let him sleep a little longer until a fire was made, for the morning wind was cold.

In spite of his mother's loving consideration, Ino suddenly started up. Clad only in his underwear, he jumped about on the bed shouting, "Don't, don't! Please don't beat my father!" He began to weep, covering his eyes with tiny hands shaped like bracken sprouts.

Startled, Onami took him into her arms. "What is it, Ino?" Even in her embrace, the child continued to cry. "No one is beating Papa. Did you have a nightmare? Look, Papa is still in bed right here."

She turned the boy's face toward the sleeping figure to reassure him. Ino stared with an air of disbelief, but seemed a little relieved.

"Nothing's happened. You just had a bad dream. Now, you'd better get back under the covers or you'll catch a chill in this cold air." She forced him down and tucked a quilt securely about him.

Wide eyed, Ino said, "I was so scared! Mama, some horrible stranger . . ."

"Oh? What did he do?"

"With a huge, huge shovel, he beat Papa on the head again and again, when he was just sitting quietly. And his head cracked in half, and I was awfully frightened."

"Heaven forbid! How horrid! What an omnious dream!" Onami knitted her eyebrows.

Just at that instant, the bean vendor passing in front of the house cursed in his familiar tremulous voice, "Damn it! The thong broke on me!" Irked all the more by this additional evil omen, Onami went to the kitchen to start a fire under the water pot, but she was infuriated by the firewood, which was reluctant to burn, and irritated at the window, which refused to slide smoothly.

"What a way to start a day! It's all in my mind, I know, but there are enough reasons already for me to fret. I'd best keep them to myself, though." She chided herself and made an effort to act cheerful. Her vivacity being mostly pretense, however, her laughter only left mournful echoes, filling the air with even more gloom.

"Is Jūbei-dono home?" A young acolyte entered the house with an air of precocious importance, seated his supercilious self, and abruptly stated a message, omitting the customary greetings: "You are wanted at the temple. Present yourself promptly."

Jūbei and Onami were equally puzzled, but a formal summons was not to be declined. Jūbei felt it useless to enter the gate of Kannō Temple again, but he went, if only to inquire why he was wanted. What awaited him was to leave him in total bewilderment. Was it a dream or was it real? Was it to be believed at all?

Abbot Rōen was seated between Endō and Tame'emon. In a most serious tone, Endō announced, "The construction of the pagoda was to be entrusted entirely to Genta of Kawagoe. Nevertheless, by special consideration and exceptional mercy, the Abbot has decided to award the contract to you. There is no need for you to decline. Accept it at once."

The Abbot himself added in his hoarse voice, "Well, Jūbei, build it as best you can. I will be pleased to see it done well."

Blessed more than he could bear, Jūbei prostrated himself on the floor, his entire body heaving. "I offer you my humble life," he blurted out before choking, speechless.

In the still of the spacious room only the faint sound of breathing pierced the air, transmitting some wordless message.

⟨21⟩

During the summer, the sweet fragrance of the white and red lotus flowers had perfumed kimono sleeves and skirts. Dewdrops rolled about on the floating lotus leaves, while the breeze softly caressed the vertical ones. Such intriguing summer scenes vanished completely as the red dragonflies came to play with the drifting duckweed and the first frost tinted the treetops in the hills. Now among the lotus stalks left standing pitifully bare in red ocher, snowy herons walked slowly and comically, seemingly wishing to remain incognito. The flying geese almost brushed their backs against the twinkling stars in the deep blue twilight sky, their cries enhancing the graceful scene around Shinobazu Pond.

In an upstairs room of Hōrai Restaurant, where customers could drink like fish and enjoy the poetic scenery of the pond, sat a man with an air of controlled elation, apparently waiting for someone. Although his speech and manners betrayed the gallant spirit of the artisan, his simple taffeta kimono and unobtrusive silver-plated pipe set him off as a man of refined taste without a touch of vulgarity about him. A woman called Den, who knew that this regular customer was a leader whom many men respectfully addressed as "Master," brought in a tray of appetizers.

"You must be getting impatient waiting for your guest," she said.

To relieve the tedium of waiting, the man played along. "Oh, I'm so impatient I can hardly bear it. What could be taking so long?"

"Well, her make-up, for one thing. You can't very well

blame her for that, now, can you?" Den responded with a teasing laugh. She was adept at this familiar game of words.

"You're so right. When my guest shows up, take a very good look, will you? I don't think you've ever seen anyone like this guest of mine around here."

"Well, well, what consolation prize would you give me for all the pleasure you're going to have tonight, Master? Is she a teacher of music or dance?"

"No."

"A young lady?"

"No."

"A widow?"

"No."

"An old lady."

"Don't be silly. Have pity on me."

"Then, a baby!"

"You are joking!"

As they were laughing, someone called Den from outside the door to announce the arrival of the expected companion. Just before pulling the door open, Den turned around for a second to shoot a knowing wink and a silent grin toward the man in the room, to add to his imminent pleasure. Unaware of Genta's mischievous amusement, she slid the door to one side. The guest who lumbered in, though, was a man, rugged and unromantic, a far cry from a charming woman. His smudged face was framed by unkempt hair and a shaggy beard, his clothes tattered and soiled. At this irksome sight, Den was too astounded to utter the customary greetings.

"Jūbei, please come right in," said Genta with a smile. "Don't stand on ceremony. Make yourself comfortable."

He forced the hesitant Jūbei to take a seat. When the table was set, Genta drained a cup of saké and refilled it for his silent guest.

"I had Tomimatsu deliver my invitation to you in the hopes of reconciling our differences," said Genta. "I wanted us to drink together and open our hearts to each other. I hope you will forget the rash words I flung at you the other night. Please listen to me. That night I was indignant, blindly blaming you for being an obstinate fellow. To my shame, I was so infuriated that I lost my temper and even wanted to break open your head. Fortunately, however, my mind was not totally taken over by the devil. When Seikichi came to my house and happened to blubber out absurd things in his drunkenness, I was amused to note how a petty man can rationalize his silly remarks so perfectly. The next moment I realized that what I had said in your house earlier was not much different. I thought to myself, 'How wrong I was! Did I forget myself in a fit of anger? Shameful! How can I call myself a man? If anyone should find out, I won't be able to keep my honor. I'll suffer the Abbot's contempt. When Jūbei has given up everything and declined, it would be a grave mistake for me to take advantage and persist in my own desire.' At the same time, I was still angry with you for being so unreasonable. I had taken every little detail into consideration, deliberating whether insistence on one point would bring about strained relations in another respect, or whether doing justice here would force a sacrifice somewhere else, and so on and so forth. I had worked my brains and discretion to the limit when I came up with the suggestion I made that night—and not solely for my own sake, either. I was painfully irked when you turned me down cold. However, when I made up my mind and reported my final decision to the Abbot, all my anguish was dispelled instantly by one word from him: 'Fine!' Now I feel as if my mind has been cleared by a cool breeze.

"Yesterday I was summoned by the Abbot and received words of commendation. He also gave me specific advice:

'I have finally awarded the contract to Jūbei. I want you to help him from behind the scenes. It will also serve you as a meritorious cause and a seed of good fortune for your next life. I don't suppose Jūbei has any helpers of his own. When he starts on this project, his crew will include some of your men. You had better admonish them not to bear him jealousy or grudges.' In awe of the compassionate Abbot, who sees through everything, I conceded with all my heart. Please forgive me for having said too much the other day, Jūbei. If you understand my feelings, I trust you will want to restore our friendly relationship. Now that everything has been settled, all our differences seem just like a quarrel in a dream. Persisting on the past issue leads to nothing but more trouble. Let's throw our grudge into the water of Shinobazu Pond, whose name means 'bear not.'

"Such business as the purchasing of lumber and the negotiations with construction workers might give you trouble until you are well established in the field. I can help you there with my reputation and influence. The big wholesalers, such as Maruchō, Yamaroku, and Enshūya, are known to snub new customers; you should make full use of my name so that nothing will go wrong in dealing with them. You know that Eiji, the chief of the M crew, is quite short-tempered, but—as he always claims—his bones are made of iron and his spirit is a fireball. He is a reliable man who will accept a sincere request in earnest; he won't fall back on his promise. The groundwork is more important than anything else for a pagoda, which must withstand the forces of air, wind, fire, and water. I have no doubt that Eiji will pour all his heart into laying the foundation more solid and stable than even the deity Fudō's pedestal, for such is the force of Fireball Eiji's spirit. I will soon introduce you to him.

"At this point, I have only one wish: that you accomplish

the task superbly. There is nothing I would like to see more than a magnificent pagoda completed, one which will stand for hundreds of years to be seen by those who would be our disciples and junior colleagues. If it should turn out poorly, wouldn't it be our dying shame? Supposing they sneered, 'It's said that in the days of Genta and Jūbei, carpenters cried and rejoiced over such a trivial structure.' Well, Jūbei, our bones and souls would be rasped into powder by the humiliation, to scatter away in disgrace. There would be less shame in failing to attain fame for lack of talent. But to leave one's work behind to be ridiculed by our juniors—wouldn't it be as pathetic as a foolish father being admonished by his own son? How much more disgraceful than a son getting a scolding from his father! It may be bad enough to be crucified alive, but imagine how much worse if our corpses were salted and gibbeted for all eternity.

"To tell you the truth, I was not all that serious about the pagoda until I felt the challenge of your earnest competition against me. 'Let me build the pagoda and I'll show you I'm your equal, Genta,' you were saying. And I said to myself, 'I'll build it and show Jūbei. How could I fall behind him?' I was seeing the future only in the light of fire flashing out of flint-sticks in my mind, but now I am rid of selfish desires. If only a splendid pagoda is built, it will be to your honor and my joy. This is all I wanted to say today. . . . Jūbei, you've been crying? I am glad, very glad." A born Edoite polished and sharpened to the core, Genta was no more sparing in his benevolence than he was in his rage.

Jūbei, who had been listening immobile, fell to the floor speechless. "Master, forgive me," he said at last. "I can hardly speak. Only like this I thank you, Master." Incongruously, yet with heart and soul, he prostrated himself, weeping.

⟨22⟩

Though he was inarticulate, Jūbei's sincerity was more than evident. Genta was pleased. His countenance took on an air as genial as the spring breeze over the lake and the sun steaming the mist. His tone mellowed in easy amiability.

"Now that we have made peace with each other, there remains no ill feeling between us. It will please the Abbot, and both our faces have been saved, too. I feel so relieved. Jūbei, let's just enjoy ourselves drinking today."

Getting to his feet, Genta retrieved a bundle that he had earlier placed on the alcove shelf. He untied the wrapping to disclose two piles of documents and set them before Jūbei.

"These are of no more use to me. One pile is the detailed cost estimates of lumber supplies and wages for laborers and porters and such, which took me several nights to prepare. The other pile consists of carefully drawn draft plans, covering each elaborate detail from corner to corner. Some of them show the distribution of lintels or lanterns for air and light. Some are designs for the lowest roof, double brackets, and triple and single brackets alone. You will also find relief patterns of clouds, waves, flowers, animals, and the like. The rest includes even the instructions on how to draw lines with the ink string and how to apply measuring sticks on everything. Not a single detail from the difficult center pillar to the lattice panels over the doorway, under the window, above the floor, or carved out—none has been omitted. There are also plans for open gallery boards and pillars, turtle-shaped supports, balustrades, rafters, cornice supports, and even ratio calculations of braces and hip rafters. Among them are plans which are not of my own making but which have been handed down from my ancestors strictly for the family use —such as copies of temples in Kyoto and Nara. I'll entrust all of these to you. I hope they might be of some help."

Genta then handed over the papers bearing his own cherished dreams.

Jūbei did not fail to appreciate genuine maganimity, yet he was also a man of integrity, and as such he refused to benefit from another's resources. "I thank you deeply, Master, but I have already enjoyed your kindness to the full. Please take back these papers," he said, answering more curtly than he had intended.

"Do you mean to say that you don't need these?"

"No use borrowing . . ." Nossori let slip the careless remark, unaware of the anger Genta was suppressing beneath his quiet surface.

Genta was no longer able to contain himself. "Out of my utmost kindness, I am offering you the plans over which I have worked my brains to the limit. How rude of you to turn them down! How well endowed are you that you can snub the kind intentions of others? I was enraged when you first turned against me, but I tolerated you without squabbling. An average man would have been driven by rage to any length—'In spite of my past patronage, you've got the nerve to stick your hand into my work? Even beating would be too good for you!' he'd say. But I was genuinely fond of you, and that's why I never spoke a harsh word against you. Have you forgotten that already? After we were admonished by the Abbot, I racked my brains once again and took the trouble to come to you. When I made an offer of compromise purely for your sake, you refused to give up your own self-serving claim. It would have strained the patience of an exceptional man, but I tolerated you simply out of my truly kind regard. Can't you see that? Do you think that the Abbot awarded the work solely on the basis of your skill or integrity? Do you think it was pure luck? Are you afraid that I might demand your gratitude for these documents? Or are you already so conceited that you can dismiss my plans as altogether worthless? I wouldn't think of forcing them on you.

"You are incredibly tactless! It would have been sensible for you to accept these with thanks, to make use of a few plans, and to acknowledge their merit afterward. But without so much as examining the bundle, you spurn them sight unseen as if their worthlessness were a matter of record. How dare you reject them outright! Do you presume that your trade skill is superior to mine? Or that I would fail to soar far beyond the bounds of your meager imagination? You may consider my plans beneath your glance, but I have already measured your competence. I can visualize your mediocre pagoda even before you build it, and I can certainly see flaws in it. . . . I've reached the end of my patience. I won't resort to ignoble means of revenge, but I won't forgo a severe reprisal when the opportunity presents itself. I've tried my utmost to persuade you, but now that I've given up on you, I no longer care to speak to you. Just beware of my watchful eye lurking somewhere, for if it takes three years, or even ten, I'll wait silently for the day when I can pay you back in full."

The wills of these two men of such different temperament clashed once, twice, and finally for the third time beyond reconciliation.

"Jūbei-dono," Genta lowered his voice, abruptly shifting to an overly polite address. "I had better withdraw the rejected plans. I am sure you will build a fine pagoda by yourself, but I hope it will not fall apart in the first earthquake or storm."

The lightly delivered yet deeply scornful message irked Jūbei into driving in his wedge of confidence: "Even Nossori has a sense of honor."

"Well, that is quite a statement. I shall endeavor never to forget it." Genta hammered in his nail of warning, glowering fiercely. Presently he arose, saying, "Damn it!

How could it have slipped my mind? Jūbei-dono, please take your time and enjoy yourself. I have just remembered something urgent I must attend to." Genta left the room like a gust of wind, paid his bill on rough estimate, and hurried out of the restaurant. Instead of going straight home, he immediately proceeded to another establishment in the same district. Upon crossing the threshold, he shouted as if spitting his words out, "Insufferable! Mortifying! Trivial, useless, and ridiculous! Bring saké, and be quick about it. What's the use of fumbling with a candle now? Do you think I can eat that? You silly thing! How can I enjoy my saké with nothing but appetizers? Go fetch some geisha—Kokane, Harukichi, Fusa, Chōko—by force if necessary. Send a swift-footed young man to my house to tell Sei, Sen, Tetsu, Masa, and anybody else to come join me in a spree."

Impatiently tossing down one cup of saké after another, Genta hurled his vexation at the women as they entered the room. "Good evening? That's putting it mildly! Drink up. Keep fresh bottles coming and circulate the cup in a whirl. Fusa, don't play coy. And don't you put on airs, Haru, old girl. Well, Chōko, don't you have blood running in your veins at all? Look alive or I'll set off a firecracker right on your head. Now, sing up a storm! Hey, you sound pretty good, Kokane. Kick your leg up higher, Kaguri. Oh, Seikichi, you've come! Tetsu, you too? Good, wonderful, excellent! Make a racket by all means. I've got something to celebrate. To hell with formality!"

With the boss in such roaring spirits, the merry mood engulfed Sen and Masa, who arrived shortly, to plunge them into bacchanalian revelry. Should the ceiling blow open or the floor collapse, repairing was their very trade anyway, so they danced about freely and vociferated. Not quite so tenderly they sang "Itako Dejima," raised battle cries to a rustic jig, and tripped over their own feet dancing.

As Tetsu tapped drumbeats on the water bowl, Seikichi sprawled alongside Fusa to play percussion for "You Are Drinking Nothing but Vinegar" with her hair ornament. In the midst of this uproar, a solemn-looking Masa was groaning out the quaint tune of "Toward the North Lie Rugged Mountains" only a shade softer than a chanting lumberjack. Toward the end of all this turmoil, even betting games became so wicked that the losing women were stripped down to impromptu paper skirts. At that point Genta issued the order, "Now let's move on." Thereupon they pulled out together, who knows whither.

⟨23⟩

When a falcon is in flight, it never lets his eyes wander. If it is after a crane, for instance, it pursues nothing but the crane through the clouds and against the wind, not once resting until it sinks his sharp claws into the throat of its prey. Ever since Jūbei received the order, he dedicated his entire being to the pagoda project; at breakfast he ruminated on the pagoda, and in his dreams at night his soul circled the top of its nine-ringed spire. Once at work he completely forgot his wife and child, never remembered what he was the day before, nor wondered about tomorrow. He charged his axe with all his strength to cut wood, and he poured his heart into drawing each plan. His mortal body existed in the mundane world where dogs bark, birds sing, and Gombei's family celebrates while Mokuemon's mourns. Yet, his heart unfettered by trivial ties, he strove and endeavored as if his life depended on it. It was not that he was undisturbed about having incurred Genta's displeasure, but being Nossori, he soon dismissed the matter lightly, almost as if it concerned someone else entirely, until it slipped totally out of his mind. His concentration on the work at hand resembled the insensibility of an asinine old bull who would run in but a single straight path.

The five treasures consisted of gold, silver, lapis lazuli, pearl, and crystal. The five kinds of incense were cloves, aloeswood, ambergris, frankincense, and sandalwood. With the additional offerings of the five medicines and the five grains, the ground-breaking ceremony was held in honor of all the guardian gods, including the Great Earth God, the Mountain God, and the Mountain Goddess. The staking and the first digging proceeded without a hitch. The foundation stones enshrining the five planets were laid one after another, counterclockwise from the auspicious direction of the month. The Adze Initiation paid homage to seven gods: Amanoma Hitotsu, the original blacksmith; Teoki Ho'oi and Hikosachi, inaugurators of carpentry; Omoikane, Amatsukoyane, and Futodama, in charge of rituals; and Kukunochi, the god of trees. The Rite of the Immaculate Plane was duly performed next.

Finally, in the pillar-raising ceremony, the four corner pillars were planted with prayers for their eternal stability. Each symbolized one of the Four Guardian Kings: Jikokuten in the east, Kōmokuten in the west, Zōchōten in the south, and Bishamonten in the north. Everlasting protection was sought from the three star gods—Tensei, Shikisei, Tagan—as well as from the seven stars of the Great Dipper. Jūbei drove three temporary wedges into each pillar and had his assistant tighten them. Now that he had accomplished this much with painstaking care, he was so elated that even his soiled face glowed with joy. "The thick pillar as immutable as the rock of Shimotsu"—the words of the old poem recited at the ceremony somehow sounded profoundly joyful to his ears, and Jūbei broke into a smile as he sang the last refrain—"is a model by which man should establish himself in the world." He then offered his prayer at the altar and concluded the final purification ritual with the clear sounds of handclapping in supplication for the success of the project.

In contrast to the scene at the pagoda site, Genta's household was cheerless. The strong-willed master kept his inner thoughts to himself, but Okichi was, after all, a woman, small-minded no matter how sensible. Every time a visitor or a workman brought bits of news such as, "The groundbreaking for the pagoda began today," or "The pillar-raising rite was held yesterday," flames of jealousy and resentment flared up in her heart: "Jūbei, you ingrate! Taking advantage of my husband's generosity, you've cunningly made your way up in the world. If you have become a success, you still owe us a thanksgiving visit. So arrogant and triumphant, you've ignored us all these days. My husband may be too accommodating, but that Nossori is detestable beyond measure." Every now and then she flew into a fit of rage and snapped at everything and everyone. She scratched fretfully at stray tresses of her sidelocks and chased away mercilessly some beggars who happened to come asking for copper coins.

One day while Genta was out, a talkative medicine man called Dōeki paid one of his frequent visits. After much gossiping on various topics, he said half out of flattery, "The other day I went to Hōrai Restaurant with someone and heard everything from a woman called Den. How remarkable the Master is! I really think every man ought to emulate him." Okichi probed for more details. Angry as she had been at Jūbei when she did not really know the circumstances, her outrage doubled and tripled when she learned what had actually transpired.

⟨24⟩

"Seikichi, you are an unreliable, insensitive, spineless young man! Why didn't you tell me about the outcome of the other night? Were you trying to spare me the unpleasantness? How inconsiderate of you! Were you afraid I would make a scene if I learned the truth? My husband considers me a mere woman and keeps me ignorant of what is going on. Well, that's *his* attitude, but isn't it unkind of you boys to have no compunctions about keeping me deaf and blind? Knowing how the Master was feeling, moreover, you had the gall to get drunk and accompany him to brothels. Is that all a man is good for? Aren't you a bit soft-headed to drop by here today so nonchalant? I always offer you something to drink even when the Master is away, but today I refuse to fuss over you. I'm not even going to parch a piece of seaweed for you or keep you company in silly chitchat. If you want to drink, go to the kitchen and turn the tap of a saké barrel yourself. If you want to chat, you'd better find a cat or something for company."

Unfortunate enough to chance by immediately after Dōeki had left, an innocent Seikichi was subjected to the full force of Okichi's fury, for which he was utterly unprepared. Faltering and stammering, he inquired and soon learned the whole story, of which he himself had been ignorant until that moment. Now he, too, was seized by a searing hatred of Nossori.

Seikichi thought to himself, "Completely forgetting his moral indebtedness, Jūbei has behaved much too insolently toward the Boss, who means everything to me. How outrageous of him to step all over the Boss, an accommodating and benevolent man—almost to an excess! What should I do? There's such a difference in status between the Boss and Jūbei that for the Boss to fight him would be like throwing a diamond against a pebble. I can see why the Boss has been discreet enough to hold his temper all this while. How heartless! Why didn't he confide in me at least, if not in the others? He has a lot more to lose than Jūbei, but I've got absolutely nothing to lose. Damn it all, Nossori, do you think I'm going to let you get away with this?"

"Please forgive me, Ma'am, I didn't know," Seikichi said. "Now that I've found out, I won't sit here like a fool and be scolded. Please wait and see whether or not Seikichi is good only for following the Boss to a brothel. So long."

With a determined farewell, he banged open the front door and dashed out faster than the wind, neither putting on his sandals nor looking back. Suddenly anxious, Okichi called after him two and three times, but by the fourth time he was already out of sight.

⟨25⟩

The crack of the axe chopping wood; the swish of the plane shaving boards; clangs and taps as holes were chiseled and nails driven in—all resounded busily and cheerily. Woodchips flew like tree leaves in a gust, and sawdust danced like a snow flurry at the construction site in the Kannō Temple grounds on this fine, lively day. Smartly engaged in their work were men sporting dashing outfits—navy blue waistcoats fastened tightly at the neck, stylish trousers, and straw sandals. Here a shabbily-dressed old man with a soiled towel flung across his shoulders squatted in the sun, unhurriedly sharpening chisels; there a little boy was floundering about in search of some tools, while a day-laborer diligently sawed wood. Perspiring and panting, everyone was occupied in his labor.

The chief duly in command, Nossori made his rounds among them, issuing the orders and instructions that would turn the model in his mind into a tangible structure. "Cut this way. Chisel that way. Make this section just so and give that section so much incline." He showed them, by ink-strings and in words, how many inches a bulge should be or how many tenths of an inch a recess. He explained complex details by drawing lines on a board. He himself worked with the frantic alertness of a falcon and cormorant combined.

Jūbei was totally absorbed in illustrating a relief design for a young workman when Seikichi burst upon him, kicking up dust faster than a wild boar. His face flame-red and his eyes contorted in rage, the young man cried, "Damn you, Nossori! Go to hell!" At the moment Jūbei turned on his heel in astonishment, Seikichi brought down a razor-sharp adze set in a handle, with enough force to split a rock. An adze is as good as a sword in a carpenter's hand, and Jūbei saw it too late to dodge. His left ear was sliced off, and his shoulder was hacked. Realizing that he had failed to kill Jūbei with his first blow, Seikichi lunged again. Jūbei threw a nail box, hammer, inkwell, and metal measuring stick at Seikichi, but the unarmed man was unable to defend himself. Whirling around to flee, he stepped into a toolbox and drove a five-inch nail right through his foot and fell to the ground. Not missing this chance, Seikichi raised his adze. No sooner had its blade reflected the setting sun to flash an artificial streak of lightning than there arose a tiger's roar from behind.

"You fool!" bellowed a man as he tripped up Seikichi's unstable legs with an easy sweep of a twelve-foot board.

All the more agitated, Seikichi tried to get up.

"It's me! Control yourself, you fool!" the man thundered again, seizing Seikichi by the neck and wresting the adze away. Then down he thrust his face as fierce as the deity Fudō's with its huge glaring eyes, tight straight mouth, angular nose, and swirling frizzled hair.

"Oh, it's you, Master Fireball. I've got a just cause. Please stand aside." Seikichi struggled and squirmed, trying to shake himself loose with all his might, but the man continued to subdue him with his conch-shell fist.

"Wiggle too much and I'll beat you to death. Fool!"

"You're not being fair. Let go!"

"Fool! Take that!"

"You don't understand. I can't let him live."

"You stupid boy. Are you going to cry now? Calm down, or I'll slug you again."

"Master, don't be so cruel."

"Shut up. Take that! I'll beat you to death yet."

"You're not being——Master!"

"Fool! Here, take this!"

"Master!"

"Fool!"

"Let me go!"

"Fool!"

"Mast——"

"Fool!"

"Let me——"

"Fool!"

"Mas——"

"Fool! Fool! Fool! Didn't I tell you? Good, you've calmed down. Now come along to my house. . . . What's this? Hey, this fellow has fainted. What a weakling! Boys, come over here. At the crucial moment you all run away. What good is it now to surround Jūbei like ants? You fools! Here I am about to have a corpse on my hands. Quick, fetch some water and pour it over him. . . . What are you picking up the ear for? What fools! You brought some water? Okay, pour the whole pailful over his face. It doesn't take much to revive this sort of fellow. Good! Seikichi, pull yourself together. What a baby. I'll have to carry you home on my back. Jubei's shoulder wound isn't serious, is it? Let me see. It doesn't look too bad. So long!"

⟨26⟩

"Is Genta home?" asked Eiji, entering the house.

"Oh, Master, please come right in," Okichi greeted him, quickly rising.

Eiji settled down in front of the brazier and drank the

cherry tea offered to him. Presently, he looked Okichi in the face and said, "You look rather pale. What happened? Isn't Genta home? I suppose you've already heard, but Seikichi has done a stupid thing. I've come to have a talk with Genta about it.... What? Oh, is that so? He's already gone to Jūbei's place? Well, well. That's Genta all right; he moves faster than I can think. Okichi, there's no need for you to worry. Genta is merely expected to bow his head a few times to Jūbei and the Abbot, apologizing that one of his men has done wrong and that he begs their forgiveness for his lack of supervision. If the other party should keep grumbling, then Genta can take up the fight himself and carry it to a finish. Judging from rumors, Jūbei might have deserved having an ear or two cut off, and Seikichi's antics may have been fitting.

"The poor boy; he's smarting from the taste of my fist all right, but his tears flow more from remorse than from physical pain. I suppose he came to his senses when I asked him what would have happened if he had succeeded in killing Jūbei. He's been crying, 'Oh, how wrong I was! I've made a reckless mistake. I've caused the Boss to bow his head. I'm sorry, so sorry.' Poor fellow. Isn't he lovable? Genta will no doubt reprimand him harshly and even tell him to apologize to Jūbei. That's socially demanded of him and there is no way out of it; but here's something you can do for Seikichi. Why don't you . . . ah . . . for him . . . you know. All right? Things like this must be quite clear to Madame Okichi, married to a man like Genta. Isn't that so? Well, with Genta away, there's no need for me to linger. I'll take a rain check on your dinner invitation. If you need me, come over any time."

The more Okichi thought the more repentant she felt. "Just like a silly woman, I spoke spitefully to Seikichi. The poor rash youth has now made his world tighter by getting into such trouble, and I've put my beloved husband in the humiliating position of having to apologize to that insufferable Nossori. The accident was caused by a slip of my own tongue as much as anything. What should I do now?" She pondered on and on, so lost in thought that her elbow slipped off the edge of the brazier. She arrived at a decision abruptly. "That's it," she murmured, rising to open a large bureau drawer, from which she took out a sash scented with musk.

"This is my most treasured sash. I wore it when I first came to this house as a bride, so happy, shy, and frightened. And I'll part with this Hakata sash and this satin sash, for which I begged my husband so earnestly. Ah, how innocent are the memories of the past that cling to this three-piece set, but its striped shantung takes too much care. I shall also let this kite-yellow silk kimono fly out of my hand. Although my mind is as confused as the pattern of this favorite paisley kimono, my love for my husband knows only one straight course. I have cherished this figured-satin sash as a keepsake of my aunt who once served a lord, but I am no longer reluctant to part with it."

She emptied the drawers and had a maidservant wrap up all her possessions. Anxious to leave before her husband came home, she gathered even combs and hair ornaments into a small box. What a pity! She took them to a pawnshop and then proceeded to Eiji's house, unmindful of the dark night.

⟨27⟩

Genta's frame of mind had taken a complete turn after the incident at the restaurant. Jūbei, whom he had at first patronized, now only grated on his nerves. How vexing it was for him to be forced to apologize to Jūbei with his head bowed and his hands on the floor! Nevertheless, should he fail to do so, he might be suspected of having incited Seikichi to commit violence. Genta fumed, "How mortifying to be unjustly accused of a crime! It's the devil's own luck that I have to suffer this humiliation on account of Seikichi's absurd action." But he knew that the matter could never be settled without his performing the role expected of him. Resigning himself to the inevitable, he paid a reluctant visit to Jūbei, expressed his sympathy for his injury, and apologized for his insufficient supervision of Seikichi.

Jūbei was wordless, as usual. But Onami, out of feminine meekness, said, "Fortunately, the shoulder wound is not too serious, so you need not worry yourself about it. We are overwhelmed by your kindness in coming personally to inquire after our condition." Although she was sociable enough to speak, sharp edges lurked beneath her unduly formal words.

It was obvious to Genta that she suspected him of having secretly ordered Seikichi to carry out his revenge. "How maddening," he thought. "Jūbei probably feels the same way. May the time come soon when I can show him what revenge is! Cutting off an ear may be good enough for a petty fellow like Seikichi, but I would never let my wrath burn up as readily as a woodchip. Today's mishap is today's mishap, and my temper is my temper, absolutely separate and apart. I'll show my way when I am good and ready, not before."

Without betraying his chagrin, he performed his social duties and proceeded to the temple, where he apologized to the Abbot for the misconduct of his man. After he got home he decided to call on Eiji to get a first-hand account of the incident and to thank him for restraining Seikichi. At the same time he intended to reprimand Seikichi severely and warn him never to set foot in his house again. As he was about to start out, he noticed Okichi's absence. "Well, she said she would be out for a few minutes," said the maid, feigning ignorance. Unaware that Okichi had instructed the maid to so answer, Genta said, "Very well. When you see the mistress, tell her that I'll be at Eiji's house."

Genta had just slipped on his sandals and crossed his threshold when he spotted a woman coming toward his house. With a paper lantern full of burn marks in one hand and a bamboo cane in the other, she was hobbling toward him, bent nearly at a right angle with age.

"You must be Seikichi's mother."

"Ah, it's you, Master."

⟨28⟩

"It's fortunate that I've caught you in time. Are you on your way out?" the old woman asked anxiously.

"That's all right," said Genta, nodding slightly. "Feel free to come right in. You must have some urgent business to be calling at this hour. I'll make time for you."

"Thank you ever so much. I'm sorry to hold you up, but begging your pardon then. . . ." She followed Genta through the latticed door.

"It's brave of you to come out in this cold. Unfortunately, my wife is not at home, and I can't offer you anything. But no need to huddle in the corner. Come over to the brazier and warm yourself."

"I'm overwhelmed by your kindness, but the portable warmer I'm carrying is quite enough for me." Her body seemed to tighten and shrink even more at Genta's considerate invitation. Wiping her nose on the sleeve of her old half coat, she backed up all the way to the doorway and squatted down, appearing anxious to speak.

The sensitive Genta felt sorry for her. Here he had been about to go to Eiji's in order to give Seikichi a tongue-lashing, but now he saw before him an old, feeble woman who had not a single close soul except Amida Buddha and her own son. He thought, "If I should forsake Seikichi now, she would feel as helpless as a bow with a torn string. With no hope or purpose left in her weary life, she would grieve and lament for the rest of her cheerless days, soaking in the tears of regret." The more Genta thought, the sorrier he felt. He was fumbling with some tobacco when the old woman edged up a bit closer.

"I'm very sorry for calling on you at this hour, but I have something to ask you. . . . That's right. You must know by now, but I hear my Seikichi has done a terrible thing. I heard most of the story from Master Tetsu. Seikichi has always been so quick-tempered. He gives me constant worry, always making remarks like 'I'll beat him,' or 'I'll slash him.' Owing to your kindness, he's now a full-fledged carpenter, but he's still naïve and headstrong. He would never commit an evil or a dishonest act, but he loses his head when he's excited. . . . That's right, he's a boy without an evil bone in him. . . . Oh, you already know that? Well, I thank you kindly, Master. I have no idea what caused this fight, but it seems that he went swinging an adze or something just as dangerous. When I heard that, I felt as if I myself had been slashed. They say that the chief of the M crew held him down. Thank heaven for that. If the injured person should die, that would make Seikichi a murderer! Heaven forbid I should lose him. I have nothing else to live for.

"The gods only know how distressed I was by his extreme peevishness as a small child, until he was cured by the grace of the goddess Kishimojin of Nakayama. I had vowed that if he was cured, I would take him to the temple grounds before he turned seven years old. But for some reason or other, I failed to have him pay that thanksgiving visit. Perhaps it is a divine retribution for my broken vow that he is so reckless, though quite healthy now. I was so upset when Master Tetsu told me what happened today. It almost broke my heart to hear that he'd even had a weapon ready. It was reassuring to know that Chief Eiji took him under his care, but when I asked if Seikichi wasn't wounded, Master Tetsu only said that he's all right and not to worry. His evasiveness made me worry all the more. He also said that he didn't think it would be a good idea for me to go to Chief Eiji's now, but that I should see you instead. After he left, my heart ached so much that I could neither sit nor stand any longer, so I asked the umbrella maker who lives next door to me to keep an eye on my house while I came over here.

"Could you tell me how to get to Chief Eiji's house—I intend to go there immediately. I wonder what state *he's* in; he may be seriously injured himself. If possible, I'd like to know about the circumstances behind the fight, too. I'm quite certain my son would never commit an evil act, but young as he is, he might have taken a misdirected revenge. If so, I would apologize to Master Jūbei with my life. I am an old woman whose life is no longer dear, and I must make sure that no one will bear a grudge against Seikichi, who has a long life ahead of him."

Genta was at a loss how to answer the tearful rambling of this old woman, who was ignorant of the circumstances, but deeply concerned over her son.

⟨29⟩

"Hachigorō, are you there? Someone's at the door," said Eiji.

"Strange. It seems to be a woman," muttered Hachigorō, opening the door. "Calling at this time of night on a man who's got no interest in womanizing. Anyway, come in."

"Sorry for the trouble, Hachi-san," said the visitor casually. As she extinguished her lantern and proceeded to take off her headcover, Hachigorō was amazed to recognize Okichi. He remembered that she had tipped him generously at the last Bon Festival and the New Year.

"Boss, this is . . . well . . . you know . . . ," announced Hachigorō hastily, trying to hide the discolored underwear that was peeking through the front opening of his quilted coat. For an Edoite, the broken phrases conveyed quite sufficient information.

"Well, well. Welcome to my house, Okichi. Please sit down over there where it looks least dusty. Watch out, though—the cockroaches may crawl toward you. It can't be helped in an all-male household where dirt is the only decoration. If and when I marry a nice woman like you, she'll clean up the place," laughed Eiji.

"Well, even then, you'll probably keep saying, 'It's so dirty,' just to irk her," retorted Okichi, also laughing.

After exchanging a bit of small talk, Okichi turned serious. "Is Seikichi sleeping? I was worried, so I've come to see how he's doing."

"Sei has just fallen asleep and is not likely to wake up for some time. It's not that he has a wound or his skull is cracked. According to the bone-setter, he fainted from over-agitation and the shock of severe beating. It's nothing serious, so you may take a look if you wish."

Okichi followed Eiji and found Seikichi fast asleep in a small three-mat room. His face and head were swollen so pitifully that she almost resented Eiji's relentless beating, but there was nothing she could do about it. She returned to her seat and faced Eiji.

"No doubt my husband is enraged by Seikichi's senseless attack, and as a matter of obligation to the Abbot and Jūbei, he will either reprimand him or remove him from his employ. But Seikichi was not driven by his own personal grudge. No, it was on our behalf that he acted out his animosity, misplaced and unreasonable though it was. I cannot, therefore, sit idly by and watch what my husband will do to him. Besides, there is a certain specific reason why I must do everything within my power to help him.

After considering the matter carefully, I have decided to send Seikichi out of Edo for a year or so. When people stop talking of the incident and my husband's ire has abated, there will be any number of ways to intercede in his behalf. I will entrust to you the money I have made ready for his trip. Please give it to him and explain the arrangement as you see fit. As you know, my husband is a forthright man. Whatever he may feel in his heart, he will make no allowance in punishing Seikichi. He will refuse to listen, no matter what the young man may have to say for himself. My intercession cannot change the rules of social obligation, which must be observed. Nevertheless, when a man is about to be made an outcast for an action which was not motivated by self-interest, I must do something about it. I can make sure that my husband looks after Seikichi's poor mother, as long as Seikichi stays out of town. But about my coming here and helping the youth behind his back, please keep it from my husband for at least for a while longer."

"I understand. Remarkable! That's all, isn't it? Go home, go home. Genta may come here any minute. You shouldn't bump into him now."

Reassured by Eiji's blunt but considerate advice, she entrusted the matter to him and went home. Just missing her, Genta next appeared to pronounce, as predicted, that Seikichi was to be forbidden access to his house and that he had severed the tie of master and disciple. Eiji smiled silently, while Seikichi apologized in tears.

After Genta's visit that night, Seikichi wept again listening to Eiji. He vowed, "Even if I must turn into a dog, I shall never forgo my ties with Master and Madame!" A few days later he departed from Edo. Hachigorō accompanied him as far as the Hakone hot springs. From there, Seikichi was to follow the Tōkaidō road toward Kyoto and Osaka, but no doubt leaving his heart behind in Edo.

⟨30⟩

The morning after he was attacked, Jūbei arose just as early as usual. Alarmed, Onami hastened to stop him. "Good heavens! What are you doing? Why don't you stay in bed and take it easy? The morning wind is especially cold today. What if you should contract tetanus? The water will soon be boiling, and I'll help you wash up in bed," she said anxiously as she started a fire under the chipped pot that hung over the broken kitchen stove.

"There's no need to treat me like a sick man," laughed Jūbei, unperturbed. "If you just wring the towel for me, I'll feel better to wash by myself." He poured water into a leaky pail and went about his morning routine with hardly a sign of distress. Unmindful of his wife's dismay and anxiety, he finished breakfast and stood up.

As he shrugged off his robe and tried to change into his workman's pants and waistcoat, Onami gasped, "Heaven forbid! Where are you going? However important your work may be, the wound couldn't possibly have healed in one night, nor could the pain have diminished. Even the doctor said to lie still and not to move. He thinks you'll be all right, he said, but until the wound closes, caution should be your utmost concern. Do you mean to go against the doctor's orders? You're too headstrong for your own good. Even if you get to the site, you won't be able to do any physical work. Who would blame you for staying home today? If you still feel obligated to go, I'll run over to see the Abbot and personally request three or four days' leave for you. There's no reason why the merciful Abbot wouldn't grant your request. He'd surely tell you to take care of yourself and not to act imprudently. No, please put these clothes back on and stay still in the house, at least until the wound is closed."

She tried her best to stop him, placating and soothing him. When she picked up the kimono he had just taken off and tried to put it back on him, he brushed it aside with his able right arm.

"I don't need that! If you want to be useful, help me into my waistcoat."

"Now, now. Don't say that. Please stay home."

She draped the discarded kimono over his shoulders, but he flung it away again. Man is a creature of pride, while woman is a creature of sentiment; no amount of bickering could bring them to terms.

At last Jūbei grew a little angry. "What an annoying, ignorant female! How dare you stand in my way! All right, I won't ask for your help. I'll get dressed by myself. How could I keep command of my men if I took time off from work because of such a slight scratch? You probably have no idea, but because I've always been regarded as a simpleton, the workmen have little respect for me. In my presence they pretend to follow my orders, but behind my back they neglect their work, speak against me, and make fun of me. Even though they assume a respectful attitude on the surface, not a single one among them works for me with the sincere intention of doing a good job. You don't know how miserable that makes me feel! When I tell them to warm up to their work and put in real effort instead of merely making a show of it, they bow their heads only to hide their sneers. If I rebuke them, they apologize in words but show defiance in their eyes. If I swallow my pride and ask them humbly, they grow presumptuous enough to take advantage of me. It's vexing, disheartening. It may sound grand to be addressed 'Boss' and 'Master' by so many people day after day, but I'm in constant agony, so much so that I think I'd be far better off employed by someone else even as a ditch digger.

"Against such odds, I've carried the work up to this point. If I took a day off now, it would bring on a major setback. The men would start neglecting their work openly, excusing themselves for leaving early because of a chest pain, or for being late on account of a headache. If I myself take days off, I won't be able to utter a word of reproach. Our progress would slow down to the sporadic pace of dripping rainwater, and my project would fail when it could be done well. If I should fail in this job, how could I ever face the Abbot and Master Genta? You see, if I can't complete the pagoda, I will be nothing, a living corpse. On the other hand, even if building the pagoda should cost me my life, I would live forever in my work. Can I stay in bed with an adze wound only a couple of inches long? Which should I fear more, tetanus or failure? Had I lost my entire arm, I would still not miss a day of work. I would get to the site every day until the pagoda is finished if I had to be carried in a palanquin or by any other means. All the more so with such a trifling scratch!"

Jūbei tried to put his left arm in the waistcoat which he had snatched from Onami's hand, but pain made him grimace. Onami was no longer able to protest. Carefully shielding his wound, she helped her husband squeeze into a short coat and workman's pants, and saw him off to work against her better judgment.

Meanwhile, taking it for granted that Jūbei would not come to work, the workmen began to straggle in around ten o'clock. But as soon as their astonished eyes alighted on Jūbei, they were told, "I'm very pleased that you are so conscientious in coming to work today." Jūbei's greeting made each one break into a cold sweat. From that day on, they all became assiduous in their work, and their attitude took a complete turn. They accomplished three times more than was expected of them and moved twice as eagerly. Nossori gained numerous other hands after losing the use of one arm, and his work made remarkable progress. By the time his shoulder wound healed, the pagoda was nearly finished.

⟨31⟩

Toward the end of the first month it was obvious that the painstaking work of Nossori Jūbei had not been in vain. The magnificent Shōun, that is, Cloud-Bearing, Pagoda of Kannō, or Divine Response, Temple was no longer a mere vision. As the scaffolding was removed, there gradually emerged a pagoda, five stories in all, towering majestically into heaven—a Deva King manifested in a hundred-sixty-foot figure erect on top of a rock, glaring at the host of devils and stamping his feet as if to shake the earth's axis.

"Splendid!"
"What superb workmanship!"
"Phenomenal!"
"Unprecedented!"
"There couldn't be another pagoda like this in the world!"

Forgetting how they had at first slighted Nossori, everyone from Tame'emon down to the gatekeeper praised and admired the pagoda. Endō and the monks of the temple all but danced in joy.

"This is a pagoda truly worthy of Kannō Temple. How wonderful! We are blessed with a mentor unsurpassed in our time; among the great priests of all the sects, old and new, competing in their virtue like tigers, leopards, cranes, and herons, Abbot Rōen is pre-eminent—a veritable King Lion or King Peacock. Now we have the most outstanding pagoda as well. In all of Edo, even in the temple grounds at Shiba and Asakusa, there is none to rival this one. By the grace of his virtue, our noble Abbot discovered a man who was otherwise destined to end his life without ever showing his glittering talent to the world. How worthy of Jūbei to have accomplished the work against all odds, as a way of repaying such noble patronage! It is a curious karma, an exquisite karma, so fascinating and heartwarming. Was it Heaven's doing, or man's? Or did the good gods of all the heavens secretly steer the course? Granted, there is the legend of Tanika, the virtuous Indian, who was skilled in the art of building; yet never have we heard of such a thrilling incident in China, or even in India during the Buddha's lifetime."

Thus the monks expressed their heartfelt emotions and went on to make commendable pledges, not motivated by their usual self-interest:

"At the dedication ceremony, I shall write Buddhist verses and tales."

"I shall compose poems and songs."

"Let us praise, extol, poetize, and record the occasion."

In contrast to the laudations of men, the will of heaven was difficult to fathom. Through the joint efforts of Endō and Tame'emon, a tentative date had been set for a grand dedication ceremony. On that day, people from the noblest down to the most humble would be allowed to view the pagoda, the surplus funds would be distributed among the poor, and Jūbei and his men would receive commendations and rewards. In addition, solemn court music was to be performed and a religious service held in honor of this rare and precious pagoda. While everyone was busy with the preparation, though, the peal of the midnight bells sounded uncommonly muffled. That was only the beginning. Gradually a strange wind began to rise. The air turned so unseasonably warm that sleeping children kicked off their bedcovers. At the same time, the rattle of shutters grew more and more violent, and through the jostling treetops in the dark, the King Demon roared out fiercely:

"Rob these human hearts of peace! Rip out the livers of vainglorious men! Awaken them from sleep! Let waves of blood surge and heave in the fools' breasts. Drain the color from the ruddy faces of hypocrites. Swing your axes! Wield your spears! Now is the time to feed the hungry swords in your hands. Man's lifeblood is a fine food; let your swords drink it to the full. Let them feed on it to the last drop!"

No sooner had the King Demon issued his unsparing command than a ferocious wind started up; the horde of demons with axes, spears, and hungry swords broke into a violent rampage.

⟨32⟩

Startled up from their dreams, the Edo residents—young and old, men and women—all were thrown into a panic. "Evil winds have come up. Latch and support the storm doors!" As distraught families floundered and bustled about in every house, the exalted King Demon bellowed:

"Demons, be not shy of humans; cause them to fear you. They have slighted us and held us in contempt too long; they have neglected to make us the offerings ordained by the Law. Dogs that walk instead of crawl, birds that make nests of extravagance and roosts of arrogance, monkeys without tails, snakes that speak, sons of the fox devoid of sincerity, female swine with no sense of shame—how long can we tolerate their contempt? How long shall we let them glory in their effrontery? The decreed endurance of sixty-four years has expired; with my powers I have broken the iron chain of destiny that has restrained us and have demolished the Cave of Mercy and Forbearance that has confined us. Rage, you demons, rage now or never! Retaliate now, once and for all!

"Fling the stench of human arrogance out of the Three Thousand Worlds. Force their heads to the ground. Test your merciless axes on their chests. Turn them into muck on your atrocious spears and wrathful swords. Thrust ice down their throats—make them shudder from fear and cold. Drive needles through their livers to cause mysterious pains. Destroy the offspring of their profligacy right before their eyes and drown their material idolatry in the ashen river of grief. They have stolen the homes of silkworms; now deprive them of their own homes. They mocked the ingenuity of the silkworm; now you acclaim their own cleverness. Applaud the schemes that they thought were shrewd; praise the hearts that they thought were great; extol the emotions that they thought were noble; eulogize the truth that they thought was attained; and admire the power that they thought was mighty. All humans are meat for our axes, fodder for our swords, and food for our spears; fatten them with compliments before feeding them to our weapons and mock them for having prepared such an excellent meal for us. Sport with them as long as you can—then torture them to death. Skin them alive one by one; peel off their flesh; make balls of their hearts to kick around; beat their backs with thorny orange branches; deprive them of the breath for sighs, the fluid for tears, the throb of blood for heartbeat, and the voice for screams—wrest them all from the humans! There is no pleasure surpassing brutality. Fail to behave violently and you will perish instantly. Raise a storm! Rampage ruthlessly! Fight against gods and strike the Buddhas! When we have smashed Reason to pieces, the world will be ours!"

Stones and sand whirled up at his every command. From two o'clock in the morning to four, six, and even eight in the evening, the King Demon carried on without a pause, arousing thousands of his kinsmen. Those crossing the water stirred up waves, and those running over land kicked up sands. Heaven and earth turned yellow with dust until even the sun was obscured. Some swung axes, sneering as they felled pinetrees carefully trimmed by men of taste. Some let spears dance swiftly to bore holes into wooden roofs. Others rocked well-built houses and bridges with their superhuman strength.

"Not enough! You are not savage enough! Come, follow me!"

The King Demon leaped to his feet, gnashing his fangs in rage and frustration. His kinsmen filling the sky raised sharp battle cries and furiously played havoc. The trees standing in the temple and shrine grounds and in rich men's gardens all groaned and shrieked. Soon the earth's hair stood on end in fear, willows sprawled, bamboo stalks cracked. Black clouds came streaming across the sky, and raindrops larger than acorns began to pelt down. All the more encouraged, the demons redoubled their unbridled destruction. Plucking up fences, knocking down walls, collapsing gates, peeling roofs, shattering the roof slates under their feet, blowing away a trashman's hut with one gust, twisting off an upper story in two whirls, and demolishing a temple after three blasts, they raised thunderous cheers of victory. They delighted in the comical sight of humans alarmed by their every cry; they rejoiced to hear men and women bewailing the loss of their homes. As the demons continued to commit every violent act imaginable, the faces of one million people in all eight hundred eight blocks of Edo turned ashen in terror.

The most alarmed among them were Tame'emon and Endō. The precious pagoda, barely completed, was being assaulted from all sides. The nine-ringed spire was swaying, its jewel top writing unintelligible scripts in the sky. The pagoda bowed and arched under the onslaught of the rock-rolling wind and the shield-piercing rain. The creaking of wood . . . the pagoda regaining its erect posture . . . arching again . . . more screech . . . leaning as if about to topple . . .

"Good heavens! Can't anything be done? What if it should collapse? Isn't there a way to support it? With the rain adding forces to the wind, there's no hope for such a tall structure to survive this unprecedented tempest! When even the main hall is shaking this much, imagine the perilous state of the pagoda perched on its narrow foundation without so much as a tree to shield it. Wouldn't magic incantation stop the wind? Genta is supposed to inquire after our safety in such a frightful storm. Hasn't he come yet? Jūbei is obligated to come, too. While even we are worried to death like this, isn't he concerned about the pagoda he built himself? Look out! There it goes, bending again. Someone, go fetch Jūbei!"

No one was willing to venture out into the street, where roof slates and wall boards were sailing through the air and pebbles dancing about. Finally, with the promise of an exceedingly generous reward, they dispatched Shichizō, an old janitor.

⟨33⟩

In addition to the quilted hood covering his head, Shichizō fortified himself with a bamboo hat to keep off the rain. Securing his workman's raincoat, he nervously ventured out into the storm, gripping a sturdy cane. He narrowly made his way to Jūbei's shack, which he found in a pitiful state. Half the roof had already been torn away by the wind; the parents and child were huddled wretchedly in a corner with an old straw mat barely able to ward off the rain that poured down from the ceiling.

Shichizō was all but shocked by Nossori's resourcelessness. "Master Jūbei, how can you be so unconcerned about the pagoda? Outside it's like a battlefield. Roof tiles are flying and trees are uprooted everywhere. Don't you wonder how your pagoda is? So tall with nothing to protect it and on a narrow foundation, it's being blasted by winds from all sides. And how it's swaying and teetering! Arching like a flagpole, creaking, crackling—it's dreadful. Reverend Endō and the Manager Tame'emon are frightened out of their wits. They are worried it may split asunder any minute. It's your duty to run over in case of such a natural disaster, even before you're sent for. Aren't you being rather nonchalant? On account of you I had to risk my life on this dangerous errand. My hat was blown away, I got soaking wet, and to top it all off, a piece of wood came hurtling against my forehead! Look at this cursed bump! I must look dreadful. Now, please come with me right this minute. Tame'emon-dono and Reverend Endō ordered me to bring you. Goodness! What was that? Your storm doors are gone! What a start that blasted noise gave me! How could the pagoda possibly be standing at this rate? Even now while we're talking, it may be toppling or breaking in half! Hurry and get ready, hurry, hurry!"

"If you're going out into the street," offered Onami, anxiously, "I'll get you a firefighter's hood. It's very old, but I want you to put it on. You can't tell what might come flying at you, and your safety matters more than appearance. Please wear the fireman's coat, too, shabby as it is."

Jūbei watched with exasperation as Onami rattled open an ill-fitting closet door. "Why make a fuss? I'm not going anywhere. Just because a little wind has kicked up, there's no reason to panic. Shichizō-dono, I am sorry you had to come over, but my pagoda will not topple. It's not a fragile thing that could fall apart in such a trifling storm. So there is no need for me to go with you. Please tell Endō-dono and Tame'emon-dono that I said so. The pagoda will be perfectly safe," he said calmly, not even budging.

"Come anyway," said Shichizō, somewhat vexed. "Come see for yourself how the pagoda is quaking and creaking. It's only because you can't see it from here that you are talking like that. Just one look at your pagoda fluttering like a banner at a temple festival, and even you will go out of your mind. There's no point in being brave in private. Now, come with me! Oh, here it blows again. Ah, so frightening! This wind isn't going to let up. Reverend Endō and Tame'emon-dono must be getting impatient. Put on a hood, a coat, or whatever, and come on."

"It's all right. Please stop worrying and just go back."

"It's not all that easy not to worry."

"Everything will be fine."

The two of them continued to repeat themselves. In the end, Shichizō became irritated. "I'm telling you to come! And don't think that it's merely my words. It's the order from Reverend Endō and Tame'emon-dono."

"I was not ordered by either of them to build the pagoda," retorted Jūbei, also changing his tone. "I don't think the Abbot would send for me just because a wind was blowing. He wouldn't be so untrusting. Should the Abbot himself say, 'The pagoda is in danger. Send for Jūbei,' then it would be my crucial moment, a matter of life and death. I would run over, wholly prepared to accept Heaven's will. As long as the Abbot utters no word of doubt about my craftsmanship, there's no cause for fear. Whatever others may say, I can rest easy now just as on a fine day, for I didn't build the pagoda with paper or by way of magic or shortcut. I'm not afraid of a storm or an earthquake. Please tell that to Endō-dono."

With Jūbei's brusque and adamant words, Shichizō gave up and ran back to the temple.

When he made his report to Endō and Tame'emon, he was roundly rebuked: "What a dull-witted fellow you are! Why didn't you say right then and there that the Abbot was summoning him? Look how the pagoda is lurching. You must have been infected by Nossori the Dimwit to be so witless yourself. Go back and tell him that the Abbot is sending for him. Trick him into coming!"

Mumbling indignantly to himself, Shichizō braved the storm once again.

〈34〉

"Now, Jūbei, you must come this time. I won't take no for an answer. It's the Abbot's summons," Shichizō shouted excitedly from the doorway.

Jūbei rose to his feet. "What? The Abbot's summons? Shichizō-dono, is it true?"

"Oh, what a shame!" Jūbei thought. "However strong the wind may be, does the Abbot fear that what I built with all my heart might prove less than perfect? How regrettable! I believed in the Abbot, whom I thought to be the only living god or Buddha in this world watching over me with compassion. But even he didn't fully trust my skill. What an unreliable world! I have nothing left to live for. I happened to be discovered by a man of incomparable wisdom and I rejoiced, believing it the greatest honor of my life. But it turned out to have been a passing dream indeed. That he should fear the pagoda I built to the best of my ability might be toppled by a bit of stormy wind! How vexing! I want to cry. Do I really seem like a man without pride or honor? Do I appear to be one who would continue living shamelessly after his work had been disgraced? If the pagoda should topple, how could I allow myself to live; how would I even want to live? How, infuriating! Onami, am I so sordid? I don't want to live any more. I am sick of my body, too. Now that the world has turned against me, the longer I linger, the more shame and agony I'll suffer. Let the pagoda collapse, and the storm grow more severe! Since the wind blowing across the sky and the rain beating down on the ground are not as cruel to me as my fellow humans are, I wouldn't resent . . . no, I would be even happy to see my pagoda destroyed by Nature's forces.

"Should a single board peel off or a single nail come loose, I would kill myself with no regret over quitting this miserable life. At least after I'm gone, people would pray for me, saying, 'The witless fellow called Jūbei was not an honorless man who kept on living merely for the love of life despite the disgrace of professional failure. He has proved himself a better man than we thought.' This is as good a time and place as any for giving up my life, which is destined to end eventually. I hate to desecrate the holy temple grounds with the taint of death, but how could I take even one step away from my pagoda if it should prove defective? All the Buddhas and bodhisattvas, please forgive me. I am ready to cast myself down from the top of Shōun Pagoda when the moment comes. This five-foot sack of flesh may be unsightly when crushed, but it holds nothing sordid inside. Out of my steadfast belief, I am going to spill my immaculate blood. Please look upon me with pity."

Whether such thoughts crossed Jūbei's conscious mind or not, he himself was not clearly aware. Following the familiar streets as if in a dream and separating from Shichizō on the way, Jūbei arrived at the pagoda.

Climbing to the fifth floor, he opened the door and leaned out. The violent raindrops pelted him like missiles, making it impossible for him to keep his eyes open. The fierce wind assaulted him as if to tear off his remaining ear and snatch his breath away. Although he recoiled instinctively at first, he fought his way out onto the veranda. Gripping the banister, he stood erect, glowering up to heaven. The sky was blacker than the darkness of the fifth month, and only the roaring wind clamorously filled the space. Solidly built but soaring so far into the void, the pagoda swayed and shook with every blast of wind, precarious as an open boat tossing on the rough waves. Jūbei was forced to confirm his grave resolve once again. At this ultimate crisis, the moment of life or death, he stood clenching his teeth, his eyes bulging wide-open and his hair bristling. With a six-inch chisel in his steady grip, he patiently awaited heaven's judgment.

Meanwhile, whether or not he was aware of Jūbei's presence above, a strange figure was circling round and round the pagoda in the wind and rain.

⟨35⟩

"This storm was the most fearsome of our lifetime." Even old folks usually given to downplaying anything new by bringing up some time-worn example broke their habit for once as they talked in awe about the storm. Lighthearted young men, ready to make fun of even disasters and strange occurrences, all the more indiscreetly and irresponsibly relished the gossip of other people's sorrows and misfortunes, such as the destruction of a certain fire watchtower or the crumbling of someone's house.

"That greedy so-and-so who put up money for his theater must have suffered a great loss. Didn't he deserve it, though! It was funny the way the whole thing caved right in!"

"And the upper floor of the house of that saucy woman who teaches flower arrangement. Granted it was a later addition, but served her right to lose it, too."

"More than that, there was a reason why one of the greatest temples in Edo fell apart so easily, you know. It's said that after they collected a large sum of money from their parishioners, the monks in charge secretly embezzled part of the funds and the builder cut corners. Even the thick column of the main hall was probably hollow inside."

And so on and so forth. Everyone, however, was utterly impressed by Shōun Pagoda of Kannō Temple, which lost not a single board or nail.

"That Jūbei is a great builder, isn't he? They say that he was resolved to die if the pagoda toppled. With a chisel in his mouth, ready to plunge a hundred and sixty feet, he was standing atop the banister like this, glaring at the wind and rain, so cool and collected in such a frightful storm. Even that determination of his alone must have protected the pagoda. The god of wind himself must have flinched before Jūbei's indomitable glare."

"He's the most expert craftsman since the reknowned master Jingorō. The pagodas at Asakusa and Shiba temples both suffered some damage, but Jūbei's did not shift out of place one-tenth of an inch. How well he has done!"

"And there's more to that story. Jūbei's master is said to be awfully great, too. I understand that he was circling around the pagoda in that torrential rain. Had he found even the slightest defect, he was going to lash out at Jūbei, 'What a disgrace! What dishonor you brought upon all our colleagues! How can you go on living after this!' He meant to rebuke Jūbei until he could never again dare to hold a hammer or an adze. He even intended to challenge him to take his responsibility in the manner of a samurai, by forcing him to commit seppuku."

"No, no, that's all wrong, he's the one who fought with Jūbei over the pagoda contract."

People talked knowingly among themselves.

On the day of the belated dedication ceremony, the Abbot climbed the pagoda with Jūbei and Genta, whom he had summoned. Dipping a brush in ink carried by an acolyte, the Abbot announced:

"I am about to give this pagoda an inscription. Genta and Jūbei, I would like both of you to witness it."

CONSTRUCTED BY JŪBEI OF EDO AND
CONSUMMATED BY GENTARŌ OF KAWAGOE

The Abbot added the date in his firm hand and turned around, his face beaming. The two men prostrated themselves, uttering not a word.

Since that day, the holy pagoda has forever soared up to heaven. Seen from the west, the high eaves have sometimes launched a clear moon; and viewed from the east, the banisters have swallowed the crimson sun in the evening. The story of this pagoda has survived more than one hundred years to this day.

❖ Selected Allusions

AKECHI MITSUHIDE (1526–82): one of Oda Nobunaga's vassals, who, disgusted with his lord's ill treatment, was driven to stage a coup d'état. (See the Afterword, p. 270.)

BON FESTIVAL: the festival of the dead, during which the spirits of the deceased are supposed to return to their former homes.

FUDŌ: the head of the Five Divine Kings serving the Sun Buddha. Their duty is to subjugate evil and desire.

GOMBEI; MOKUEMON: two Japanese names used in a manner somewhat like the phrase "every Tom, Dick, and Harry."

HAKURYŪ (Kanda Hakuryūshi, 1680–1760): a professional storyteller who specialized in tales of war.

JINGORŌ (Hidari Jingorō, 1594–1651): a carpenter-sculptor of legendary fame. The famous "Sleeping Cat" on the Yomei Gate at Nikkō, erected in honor of Tokugawa Ieyasu, came to be attributed to Jingorō by storytellers.

KISHIMOJIN (Skt., Hāritī): a Buddhist goddess, in Japan worshiped as the patroness of children.

MORI RAMMARU (1565–82): a handsome and valiant young page in Oda Nobunaga's service. (See the Afterword, p. 270.)

ODA NOBUNAGA (1534–82): a warlord who was on his way to unifying Japan when he died in fire surrounded by Akechi Mitsuhide's army.

OKANE OF ŌMI: a young woman who stopped a runaway horse, according to Legend 381 of *Kokonchomonjū* (Collection of hearsay stories from past and present, 1254). She was made famous in the Edo period through a Kabuki dance called *Sarashime*, also known as *Ōmi no Okane*, first performed in Edo in 1813.

ENCOUNTER WITH A SKULL

~1~

IT HAD NEVER BEEN in my nature to affect dandyism or to pursue elegant avocations. I was merely a five-foot snail gadding about in all directions, driven by a desire to see as much of the world as could be perceived with the uncertain eyes of my antennae. So I started out on a journey, not caring whether a present-day Lady of Eguchi refused me a night's lodging, or a nobleman of Uji begrudged me a fragrant cup of parched-rice tea.

> Far from towns,
> I share with the dew
> A pillow of grass.

I had composed this haiku as I lay wayworn in a field late one night on a lonely trip through the northern provinces. Having made myself "a companion of the dew," a *rohan*, destined eventually to drop from the branches, I entertained no more wish than to die by the wayside only to fertilize useless green moss in the gloomy shade of a large tree good for nothing but kindling. My daydreams, however, had been embracing an inane, audacious ambition: "I shall endeavor to purify this frivolous world." My soul, possessed by such a wild fancy, roved in vain for the past thirty-some years. "There is no tranquillity in the life of a self-mocking man, and most of his actions are swayed by the winds of karma." Recalling such proverbs, I would feel my heart chill and bones burn on a wintry night of the year-end fair, or on a summer evening when bats fluttered about. Nevertheless, such a sober state of mind would last but for a few days; I otherwise whiled away the time in idle relaxation.

In April 1890, I was at an inn by Hot Water Lake beyond Chūzenji at the foot of Mt. Shirane, nursing an illness and practicing five-stone checkers. As soon as I had recuperated, thanks to the healing power of the spa water, I was plunged into a state of euphoric animation, lustily quoting such sayings as "A heroic man is possessed of a soaring spirit that can challenge even Heaven." Feeling venturesome enough to disdain taking the same road back, I asked the innkeeper if there was a path leading forward.

"Well, we're at the end of the road," he replied. "As you can see, Front Shirane and Rear Shirane tower high above the clouds, so climbing them would be impossible even in the summertime. Next to them rises Wildwood Pass, commonly known as Spirits Pass, whose head marks the border between Kōzuke and Shimotsuke provinces. Mountains rise up one on top of another, and there's not a soul to offer you a drink of boiled water within fifteen miles of here. The climate varies so much from place to place that the famous *yashio* flowers may be in full bloom in Ōsawa and Tokujira, while the buds are still tight around here. Besides, the Pass is totally covered with snow, as much as five or six feet deep in the valley, so you'd hardly be able to find the trail. Only a handful of travelers have crossed these mountains since the beginning of the year—it's not a place one ventures into merely for fun. You have no choice but to return to Chūzenji. You'd be better off traveling to some smaller mountain near human habitation, like Mt. Ashio or Mt. Kōshin."

"Does he take me for a city-bred weakling?" I fumed to myself. "I'll show him the cantankerous temper and the stubborn pride of a contrary man." In a sham display of courage over such an obviously trivial matter, I stood firm on my cold thin legs (I despised long underwear) and insisted, "The Pass doesn't scare me. Prepare some grilled riceballs and go buy a pair of grass sandals. Slight hardship would be a small price to pay for the excitement of exploring a new trail. I'll entertain the mountain gods with my humming as I cross."

"Really now! That's preposterous! Without snow boots you'll surely freeze. You should at least hire a guide to take you to the border if you're that determined to go. If you're planning on collecting the local *nikujuyō* plant for kidney medicine, this isn't the season for it. As the saying goes, 'A whimsical action is useless.'"

"Don't give me such nonsense," I snapped at him. "Just do as I say. Go hire a guide and buy a pair of snow boots for me."

Tucking up the hems of my kimono and tying on my boots securely, I started out valiantly to climb the mountain with my guide, a six-foot-tall woodcutter. After trudging on several hundred yards, I was forced to concede that the innkeeper had been right. The snow was frozen hard on the surface but quite soft and loose beneath. The ascent became steeper and steeper, while my feet kept slipping. A bit discouraged, I spied my guide. To my annoyance, he was steadily gaining ground in his boots of wild boar fur and iron snowshoes.

Spurred on by my own ruffled pride and competitiveness,

I had just caught up with him when the huge man turned on his heel and said, "It's impossible to find the footpath in this snow, so we almost have to follow the valley downward. But if you're willing to chance a little difficulty, we can take a shortcut to the peak, even though the climb is rather steep."

"Might as well," I replied, resolved to proceed.

We climbed on for about another three miles. It was dark under the thickly grown firs, pines, boxtrees, and willows. The mountain lived up to its name, Wildwood, so dense and ghastly was the forest. As the winds rustled in the treetops, the water droplets fell from the branches onto my neck, and the moist mountain air assailed my face and filled my lungs, sickening me. The rabbit and deer tracks in the snow gradually disappeared, and little by little, the bird calls ceased to sound. Although my body was damp from the ordeal of climbing, I felt as if the defiling robes of the Five Desires shrouding my mind had begun to peel off, one after another. The Devil of Consciousness, who had raged unchecked in all his supernatural glory until the day before, now seemed lonely, deprived of his allies and kin. I was humbled; I felt as if I were a fugitive from the world.

"If a man should find himself in such a state of mind when he's nearing his end in decrepit old age, his senses almost gone, how wretched, how helpless and forlorn he must feel," I thought with unaccountable sorrow. At that very instant the cry of a bird sharp enough to pierce a rock burst forth from the treetops. Ducking in fright, I saw an arabesque pattern of fear swirl before my eyes. "I'll take my leave now," I then heard the guide say. "This is the peak separating the two provinces. Bear left as you descend through the valleys down to a marsh and then walk along its left perimeter until you find the headwaters of the Katashina River, which they call the Toné River downstream.

Its flow will lead you to the hot spring village of Ogawa, which is over ten desolate miles from where we are now. Be careful not to lose your way. Now, farewell."

I was left alone, feeling doubly forlorn. The false courage I had displayed in the morning had already shriveled. I looked vacantly down the mountain. The sunlight was weak under the leaden sky, and the Aizu Mountains, said to be visible on most days, were hidden behind clouds. The tips of my toes were turning cold even as I stood there. I descended the mountain, alone and apprehensive. My snow boots kept slipping, my shins were buffeted by sharp jags of ice, my cheeks brushed against rocks, and my clothes tore on tree branches buried under snowdrifts. I walked and walked, but the marsh was nowhere to be seen. I began to wonder if I had lost my way. Breaking off some birch twigs, I made a fire to warm myself and ate the riceballs. They were as tasteless as wood shavings, but they served at least to stave off hunger. Somewhat fortified, I proceeded, carefully studying the terrain and correcting my direction. Since I disdained to own a watch, I could not even tell what time it was. To my horror, darkness was swiftly descending. I groaned. The same thing had happened to me once before, on my last trip to Mt. Ara. Not another ordeal like that, I prayed, hurrying on.

At last I found myself at the edge of a marsh. Leaving me no time to savor my relief, the sun set quickly in the valley. The ground was no longer snow-covered, but my feet hurt in the already worn-out boots. To add to my chagrin, one of the boot-strings snapped in half. As I sat down along the path pathetically trying to repair the string, I caught sight of a light flickering faintly in the distance. Elated, I trudged toward the glimmer and came upon a small bamboo-thatched log hut standing beside a large cherry tree. To my surprise, the buds on the tree were still shut tight, indicating how late the spring was in coming here. The hut was extremely simple, without so much as a crude fence, which obviously dispensed with the nuisance of a garden gate. With a stream about six feet wide running alongside, there was no need for the customary bamboo pipe to bring water into the hut.

Marveling that someone was able to live in such an austere fashion, I stood by the door, through which the light was filtering, and said, "I am utterly exhausted and quite lost after crossing the ridge from the hot spring of Chūzenji. How far is Ogawa? I'm also having trouble walking, since my boot-string broke. Would you be kind enough to spare me a pair of straw sandals?"

"What a pity." The reply came, strangely enough, in the charming voice of a woman. "Ogawa is about a mile and a half ahead. You can't miss it if you go along the stream. I can well imagine how distressed you are with your footgear worn out, but alas, I have not even a single new pair of straw sandals. If you don't mind my old ones, I would be glad to offer them to you."

This was strange indeed. A woman in such a mountain hut? I surmised that she might be a hunter's daughter. "My soles are aching," I thought busily, "and the nails on the right small toe and the left big toe are torn. I couldn't possibly walk another mile and a half. I'd better see if I can get a night's lodging here."

"I hate to impose upon you, but now that I know it's another mile and a half to Ogawa, I realize I couldn't drag my tired body any farther. Please take pity on my aching feet and let me stay for the night."

"That's out of the question! We have no man here...."
So saying, the woman opened the door and leaned halfway out, silhouetted against the glow of the light from behind. She was about twenty-five—a veritable heavenly maiden adorned with a halo—fair of complexion, eyes clear and large, eyebrows long and soft, mouth small and tight; her

straight and abundant hair, obviously washed recently, was casually thrown back with only a paper string loosely holding the ends. Startled by her ethereal beauty, I moved a few steps back and stared hard to see if she was not a specter.

"What a sorry sight you are!" she exclaimed, studying me. "Have you hurt your feet? I see some red stains here and there. And your sleeves must have gotten torn on the twigs and grass blades. You look terribly pale and weary. You certainly will have difficulty covering even the short distance to Ogawa. I really shouldn't let you stay here, you know. Nevertheless, you're not a monk, so I can't very well advise you 'not to leave your heart at a temporary lodging.'* I'll bend my principles this once and let you spend the night here—I don't have the heart to say no."

She somehow gave me an eerie feeling, but at that point I was in no condition to bring myself to flee. "What else can I do?" I said to myself and sat down. While I was still thanking her, she fetched a small pail of hot water and started washing my feet assiduously.

"This is embarrassing! I can do it myself."

"No need to be embarrassed. Now, stretch out your legs."

As we exchanged such remarks, my feet were cleansed even between the toes. I stepped up into the matted room and exchanged formal greetings with her.

"Living in the mountain as I do, I haven't much to offer," she explained with a smile. "Fortunately, however, at the back of the house is a hot spring whose source is the same as that of the spring at Ogawa. Why don't you take a bath and recover from the day's fatigue. Here, follow me. If you like, I can scrub your back."

---

*See Eguchi, Lady of, in Selected Allusions (p. 146).

I was afraid that a fox might be playing a trick on me, but I let the woman lead me by the hand to the bath.

"I call it a bath," she said, "but it's actually a modest lean-to, barely adequate to keep off the rain. The hot water, though, is from a miraculous natural spa. It will warm you to the bones."

The tub looked clean and safe enough, so I soaked in the clear hot water, which proved even more satisfying than the famous Chūzenji hot spring. Having shed the miseries of the day, I emerged quite contented.

The woman was waiting for me. "You may not like wearing such things, but please put these on while I mend your clothes."

She helped me into a light flannel kimono and a black cotton-padded silk robe. Being women's wear, they were too short in the sleeves, so my arms jutted out comically. But I appreciated her kindness and expressed my gratitude. To be honest, I was more than a little bewildered, wondering what karma had ordained my encounter with such a mysterious hostess.

"Since the moss on the rocks has soiled your sash, this will have to do for now even if it looks somewhat improper," said the woman, smiling as she handed me a thin scarlet crepe belt. I obediently wrapped it around my waist, resigned to the possibility that it might be made of bewitched wisteria vine. When I sat down by the hearth, she slipped a warm gray-checkered nursery coat over my shoulders.

"Heaven forbid I should let you catch cold after a bath! I would surely be held accountable by a certain lady somewhere, wouldn't I?" she said with a knowing smile, adding large quantities of wood to the fire. Presently an iron pot hung there came to a brisk boil, and she took it down from its hook.

"You must be famished by now. Supper is ready. I'm

sorry that it's only rice mixed with barley, but at least it's hot. Please excuse the inconveniences of mountain living."

She set up a square butterfly-legged tray and served a bowl of bean-paste soup overflowing with the delicious aroma of mountain asparagus. Gratefully I proceeded to eat every bit of it.

"Perhaps I'll join you and finish my supper." Without ceremony she began to eat. Lacking her own tray, she was about to place her bowl on the wooden frame edging the hearth cut in the floor, but she hesitated for a moment, obviously unaccustomed to such an arrangement.

"Please use this for yourself," I offered, pushing my tray toward her.

"In that case, let us try what they call the 'tête-à-tête.' Allow me," she said without even blushing.

I found her behavior since my arrival quite beyond my comprehension. After supper, she quickly cleared the tray and dinnerware, sat close to the lamp, and set about mending my torn clothes by the flickering light. It was most baffling to see a woman behave without pretense or coquettishness—as though she were my wife of ten years.

"What or who could she be?" I wondered inwardly. Her black hair was too long and supple for a religious recluse, and she was obviously not a nun. Then why should she be living deep in the mountains all alone without a man to appreciate her beauty? To my own vexation, I was such a poor conversationalist that I was still struggling to get out a question when she finished mending my clothes. Leaving them neatly folded in a stack, she came over and sat facing me across the hearth, smiling.

"I have no idea why a young man like you would take a trip like this, but you must have had some interesting experiences in your life."

"Not at all. Much as I enjoy traversing the mountains, I can't even compose a poem worth reciting, for I simply have no literary talent. From what I've seen so far, you yourself seem to be leading an idyllic life, so I presume you are well born. Yet, you, a young woman, are secluded in a desolate mountain hut. If you could tell me about the circumstances which must lie behind this . . ."

"Far from it!" she laughed. "What momentous circumstances could possibly affect the life of such a humble person as myself? I am just a carefree woman called Tae, who moved here only last year. And you?"

"A carefree man who calls himself Rohan."

"Oh, you declare yourself to be carefree?"

"That's right."

"On what basis are you carefree?"

"It is simply that I feel merry over mountains and rivers without knowing why. What about you?"

"Carefree merely from renouncing the world."

"I don't believe it! If you had really renounced the world, you'd be dressed in a black robe. Your head would be shaven. You'd be gathering flowers by the mountain path in the morning and dipping the pure water from the valley stream in the evening to offer before the Buddha's image. And you would most certainly perform religious services every day, reading sutras and chanting the Buddha's name. But I see no rosary in your hand. And for whose sake do you keep your black hair so long and abundant? Some women of the distant past are said to have gone so far as to burn their own faces with a hot iron upon forsaking the world. And, though it lacks red, your silk undergown does show sensuous gay shades. I can hardly believe what you say. Aren't you merely pretending to hate the world? Perhaps you had some reason to spite your lover and, in the course of a quarrel, you hid here to sulk. It is a well-known scheme to recaptivate the heart of a man who is showing the signs of growing weary of his love.

Right? . . . Oh, I beg your pardon. I seem to have gotten quite carried away by my own imagination."

"My, my! How dreadful! It is not for any such frivolous reasons at all, but honestly to escape from the world that I——"

"You are being facetious. Otherwise, you could tell me the exact reason why you left the world."

"While you are asking needless questions, the night grows late. It's time you went to bed," she said, reaching for the closet to take out the bedding. I expected thin cotton mats, but to my surprise she spread a mattress of scarlet damask silk and a sleeved coverlet of blue figured-satin, replete with a red silk lining and a sea-otter fur collar, all prodigiously opulent.

"Now, please lie down." She pushed me toward the bed and set up a small folding screen around it.

"Well, then, with your leave I will." I lay down, forced to break off our conversation.

The round brocade pillow graced by the cranes-riding-the-clouds pattern would no doubt inspire a dream of the supernatural Mt. Hōrai. It seemed to be stuffed with tea leaves; with such an elegant aroma and the unresolved suspicion lingering in my mind, I found it impossible to fall asleep despite all my effort. I peeked from behind the screen and saw the woman sitting like a beautiful doll, reading something by the sunken hearth.

Still wakeful after an hour had passed, I peered out again and found her in the same position. Two hours later there was still no change. By midnight I was wide awake, recounting in my mind everything that had transpired since my arrival. When I looked once more, she was stirring the ashes with iron chopsticks. The logs had already been quite consumed, so the hearth no longer provided much warmth. She must have felt the chilly wind from Wildwood

Pass, for mumbling that she would take a bath, she disappeared toward the lean-to. In a little while she returned and sat up by the hearth, whose fire was by now almost extinguished. She seemed to have nothing particular to do. By then it was quite clear to me that there was no other bedding in the house. As a man I felt ashamed to be lying under warm covers. Pretending to have just awakened, I quickly slipped out of the bed.

"Washroom?" she asked, and showed me the way.

Upon returning I assumed a surprised expression and said, "Miss Tae, haven't you gone to bed yet?"

"No, I haven't."

"I don't know whom you are expecting to come courting, but it must be quite late by now."

"Stop teasing me and go back to sleep."

"Well, I apologize if I'm wrong, but you seem to live alone. In begging for a night's lodging, I'm afraid I robbed you of your own bed. If that's the case, I'm a man who has slept in the open before, so it would be nothing for me to spend a night just leaning against a post. But it pains me to see you sitting up like this. You might find my remaining warmth disagreeable, but please take this bed."

"True, I have no other bedding, but since I agreed to put you up, I am determined to stay up through the night. Please don't worry about me," she said, blushing slightly.

"No, no, that's not right."

"Please don't say no."

"You're giving me a hard time."

"You, sir, are giving *me* a hard time."

"No, please take the bed, Miss Tae."

"You take it yourself. I insist."

"Well, this could go on forever," I said. "I'm a man and therefore will take my leave this minute to face whatever hardship lies outside. It would be an eternal disgrace for me to sleep comfortably while leaving a woman to suffer privation. I'd be ashamed to face my mother and friends. A night journey would be much easier to bear."

"If you insist that strongly, I can hardly argue with you. Yet if I let you travel in the dark now, my good intentions would come to no avail. I therefore will comply with you. But it's as if I had you warm the bed for me, isn't it? How could I let you sleep on the floor by the fireless hearth and tuck myself cozily under the covers? Even if I see my love in a dream, I couldn't possibly enjoy the meeting. There is also such a thing as female pride. I must have you sleep comfortably or I would be ashamed before the Buddha in *my* eternal disgrace."

"When you put it that way, I don't know what to do. I'm just a simple unsophisticated soul."

"In that case, please take my advice and go back to bed."

"No, you take my advice."

"You need not insist so stubbornly."

"Stubborn or not, you should listen to me, Miss Tae."

"Very well. I can't fight your stubbornness. I shall obey you. What a frightful face you're making," she laughed.

"I was born with a frightful face."

"Are you angry now?"

"Why should I be angry with your kindness? I've just become a little serious; that's all."

"How sweet. Serious, you say!" she laughed again.

"Yes, serious."

"Well, then, I will speak seriously, too. Mr. Rohan?"

"What?"

"Do you think that as long as a man gets his way, a woman's wishes need not be granted?"

"What do you mean?"

"You force a soft-hearted woman to accept your way, and do you mean to declare heartlessly that it does no harm to her pride?"

"I don't know."

"You don't know? That's a cowardly answer. Now, come this way and get in bed with me. I honor your wishes, and you honor my wishes in return. It wouldn't contaminate or dissolve your body, would it? Why are you resisting me so? It's very unfeeling of you."

Her soft hand clasped mine firmly. She was beautiful and at the same time almost menacing as she pulled at me with unabashed composure. Chilled with terror to the marrow, I closed my eyes, clenched my teeth, and mentally recited the Chinese poem "Elimination of Desires" by Emperor Wen of Wei:

In the boundless ocean of sin there is no greater evil than carnal desire. In the tumultuous world of dust there is no sin easier to fall into than lascivious pleasure. Captivated by it, dauntless heroes destroy themselves and cause the downfall of their countries. Great men of letters violate their integrity and disgrace their names because of it. In the beginning it is a simple matter of one's willpower; but in the end, one is beyond redemption for the rest of one's life. Why is it? When the wind of lust grows in its force by the day and Heaven's Law perishes, men take pride in committing deplorable misdeeds without shame. They practice vice that ought to outrage everyone and ought to be despised by all. They write lewd stories and comment upon female beauty. They rivet their eyes on the charming women on the streets and break their hearts over the graceful radiance of noble ladies. Whereas they should praise and respect women chaste and virtuous, they seduce them into transgressions. When they should be compassionate and judicious toward maidservants and female attendants, they resort to force to dishonor them forever. They bring shame upon their relatives and disgrace upon their descendants.

Men behave thus because their minds are ignorant and

their spirits impure. The wise shun them, while only cajolers fraternize with them. How can they fail to see it? Heaven never sanctions their behavior, and gods tremble in wrath. Some of their wives must atone for their sins, and sometimes their offspring suffer the retributions. There are no extinct family tombs that are not of the lunatic followers of sensuality; the ancestors of prostitutes were debauchees without exception. Those who could have amassed wealth find themselves excluded from the noble palace, and those who could have attained honor find their names eliminated from the golden roster. In life they meet with all five penalties—lashing, clubbing, labor, exile, and capital punishment. After death they suffer the agonies of the Three Spheres—Hell, Beasts, and Hungry Demons—where the beneficial effects of their previous good karma is exhausted. Of what use is the romantic life of the past, then? Which is better—to disregard advice only to later regret having done so, or to have sense enough not to fall into sin in the first place?

I respectfully counsel good young men and the eminent persons listed in the golden roster to break the spell of the demon of lust by exercising the power of determination. The fair face of a flowery beauty is nothing but a flesh-covered skull, and gorgeous make-up and adornment are lethal weapons. Even if a woman has a face as beautiful as a blossom or jewel, one should be prepared to regard her as one would one's own sister. Those who have not yet transgressed should guard against taking wrong steps, and those who have already fallen onto the deadly course should lose no time in reversing their direction. It is my hope that my advice will be widely observed and that men will lead one another out of the labyrinth onto the path of universal awakening. With the greatest evil eradicated, all other evils will vanish of their own accord. Only then will the spirit be free to enjoy the eternal glory of life.

~2~

Not nearly as saintly as Liu Hsia-hui, I was nervous enough merely being under the same roof with a woman in the bloom of her youth, as beautiful as a profusion of blossoms in spring. At first I had said to myself, "No matter how many million worldly men should reproach and criticize me, I have a clear conscience. Why should I be troubled by the harmless buzzing of mosquitoes?" And I stayed at this house, sharing the supper tray and conversing with this woman. Although I am by nature quite unperturbed by gossip and criticism, how could I allow myself, with only Heaven as a witness in such a remote mountain, to sleep under the same cover with a woman who is a stranger to me? Even if my conscience is clear, how could I possibly fall asleep with her soft body so close, our warmth passing through the scant folds of our clothes? As it was, when she merely made the suggestion, I had to chant the "Elimination of Desires" under my breath, for my mental state was not exactly as dispassionate as it would be if I were pondering the Zen riddle of "an old woman burning down a meditation hut." If I should actually share a bed with this enchanting woman in this mountain hut far from any censuring eyes, could I remain as imperturbable as a withered tree leaning against a cold rock? To be sure, even the eminent Abbot Ikkyū of Daitoku Temple confessed that if an attractive woman promised her favors for a night, a withered willow in its old age would produce an offshoot.

Be on guard, I warned myself. Only on the mountainside uninhabited by women can one remain as enlightened as an arhat. The saintly Wizard of Kume is said to have fallen from a cloud when he caught sight of the fair legs of a young maiden. Had he slept with her in the same bed, he would have plummeted right through the depths of the bottomless hell!

Even if I tried to behave myself impeccably while lying

pillow to pillow under one coverlet with this lovely tenderhearted woman, spending the night without mishap might be far from easy. "We are getting chilled as the night wind from the ridge goes through the space between our backs," she might say. Pulling the cover gracefully over my shoulders, she might entreat, "Please turn toward me to keep out the draft." It would be difficult indeed for me to keep calm under such circumstances. It would be nearly impossible with her downy locks brushing against my cheeks and her radiant face right in front of my nose. Where would she put her exquisite arms? Where could her breasts hide? This is indeed a serious situation. How could I manage to sleep as placidly as if I were merely holding a female cat in my arms? Oh, no! Suppose our clothes accidently became undone through the casual movements of our bodies, unseen under the covers? And what if her well-contoured legs or shapely feet happened to touch my own hairy shins? Good heavens! That would be a moment of life or death! Being a mediocre man, one basically shaky in willpower and always remiss in observing the moral commandments, I would certainly lose a peaceful night's sleep—that is, if I were able to control my baser instincts.

Besides, is she really a human, or a fox or a badger in human disguise? Her behavior has been altogether suspicious. She shows no sign of embarrassment in saying things that ordinary women would be unable to mention. What else could she be but a goblin? I have heard that a petty man often makes his approach in a humble attitude, and the devil always seduces with kindness. Well, come now, you devil! An iron fist knows no ambiguous human emotions. I will bring it straight down over your head to show my fearsome strength! Then again, it may not work. While I am a mere mortal, not nearly as powerful as the deity Fudō, the devil may have the might and main of Mahesvara, who challenged Brahmadeva himself. It would be the poorest of poor tactics to slap the water only to get soaked, or to beat the grass only to rouse a snake. How should I answer her? What should I do?

Oh, I remember now. Sometime ago I heard an anecdote about Bashō. When the renowned haiku poet had his sleeve caught by a woman, he remained immobile and silent. As the dejected woman turned at last to leave, Bashō caught her sleeve from behind and surprised her with a haiku, "Turn toward me. / I too am lonely / This autumn evening."

Following Bashō's example, I decided after all to remain silent. Practicing in my mind the "Contemplation of the Nine Stages of Human Corpses," I sat down with a thud loud enough to snap apart heaven and earth.

Quite impatient by now, Tae increased the pressure of her grasp on my hand. "Why are you hesitating? Please come this way!" She began to pull at me, tugging all the harder as I strained with all my strength and determination to resist her. "I'm asking you to come this way. What an obstinate man you are! You certainly don't act like one who is used to making merry over mountains and rivers."

"How ghastly if I would be forced to take even a single step by this goblin," I thought, greatly alarmed. I turned myself as rigid as a stone statue of Jizō, but still she tried to drag me. My guard weakened for a second. In spite of myself I let out a scream, shook my hand loose, and ran away. She came after me and caught my sleeve.

"Now I see! You must take me for a goblin or a specter to loathe me this much!" she laughed. "I made the offer believing you were a man of stout heart and venturous spirit. It is my fault that my kindness worked against itself to cause you such a scare. Honestly, I am neither an evil specter nor a nun shamefully driven by amorous desires. And anyway, I would not force you to do what you detest so much. But if I let you make your journey at night now,

I would fail as a hostess, which would be to my immeasurable regret. So please sit down."

Afraid to refuse outright, I took a seat on the other side of the hearth. She picked up a hatchet and stood up. Again I was startled and mystified. Noticing my expression, she laughed, put on sandals, and went out through the front door. Soon I heard the sharp sound of cracking wood. I hurried outside to help her, relieved to realize that she only had gone out to gather firewood.

"If you're chopping firewood, let me lend you a masculine hand," I offered and borrowed her hatchet. Cutting down some nearby trees, I brought an armload of logs into the hut and closed the door tight. As I sat down facing her, she raked up the embers and added the new wood. Before long a fire was burning briskly, and the warmth filled the room.

"As you can see, it will be quite comfortable for me to stay up alone by the fire. So please rest your mind and go back to bed. I apologize for having frightened my timid guest. You can go to sleep without fear now." Tae said with much laughter.

"No, no. As I said before, I want you to take the bed."

"Are you being stubborn again? Well, then, shall we sleep together?"

"I would rather not."

"If you don't like me, there's nothing I can do about it," she laughed again. "To be honest, since there wasn't much else I could offer you by way of hospitality on a cold night in the middle of the mountains, I thought I would hold you tightly and warm you in my bosom, just as your wet nurse used to lull you to sleep in her arms. I meant well. In the sight of the Buddhas and bodhisattvas, I swear that I haven't the slightest design of a questionable nature. But a fine specimen of a man you are. I didn't think you were the kind of weak-willed man who would worry about becoming emotionally involved with a woman who happens to spend a night in his arms. You are indeed cowardly and unsure of yourself. . . . Oh, pardon my tongue. . . . Well, you do what you like. As for myself, I as a hostess can't very well allow myself to monopolize the bed, can I?"

Struck dumb with amazement, I listened and reflected deeply. Not only did she seem indifferent to worldly conventions, but she even behaved as if I were a three year old. She appeared, moreover, as self-assured as a great wise man who is so enlightened that it is always springtime in his heart. I grew all the more suspicious of her. Whose daughter is she? What specter's disguise? She could not be an ordinary woman. What personal circumstances forced her to retreat to such a mountain hut with all her fine looks and tender heart? Is she a present day Kogō, Hotoke Gozen, Giō, or Gijo? Or is she altogether a goblin?

Increasingly frightened, I said, "All right, then. You are free to do what you like, but I for my part will take the liberty of spending the night by this hearth."

"I don't mind keeping you company, either. In fact, I would feel much better that way," said the woman.

Now that our bickering was over, I felt relieved enough to be able to scrutinize her more carefully from head to toe. She was like a flawless jewel, a goddess shimmering in and out of the fire's flames, whose beauty and graceful dignity surpassed anything that could be depicted by a human artist.

One would hate to place a deer in thorn bushes, and one would expect a crane to perch on an old pine tree. It must be human nature to wish an extraordinary person, a noble person, a lovely person, and a beautiful person to find the places they deserve in the world. An excellent horse ought to carry a hero, and a butterfly ought to sleep in the garden of celebrated flowers. Once at an inn, I saw a janitor drop a copy of *A Political History of Japan* out of his pocket as he was cleaning the floor on his knees. It brought tears to my eyes to imagine how mortifying it must have been for him to be wasting his lofty ambition in such menial service. Even more so in this woman's case. How pitiful that she should bury her natural beauty in obscurity, like a tree in the remote mountain valley whose blossoms are never to please any human eyes! Heaven works in heartless ways, denying a beautiful woman her deserved lot and placing her in a sooty grass hut. Just as a man of conviction would rather cast himself into the vast ocean if his beliefs are rejected by the world, this woman of refined taste and dignity, transcending mundane emotions almost to the point of perfect enlightenment, perhaps intends to end her life on this distant mountain away from the multitude. If so, how inexcusable that she, as a woman, should behave like a man. A woman being unfeminine and a man being unmanly are both against nature and utterly repulsive.

On the other hand, when a woman acts unfeminine and a man unmanly in an almost divine way, they have both attained the sphere of the holy. What this woman says is no longer feminine. It must be most difficult for her to propose sleeping with me in her arms, a man whom she has just met for the first time. Moreover, if she actually meant to hold me as a wet nurse would a small boy, she can't be a masculine woman but an extraordinary, superior being. Yet common mortal that I am, I would rather see her suitably married, making a happy home in the mundane world, than to find her here, so noble and saintly.

I glanced up at her once again. To see the way she sat there upright, almost majestic, I could not believe that she was one of those avarice-driven mortal women who suffer in love, fret over whether or not her clothes match, or fuss with coral beads and tortoise-shell combs. Her clear eyes betrayed that she was undisturbed by the trivial matters of the world. Her freshly glowing complexion revealed that far from finding her present lot distressing, she was fully satisfied with it. And her firmly set lips attested to the keenness of her wisdom in discerning right from wrong. Absolutely mysterious! No longer able to bear it, I began carefully to express my thoughts.

"As I mentioned before, I find it strange indeed that you, a young woman who is not a nun, should be living in a mountain retreat. For one thing, it seems lamentable that despite such charming features and tender heart, you should be hiding in a remote place populated by wolves and wild boars. If you don't mind telling me, I would like to know why you live here."

"Well, now," she laughed. "Do you intend to write me up in a novel, which I hear is a very popular form of entertainment nowadays? Or perhaps you wish to take my story back to the city people as a souvenir. There is really no sense in revealing my shameful background, but I'll be consoled if people hear my tale and if anyone happens to feel even a little sympathy for me. So I'll tell you the story of my unworthy life. I was led to weep and laugh by causes not of my own making. But all that is a mere memory of a long-ago dream. I now know that confession marks the end of love affair, so I shall not hide anything," she said, adding more logs to the fire.

~3~

The expression on Tae's face at that moment was divinely animated yet gentle, like the moon afloat in a dreamy spring sky over the Yangtze River after a gentle breeze wafts the clouds away. Her eyes radiated happiness, like a pair of precious stones glimmering in the sultry mist around Mt. Randen. "Please listen to my story, Mr. Rohan," she began.

I was raised in Tokyo by my parents, who were not exactly destitute. As much as our ample family resources allowed, I was treasured like a butterfly from the time I was young enough to ask if the dewdrops were hair ornaments for the pampas grass, and cherished like a flower when old enough to shelter my long crepe sleeves from the breeze. The three of us enjoyed a peaceful life as the years came and went. I grew taller with each new battledore given to me at the New Year. After the untimely death of my father in my thirteenth autumn, however, there was to be no end to my sorrows. Having seldom wept before then, except over sad plays, I became constantly given to tears. After we sent my father off with a streak of crematory smoke in a desolate field, three times daily his seat at the table was vacant—it was as if a front tooth was missing from an otherwise perfect set. There was only my mother left, crestfallen and cheerless, picking at the food as if she hardly had the strength to lift her chopsticks. I was disconsolate to see her grief, but the sight of her sorrowing daughter must have burdened her careworn heart even more. She seemed to subsist almost solely on warm water. As her eyes moistened with suppressed tears, food would lose flavor in my mouth, and I found it hard to loosen my clenched jaw.

I kept to the house more and more, abandoned the samisen which I used to enjoy playing, and failed to resume my koto lessons after the mourning period was over. I spent my time reading and derived some pleasure from my mother's storybooks, which described many things real and unreal, until reading became a habit with me. I went on to consume the classical tales such as *Usuyuki, Sumiyoshi, Ise, Taketori,* and within three years even *Genji* and *Sagoromo,* which were quite beyond my comprehension. The tales made me ponder on the kindness and coldness of human nature and taught me to discern truth from falsehood in worldly matters. I also observed that since olden times men have always been superficial beings who love and care but for a time, their desire intense but their patience thin. They delight in meeting women but never grieve over parting, prefer coquettish flatterers, glory recklessly in love conquests, and admire a woman for the beauty of her appearance just as they would cherish a dog or cat for its fur markings. Although I had nothing personally to do with them, I vehemently loathed amorous men like Prince Genji and the poet Narihira, and far from being jealous, I felt impatient contempt for the foolish women who were infatuated with such profligates.

When I was eighteen, my aged mother was taken seriously ill. Being an only child, I was totally helpless. Tearfully praying to gods and Buddhas day and night, I looked after her, but all to no avail. "When I am gone, open this box and learn your place in this life," she said and then bequeathed to me a small black-lacquered box with a blue shell-inlay design of petals floating in a stream. I was so anguished and overcome by her death that I could find no words to express my grief. After the funeral I opened the box and found a farewell letter that my mother had written without my having known it. I read it with tears of gratitude for her profound love.

But how excruciating even now to remember the shock! Horror, grief, resentment, despair, despondency, repulsion, humiliation, helplessness—every abominable feeling there is in the world welled up within me. I felt as if ice-cold water had just been poured over my head and, at the same time, as if my eyebrows were being seared in a fierce flame. Cold perspiration drenched my sides, causing me to shiver uncontrollably. Only darkness lay before my eyes and in my heart until my flickering life seemed about to expire then and there. From that moment on, I shunned the outside world all the more resolutely.

"I'm sorry to interrupt." I said, "but why did the message in the letter terrify you so much?"

"It's too painful for me to mention what was written in that letter. Let me get back to my story," Tae continued.

I turned nineteen, growing older, of use to no one. Close friends of my late parents offered to arrange my marriage to their sons or acquaintances. "How shamefully hypocritical of them, and so soon after my loss!" I thought suspiciously to myself. "They are merely attracted to my looks, which will bloom but for ten years, and my wealth, which can be spent but once." I gave my servant strict orders to decline every proposal. With all my heart I longed for my mother and prayed impatiently, "May my body dissolve soon, so that I may turn into an ethereal spirit and join my mother."

Life was no longer dear to me, and I found no pleasure in this world. I left untouched the numerous booklets that I had once read with such absorption, and I came to abhor meeting a man face to face. I was offended even when naughty maidservants gossiped about handsome young actors. Naturally, my hair was without the fragrance of hair oil and was arranged with no style. Much less did I concern myself with the quality of a tortoise-shell comb in my forelock, or worry over the suitability of dappled cloth for tying my hair. Rouge and powder were completely forgotten. I no longer took pains to pick out the right sashes, to select the right thongs for my clogs, or to coordinate my wardrobe. I was rid of all feminine discretion. Through the tears filling my woebegone heart, even heaven and earth looked dusky. Flowers bloomed, but I was wilted. Birds sang, but I was silent. The silvery moon cast no reflection on the turbid waters of my heart. I merely slept, woke, and ate in melancholy indifference. In my anguish I resented gods, Buddhas, people, and even heaven and earth. My agonizing rage against the gods and Buddhas intensified to such an extent that I would have stabbed them with a needle had they but manifested tangible forms. I was no longer bound by the rules of propriety, which are as perishable as a lamp wick, nor did I find any comfort in human sentiments, which are as evanescent as colors reflected in icicles. Frost and snow weighed cold in my heart, and tragic thoughts never left my mind.

Then, one day, a finely lacquered ricksha stopped at my gate, and out stepped a man with an imposing mustache, apparently a government official. According to his calling card, he was director of a certain government bureau, an imperial appointee of the first rank, reputed to be a man of great influence. My old butler, who had been managing the household as my guardian, received the visitor and asked the purpose of his call.

"I apologize for this sudden visit," said the man, "but, in the absence of a suitable intermediary, I must make this proposal directly. Excuse me for asking such a personal question, but is the young mistress betrothed to anyone? To come to the point, the young son of my former lord has fallen in love with the young lady, though he has never met her. Let me try to explain.

"While the young lord was taking a stroll in the country last spring, he passed by a certain cemetery and heard some beggars talking. One said, 'That young girl who just left, she's beautiful, isn't she? But what's especially touching is her filial piety. She was crying her eyes out as she knelt before her mother's tomb. Such a young thing, yet only lamenting that life was dear to her no more and that she wished to join her mother. Such a tender heart is rare in today's women, isn't it?' 'Did you just notice her today for the first time?' another beggar went on to ask. 'Since last year, when her mother was buried here, she's come every month to mourn in the same manner. She hasn't missed a single memorial day. She must be a pathetic figure even outside the cemetery. Her face looked emaciated and awfully pale today. She looks like she must weep constantly at home.' Listening to their gossip, the young lord was so moved that he shuddered and shed a tear. That, you see, was the headwater of love and the fountain of longing. He searched for her, not out of frivolous interest but out of sincere affection. In time he learned her name and address. Consumed by the flame of love, he at last asked his father's permission to marry her. That is how I have come to call on you on his behalf. As far as we know, your mistress has not been promised to anyone yet. Would you kindly consider our proposal?

"I do not mean to be presumptuous, like some glib-tongued intermediary, but you must have heard of the eldest son of my former lord, his title and estates, if only through rumor. Having recently earned a degree in Germany, moreover, he is assured of a bright future among the ranks of young noblemen. He is neither asking for a frivolous temporary arrangement, nor is he making his marriage proposal in a condescending manner. In fact, in this age of equality among the four classes, all of us intend to pledge our respect to the lady as our future countess. I hope you will consider the circumstances and grant us a favorable reply."

After the man left, my butler was almost dancing with joy. With his wrinkled face aglow, he tried to persuade me to accept this proposal. Although at first it made me dizzy to hear that a person of high rank was in love with me, I soon dismissed it as merely a fleeting male fancy and an ignoble pursuit of beauty. The next moment, however, I recalled my mother's last letter and was instantly sobered. "No, no, no! I have no ear to lend to any marriage offer," I said emphatically. The astounded butler remonstrated with me, sparing no word or point of logic in arguing that it was absurd to decline such a splendid offer. I remained adamant nonetheless, and he had no choice but to decline the proposal. I was unperturbed by the public gossip that I was cold-hearted. After that incident, though, I somehow underwent a change of heart. I no longer abhorred men as intensely as I had before. In time I even became more careful about my appearance.

Three months later, the same bureau director called on us again.

"Since our marriage proposal miscarried last time, our young lord has changed completely from his cheerful and intellectual former self. Now he seldom ventures from the house, and he leaves his favorite books untouched. He is grief-stricken at the sight of flowers or the moon, lamenting, 'It is my greatest sorrow that my life lingers in this world, where my hope is no more. For whose sake should I prolong my useless existence?' He eats less and less, spends the day dozing, and tosses and turns at night. His attendants try to comfort him, but he is wretchedness personified. His father counsels him that his behavior is sheer folly, but he only talks to himself day and night, saying things such as, 'If I were to evaporate like a dewdrop, would she take pity on me? I feel no bitterness toward the heartless lady, but I loathe myself for having been detested by her. I wish to give up my life swiftly.' Unable to bear his lamentations, his mother dispatched me again on this mission. Please try to understand the situation and tell us what it was that you found unsatisfactory in our proposal. We will follow your every instruction in the hope that his love may be requited."

The director made his impassioned plea, appealing both to reason and emotion. Listening behind sliding doors, I was moved to tears in spite of myself. When my butler-guardian came to consult with me, however, I again recalled the letter and flatly declared that I did not wish to consummate this match. I cared not if I made enemies of the many persons involved.

I thought that was the end of the matter, but the man called again one month later.

"My young lord has reached the point where he has finally taken to bed, and he has been unable to recover. There is no treatment for such an illness; both his parents are so careworn and aggrieved over the state of their beloved eldest son that it breaks our hearts to watch them. I beg you to use your good offices to intercede with the young lady. This is merely a note that my young lord scribbled in his sick-bed, but his heart-rending love cannot escape anyone's notice. I have brought this in the hope that it would appeal to your lady's compassion. I will also leave this photograph of the young lord before he was taken ill. I shall return tomorrow. No matter what your reply, we would very much like to have a picture of the lady whom my young lord loves at the cost of his health."

After he was gone, my old butler counseled me with tears in his eyes. "This match seems to have been ordained by fate. You must accept it." But I obstinately refused, and he went away somewhat vexed, leaving behind the photograph. At the sight of his noble and handsome face, I began to feel tenderly toward this young man; furthermore, my heart was stirred by his forlorn poem written in unsteady hand on a strip of paper:

> In the dead of night
> When even the lights grow dim,
> Lying with a faint and fading heart,
> Oh, how I languish for my love!

But my mother's letter helped me resolve firmly not to go near such a noble person. The next day I had my butler deliver a hard-hearted reply, without my photograph.

About ten days later a carriage came to our gate in a flurry, and the same visitor practically tumbled out. With a tearful look on his tense face, he said, "Dear, beloved, cold-hearted lady of the house, today you need not reply. You simply must come to my lord's residence. The doctor has pronounced that our young lord will not last the night. Please imagine the grief of his parents, as well as ours. This morning, he composed a poem:

> Full well I know
> My detested self is beyond hope.
> Still so hard to forsake is . . .

Without finishing the last line, he coughed up blood. What a woeful sight it was! After all, the sickness in his lungs was caused by his consuming love. Even if the lady were a demon, should she behave this cruelly toward the man who loves her so?"

In his resentment and anger, he tried to carry me off by force. I felt more agony than I would have if I were being torn to pieces, but still I resisted. At that moment another carriage clattered to a stop. Followed by an attendant, a graceful lady came rushing in without any pretense of ceremony.

"Are you Miss Tae?" she asked frantically. "My son has made his deathbed request, out of his almost paralyzed lips, to have one glimpse of you in person. I entreat you, with my hands folded in prayer. You may be loath to, but please, please come with me!"

Implored by an august countess, I felt as if my mind were being tossed about in flood waters. I was taken semi-conscious into the carriage and soon arrived at a grand mansion, which echoed with desperate cries and the sorrowful weeping of women. The lady swept through a number of rooms. Unable to shake myself free of her hand,

I followed her into the sickroom, where the young lord, worn to a shadow, had just been called back to consciousness. Upon seeing his mother, he wept piteously. Knowing that I was the sole cause of this tragedy, I wished I could dissolve on the spot. The countess pushed me toward her son. No longer able to hold back my surging tears, I held his hand and wept without knowing why. The young lord looked at me, also in tears, but responded only with a feeble movement of his hand held in mine. At that point I collapsed in a swoon. When I came to, the young lord was gone, never to revive again. I returned to my house feeling that I could hardly linger in this world.

Thereafter, I was haunted by his memory. I regretted having survived him at all and almost lost my reason, raging against heaven and earth. On the seventh day after his death, his shadowy phantom appeared while I was chanting sutras before our family altar. Mindlessly following the ghost, I left my house to wander about blindly in strange places, until I chanced upon this mountain in a state of delirium. Through a providential encounter with an enlightened priest, I was steered toward religious pursuits and settled in this little meditation hut here.

In my new abode, the rising water in the valley stream announces the coming of spring, and the falling leaves in the hills foretell the approach of winter. I am able to contemplate an infinite number of wondrous things in my quietude. As I turn my thoughts to the mundane world, I find all people fascinating in their own ways. The ice from the horrible past has melted in my heart. Now I am even amused by my own existence, which is as ephemeral as a gossamer in an easterly breeze. I love Buddhas, I love ordinary men, and I truly love you too. There is not a single thing in the word that I hate. I love the birds nesting in the trees, and I love the foxes in their holes in the ground. The flower of my heart has blossomed to fill the Ten

Thousand Spheres with its fragrance. More keenly than ever do I appreciate the mysterious truth of the Consciousness Only Doctrine. Dissociated from mud, the water is now so clear that the heavenly moon rests on it, and the glistening jewels of the Keyura Sutra are all the more appealing. It is delightful to be pitied and amusing to be detested.

It is rather amusing also that you should have abhorred me when I love you enough to hold in my arms. In the past I behaved cruelly even toward a man who loved me at the cost of his life, and now I love a man who loathes me unto death. How wondrous that through the changes of heart, one can resent or enjoy the same heaven and earth!

Thus she concluded her long story. Yet I still failed to comprehend its true meaning.

"Miss Tae, what was written in the letter in the small black box with the blue shell inlay of petals flowing in water? Unless you make this crucial point clear, I shall not be able to make sense out of your story."

"How unperceptive of you! You have yet to learn about human sentiments. If I tell you that the letter made me heartless, you should require no further explanation. It contained instructions for me to forsake the world and the reason why I must do so."

"That's ridiculous! There could be no possible reason why anyone must forsake the world."

"But there is," insisted Tae. "All my relatives are compelled to forsake the world, for we can find no peace of mind otherwise. That is why at first I resented the gods and Buddhas."

"Preposterous!"

"On the contrary, it makes perfect sense. Our fate is to perish in the remote mountains. People of the mundane world are lacking in insight: while they perceive the various kinds of pathos in life, they fail to realize that to those of us in our accursed lot, even the sun and the moon appear utterly dark, and flowers and birds bring no pleasure whatsoever. I didn't submit to the young lord's love because I wanted to spare his offspring the same wretched fate. You cannot imagine my anguish of those days."

Suddenly breaking her somber tone with a laugh, she said, "Well, I should end such a long and boring tale now. It's tiresome to tell stories, and mine is without an end. Love and resentment are actually neighbors. That's that. And this should be the close of my useless rambling." As she fed some more wood to the fire, her beautiful face looked, not as crystal white as that of the sober Ch'ü Yüan, but as ruby pink as the inebriate T'ao Yüan-ming.

Presently she glanced at me and said, "It is unfortunate that the night is so short! As the day is breaking, our brief encounter must come to an end too. You are a petal floating on the Katashina River whose scent swiftly travels ten miles along the rapid stream. I am a willow standing on the riverbank whose reflection sinks to the bottom of the water, unable to move a step. The happiness of meeting and the anguish of parting are not reserved exclusively for the morning after love-making, you know."

No sooner did the sun rise bright and radiant than the house and the woman vanished like a cloud of mist. Alone among the withered pampas grass left standing since last year, I found myself with a boot-string half tied, a bleached white skull at my feet.

What one cannot understand by sight, one should learn by inquiring. What cannot be learned through inquiry, one should comprehend through intellection. What cannot be comprehended by intellect, one should perceive through feeling. If I feel compassion for another, he will love me in return. If love and compassion are mutual, I am within him, and he is within me. With no distance between us, we perceive each other's emotions and share our boundaries. A skull in a secluded valley attracted the mind of a solitary wayfarer traveling in the present, and that traveler in the deep mountain perceived the former life of the skull. Our karmic paths happened to cross, and we chose not to forgo a momentary encounter.

With water from the river I consecrated the ground under the tree by which we had spent the night together, and there I buried the skull left behind by the spirit who had communicated by the vibration of my heartstring in the absence of a divine bow. With my hands folded in prayer, I extended my gratitude: "Hail, Amida Buddha! Thank you for a wonderful night!" Hugging the stream, I made my way to the village of Ogawa and headed for a hot spring inn.

"Do you know of someone who has disappeared into the mountains lately?" I asked the innkeeper there.

After pondering a bit with a puzzled look on his face, he said, "It's strange you should ask. Yes, only last year a mad beggar woman strayed into the mountain. We heard later that she never reached Nikkō. Even now people are wondering whatever became of her. Is she the one you're asking after?"

"That's the one. Tell me all you know about her."

Eyeing me sourly, the innkeeper began, "She was a stranger some twenty-seven years of age. Barefoot and clad in filthy rags, she was leaning feebly on a bamboo cane, a broken hat slung on her back. It was a sight too loathsome even to describe. Her entire body looked grayish red with an uncanny purple shine here and there. Her fingers were as crooked as ginger root, swollen into sinewless lumps. Her left foot barely retained three toes, one of which was bloated to twice its normal size all the way up to the instep. Her right foot showed a faint scar where the big toe used to be. Her right little finger was like a huge boneless silkworm repulsively flaccid, and her left hand was a round, fingerless fist.

"Her face was even worse, as abominable as a melting statue of a copper lion. Her browless forehead bulged prominently and was full of purplish hollows oozing a gray-yellow liquid just like rotten oysters filthier than gutter sludge. Any part of her flesh not coated with pus was exposed mercilessly, as red as a baby's tongue. Her sunken nose was an infected sore, and her upper lip had melted away, baring sparse yellow teeth in horrible contrast to her shriveled colorless gums. The mouth had festered toward the right side, leaving her cheek ripped halfway open and the molars glaring out. Her hairless head glistened weirdly like a well-polished red gourd or a ripe persimmon about to break. Her right eye was merely a wet crater, and the left underlid was turned inside out vividly displaying red veins. Her remaining eyeball protruded out of the socket, its glazed umber pupil almost immobile, glaring up at men, the gods, and Buddhas. From time to time she would heave a sigh as if to vent a bodyful of venomous air —so repulsive that even dogs and birds fled. One look at her and we all felt sick. Even just recalling her foul odor at mealtimes, we were unable to enjoy our bean soup; reminded of her loathsome condition, we were forced to throw away the delicious salted fish guts. So we avoided her, no one offering her as much as a riceball.

"We heard her pitifully groaning out something like a song—she seemed to repeat under her feeble breath, 'Abandoned by the world, I abandon the world.' She would glower at the heavens, wildly swing her bamboo cane, and strike stones and trees by the wayside in a crazed frenzy.

"Seared by the flames of fury in her heart, she vanished, raving, into thin air."

❖ Selected Allusions

BASHŌ (Matsuo Bashō, 1644–94): poet, one of the most renowned haiku masters of Japanese literature.

BRAHMADEVA: in ancient Indian religion, the main deity and the creator of all things; the personification of the essence of the universe. Known as "Bonten" in Japanese Buddhism, he is the lord of the Pure Realm and guardian of the Sacred Laws.

CH'Ü YÜAN (340–278 B.C.): a southern Chinese aristocrat and poet known for his serious poems and tragic life, which ended in a suicide by drowning.

CONSCIOUSNESS ONLY DOCTRINE: the Buddhist ontology that holds that the only real existence is the mind, for everything in the universe is a mere reflection of the mind. By extension, the spirit of a dead person can communicate with the living.

EGUCHI, LADY OF (*c.* 1200): a courtesan and poet whose given name was Tae. It is said that when the renowned monk-poet Saigyō (1118–90) visited Eguchi, the following poetic conversation took place:

> It would not be difficult
> To forsake the world,
> Yet how you begrudge me
> A temporary lodging. *(Saigyō)*

> Since I understand that
> You have forsaken the world
> I can only say that
> You must not leave your heart
> At a temporary lodging. *(Tae)*

FUDŌ: the head of the Five Divine Kings serving the Sun Buddha. Their duty is to subjugate evil and desire.

GENJI: the hero of *The Tale of Genji,* a prince who loved numerous ladies. He is generally regarded as a paragon of *mono no aware* (the pathos of things) with the aesthetic capacity to be

moved by the quintessential beauty of all things and people.
HŌRAI, MT.: in Taoist legends, a holy mountain inhabited by immortals.
IKKYŪ (1394–1481): poet and priest of Rinzai Buddhism, the forty-sixth head of Daitoku Temple in Kyoto. He is the subject of legends containing humorous and epigrammatic episodes.
JIZŌ: a bodhisattva who manifests himself in the form of a child, and therefore believed to be the guardian of children. Jizō also came to be identified with local deities, thereby taking on the power to make travel safe.
KOGŌ, HOTOKE GOZEN, GIŌ, GIJO: twelfth-century courtesans who, according to *The Tale of the Heike,* became nuns after the deaths of their samurai lovers.
KUME, WIZARD OF: according to several old Japanese legends, a hermit who lost his ability to fly when he caught sight of the legs of a woman who was washing her clothes on the bank of a river.
LIU HSIA-HUI: a wise man of ancient China who is said to have proved himself impervious to women's amorous advances.
MAHESVARA: also called Siva, the supreme deity of Brahmanism. In Buddhism, he is depicted with eight arms and three eyes, holding a three-pronged spear and riding a white ox.
NARIHIRA (Ariwara-no-Narihira, 825–80): nobleman, poet, the hero of *The Tales of Ise.* He is considered to be one of the models for Prince Genji.
RANDEN, MT.: a mountain in China famous as a source of beautiful precious stones.
T'AO YÜAN-MING (376–427): a southern Chinese poet noted for his idyllic nature poems depicting a Taoist paradise called the Realm of Peach Blossoms.
TEN THOUSAND SPHERES: a Buddhist term for the entire universe.
Usuyuki, Sumiyoshi, Ise, Taketori, Genji, Sagoromo: tenth- and eleventh-century works of fiction; properly cited, all have *Monogatari* (tale) after the title given here. *The Tale of Genji* is noted as one of the earliest novels in existence.

WEN OF WEI (r. 220–26): founder of the Kingdom of Wei (220–65) of China, he wrote a highly acclaimed book of literary criticism, which includes the famous passage "Literature is a great feat of living, an immortal accomplishment."

THE BEARDED SAMURAI

[1]

ON FOREIGN SOIL thousands of miles away, our troops a hundred thousand strong demonstrate their valor by winning glorious victories. Within our empire, however, not a speck of dust is disturbed. Dogs slumber untroubled beside willow trees, and chickens cluck idly under thatched eaves. A picture of halcyon peace itself.

In contrast to our wondrous Meiji period, all sixty-four provinces of Japan writhed in chaos in the mid-sixteenth century, a scant three hundred years ago. Avarice-bred squabbles and blood feuds knew no end, and a darkness as murky as the night of the fifth month blotted out the light of universal justice and humanity. From the cream of the population down to born mediocrities, men were totally villainous and women thoroughly shameless. A man's pledge was not to be trusted unless he submitted his own father as a hostage, and even the black robe of the Buddhist nun assured women no protection from ravishment. The virtues of loyalty and benevolence were nothing but relics, and the teachings of compassion went unheeded.

Consequently, no one listened to the will of Heaven, observed the Sacred Law, or endeavored to correct and perfect himself. Men competed for fame and fortune by any means available—the sharp-witted by their wits, the strong by their strength, estate owners by the strategic advantage of their castles or the solid defenses of their domains, nobles by the prestige of their lineage or the privilege of their titles, and the plain samurai by a three-foot sword and his own two hands. They feared no god other than the blazing fire of their lust and let no needless Buddha stand in the way of their obsessive delusions. They staked their lives upon the ceaseless, desperate contention that "if I lose, I give up my life, no more than sixty years at the most; but if fortune rides with me, I can savor glories and riches that would satiate any man's appetite." Alas, it was a veritable scene from the Sphere of Asura.

Yet the cherry tree, even in a chaotic age with no one to cultivate it or appreciate its beauty, bursts into magnificent bloom in this wondrous country of ours. It is our pleasure, therefore, to find in such times of hopeless moral chaos a few men and women who left indelible marks through their uncorrupt hearts and noble conduct—shining stars to brighten that part of our history shrouded in black clouds.

The story I am about to unfold concerns one such man, unknown until now, but quite intriguing, nevertheless. The events might not have taken place in actuality, but I hope the reader will allow that the sentiments could very well have played their role at a given time in history, for a mere reiteration of historical facts is not my intention here.

[2]

Long ago, in the summer of 1575, Takeda Shirō Katsuyori was angry. While he was resting in imperious arrogance upon the hegemony established by his late father, Shingen, a certain Okudaira family in the Mikawa border area had had the audacity to declare its rebellious intentions. If he let them go unpunished, he would be courting open disrespect from other ambitious warlords, while undermining the confidence and reliance of lesser allies. Almost certain that Nobunaga, and Ieyasu in particular, would lose no time in building a cause around this incident to raise an army against him, Katsuyori promptly made an object lesson of the Okudaira by executing their youngest son, who had been kept as a token of their homage in the Takeda domain of Kōshū.

Katsuyori reflected, "The youth has been transported directly to his own native province of Mikawa and crucified there at Hōrai Temple, but I have yet to see the severed head of his brother, Sadamasa. I shall lead our army into Mikawa in a show of force, for I must impress upon my potential enemies that I am no less a leader than my father. If Ieyasu comes to their rescue, I'll be glad to cut off his head; if he doesn't have the courage, that's just as well also. My campaign will still serve a dual purpose: to carry on my father's ambition to cut a swath all the way to the capital, and to secure the fealty of all other warlords with the gibbeted head of that hateful Sadamasa."

On such a reckless impulse, Katsuyori led his fifteen thousand men through the northern tip of Enshū Province and set up camp in Mikawa. His grand scheme went awry, however, when a certain Ōga, a retainer of Ieyasu's who had agreed to conspire against his master and help Katsuyori, was betrayed by a double agent. Ōga was subjected to the extreme penalty of slow execution by the bamboo saw, and his family of eight was crucified. Frustrated and enraged by the collapse of his plot, Katsuyori ordered a raid on a small nearby fort, which was hardly enough to sate his aggressive appetite. By the first of May, he had laid siege to Nagashino Castle, which was under the control of the Okudaira. He deployed his generals along the Iwashiro River, installed his uncle atop Hawk's Nest Hill, fortified such strategic spots as Inner Mountain, Lord's Chamber, and Crone's Bosom, and positioned his field headquarters on Medicine King Ridge. Expecting little trouble in taking the modest castle, he mounted simultaneous assaults on a few other targets as well. Katsuyori then brazenly challenged Ieyasu to come out and rescue his confederates besieged within the latter's own domain of Mikawa.

Tokugawa Ieyasu, widely acclaimed to be the ablest lord in the region, had no intention of ignoring Katsuyori's challenge, yet he found himself restrained by a rational assessment of the situation. The Takeda army had earned its formidable reputation through numerous battles fought under Shingen's leadership. The Tokugawa legion was outnumbered three to one; furthermore, it had tended to be unmanned by the mere mention of the Takeda name ever since its defeat in the battle of Mikata-ga-hara in Enshū in 1572. Even if his men were inspired enough to make a desperate charge to save Sadamasa in the name of justice and samurai honor, such a move would be nothing short of suicidal, like eggs throwing themselves against a boulder. Attack was out of the question. On May 6 and 7, he had risked skirmishes with five eager Takeda regiments commanded by the feared General Yamagata, and even there he had narrowly averted a distinct defeat.

As a last resort Ieyasu decided to turn to Nobunaga for help. Twice he dispatched a messenger to explain the situation and request military aid under their mutual assistance pact. But Nobunaga procrastinated, understandably reluctant to sally forth against the Takeda army. Ieyasu finally sent Sadamasa's aged father, Sadayori, to plead for help; along with him went an emissary who was to convey the implied threat that if Nobunaga refused to honor the pact, Ieyasu would have no choice left but to give Enshū

Province to Katsuyori as a tribute and join forces with him in attacking Nobunaga's domain of Owari instead. Fully prepared to take further action should Nobunaga fail to respond to his veiled ultimatum, Ieyasu waited anxiously.

[3]

In the meantime, Oda Nobunaga was doing some busy thinking of his own:

"Now that the redoubtable Shingen is dead and buried, leaving that callow and reckless boy Katsuyori to carry on his ambition, I can afford to feel much more at ease, but the Takeda are still a mighty power to contend with, boasting loyal generals and a horde of valiant and seasoned warriors. If I fail to come to Ieyasu's aid, however, my cowardice will be held up for ridicule, and I might as well abandon my cherished ambition of conquering the entire nation. It's common knowledge that I owe Ieyasu a favor for his crucial assistance at the battle of Anekawa back in 1570. Worse yet, the Okudaira rebellion was touched off by my suggestion to have one of Ieyasu's daughters marry Sadamasa. When I am to blame for the death of the young hostage, how can I ignore the father's plea, leaving his other son to die, alone and helpless? It was indeed crafty of Ieyasu to have sent me the father of the very man who is suffering at this moment in the besieged Nagashino Castle. Ieyasu must have also instructed his emissary to tell one of my vassals that my refusal to help him would lead to a Tokugawa-Takeda alliance. Although still a lesser power, Ieyasu is clever enough to use the old man Okudaira to play on my emotions, and he is highly ambitious to boot. I don't doubt that he'd consider allying with Katsuyori against me. Katsuyori's raw courage combined with Ieyasu's military acumen would certainly pose a threat. Having survived through all those battles, I'm not foolish enough to let such an alliance take place.

"Even during Shingen's heyday, it was not fear of the Takeda army but my own discretion that had kept me from advancing into Kōshū. My policy is never to make a move before I am dead sure of favorable answers to a few critical questions: Is it worthwhile to engage in battle right now? Do I forfeit anything by backing out? Will the enemy retreat before my advance, leaving me empty-handed? Will my move guarantee definite profits? Judging the extent of Ieyasu's present predicament as well as Katsuyori's maneuvers from the repeated entreaty of Ieyasu's emissaries, I probably stand to gain from a battle at this point. But if the dauntless Takeda warriors are effectively deployed under experienced field commanders, our side can't expect to come out unscathed, even if we ultimately win because of Katsuyori's recklessness. If the enemy retreats too fast, my own reward probably won't be worth my effort."

Thus agonizing and deliberating, Nobunaga postponed his reply to Ieyasu until the last possible moment. At last deciding to take to the field for now and put a certain operational tactic into effect later if need be, Nobunaga ordered the mobilization of soldiers from all his provinces. Each man was to bring a fence post and a rope with him. For his commanders, who were eager to slay their leonine counterparts in the Takeda camp, Nobunaga hosted a party to compose linked verse in celebration of the anticipated victory.

Nobunaga recited his opening composition:

> *Matsu takaku*
> *Take tagu(h)inaki*   [*Takeda kubinaki*]
> *Satsuki kana*

Pine is tall and
Bamboo incomparable   [Takeda is headless]
In the fifth month.

One called Sekian carried the theme into the second link:

> *Shirō wa mienu*
> *U no hana no kaki*
>
> Not visibly white [Shirō is nowhere to be seen]
> Is the deutzia flower fence.

The poet Jōha added the third, wishing the demise of General Yamagata, known as the Demon:

> *Iru tsuki mo*
> *Yamagata usuku*
> *Kiehatete*
>
> The setting moon
> Vanished, [Yamagata
> Pale behind the mountain. faded away.]

And Oda Nobunaga concluded the sequence:

> *Oda wa sakari to*
> *Miyuru akikaze*
>
> The small field *(oda)* seems
> To thrive in the autumn wind.

Nobunaga meanwhile had adopted a secret plan proposed by one of his commanders, Sakuma Nobumori, whereby a false promise was made to a certain Chōkan, a retainer of Katsuyori's.

On May 13, the massive Oda army marched out along the Owari road; they boasted countless commanders with illustrious military records, including Akechi Mitsuhide, Hashiba Hideyoshi, and Nobunaga's two sons. Some fifty thousand troops radiated the fighting spirit of twice that number, uplifted all the more by the blare of conch horns and the stirring flourish of drum beats.

[4]

From May 10 to 14, the Takeda's continuous assault on Nagashino Castle steadily increased its ferocity. The garrison commander, Okudaira Sadamasa, remained resolved never to yield to the hateful enemy who had sent his wife, children, and young brother to their excruciating deaths. Expecting no quarter upon surrender, even the rank and file had no intention of awaiting their end without resistance. Determined to display their last acts of bravery with the sword before sharing the fate of the castle, they succeeded in repulsing charge after charge. As the siege dragged on, however, dwindling provisions threatened to render the garrison untenable. Sadamasa dispatched Torii Suneemon to deliver a message to Ieyasu, who was then at Okazaki Castle in Mikawa. Slipping through enemy lines, the messenger reached Okazaki on the fifteenth of the month and gained an audience not only with Ieyasu but also with Nobunaga, who had just arrived. After accomplishing his mission, however, the ill-fated Torii fell into enemy hands and was crucified.

Meanwhile, Nobunaga concluded a personal conference with Ieyasu, and during the next three days moved his army closer and closer to Nagashino. By May 18, after careful reconnaissance of the area, he had established his command post on Paradise Temple Hill in the town of Hidara, to the forward left of Nagashino. With his eldest son, Nobutada, occupying Heavenly God Hill, his second son, Nobukatsu, on Sacred Hall Hill, and Hideyoshi and others on Tea Mortar Hill, his crack troops formed thirteen layers of fortification. The Oda lines were secured tight enough to discourage any assault, even if the Takeda warriors were capable of feats rivaling those of demon-gods.

Ieyasu was even more resolute. He was the principal in this conflict, and this was his chance to avenge the recent affront and to put an end to a feud besides. A long-standing enmity flaring with new heat in their breasts, the Tokugawa warriors rose to the occasion despite their small numbers. Ieyasu allocated his forces into nine sectors, setting his camp on Tall Pine Hill further forward than Nobunaga's. The nearby Pine Ridge was fortified by his eldest son, Matsudaira Nobuyasu. The Tokugawa troops were roused to a seething impatience for battle by Ieyasu's unsparing command: "Don't bother collecting enemy heads to prove that you've killed. Just kill, kill, and kill to the bitter end."

Nobunaga for his part promptly put his plan into action. Under his orders all units began building barricades with the post and rope that each soldier had brought with him. Two to three terraces of fence along the gradually descending hillside in front of the entire encampment were to be manned from corner to corner, except where an open space had been provided every thirty feet to lure enemies in. The sizable army soon completed a line of defense as long as the Great Wall of China. Behind this impregnable barrier the Oda force stood arrayed, ready to welcome enemy assaults with devastating showers of missiles.

[5]

"I had half anticipated that Ieyasu would come out, and I even looked forward to dealing him a death blow. But in addition to Ieyasu, even Nobunaga has hauled his grand army all the way out here—the last thing I would have expected from that weak-kneed fellow. Well, so much the better. I won't have any trouble stampeding a flock of glib-tongued, soft-boned, urbanized men from the Owari Plain. Ever since my father died, Nobunaga has seized every opportunity to spurn me. He may be itching to try one of his clever little tactics that worked on those spineless neighbors of his, but what can he possibly do to me? I shall strip him of his armor once and for all and laugh in his face, or behead him with my own hand. Uesugi Kenshin, who is second only to my late father in military reputation, once struck camp in deference to me without giving battle when I was still a mere youth. How foolhardy and audacious of Nobunaga to show his face around me, when he isn't fit to dust the great Kenshin's sandals! I'll teach him the consequences of his flagrant disrespect."

The day after Nobunaga arrived at Paradise Temple Hill, Katsuyori assembled his commanders and made an announcement:

"As you already know, the enemy has advanced to Hidara Field. Clearly they intend to come to the rescue of Nagashino Castle. Our luck has it that both Nobunaga and Ieyasu have kindly aligned their heads for us to take at one time. The castle is harmless enough; it can be kept in check by a small contingent guarding the supplies at the outpost on Hawk's Nest Hill. Two thousand troops will be left to secure Nagashino Field. I shall cross the Cascade River by a bridge which we will build at Cormorant's Narrow and set up my command post two miles forward in Pure Well Field. The rest of you can ford the Iwashiro River and fan out to form giant wings. With our backs to the vast river, we shall slice our way through enemy lines." Katsuyori explained his plan of action with bravura, his voice crisp and vibrant.

Flanking the commander-in-chief sat Nagasaka Chōkan and Atobe Katsusuke, their shoulders squared and their brows arched smugly in silent but unconcealed admiration for the young master, as if the battle had already been won. None of Katsuyori's commanders, however, uttered a sound as their leader declared his intention to court disaster by this foolhardy offensive. Inwardly appalled by the reckless plan, they maintained a deathly silence under knitted brows. Quick-tempered Naitō, the most volatile of the famed Kōshū Four generals, though, was too forthright to hold his tongue, no matter what the consequences. He, if anyone, would refuse to consent to such a preposterous maneuver. Intransigent determination flushing his face, Naitō inched forward on his knees and swept scathing eyes over his colleagues.

"Does your silence mean that you're ignoble enough to do our lord's bidding blindly without assessing the tactical feasibility or possible outcome of his scheme? Have you forgotten our clan's tradition to deliberate thoroughly on all military decisions, which rules out thoughtless compliance? This is no trivial matter. I find your silence before such a momentous battle disgraceful. In fact, is it not most disloyal and dishonorable of you to suppress your disagreement, concurring with the lord in false obedience? I shall state my candid opinion in the hope that all of you will follow my lead."

After glowering at his speechless comrades, Naitō inclined his head slightly to address Katsuyori:

"My lord, please listen to me for a moment. You have just outlined an extremely drastic plan of combat operation, but, with all due respect, you seem to have made a quite uncharacteristic error in judgment. The decision to advance or retreat depends entirely upon the tide of battle, and it is no honor for a samurai to be driven by reckless courage. Take your late father, whose valor was probably unparalleled in our country. We have all witnessed Lord Shingen's timely decision to evade battle if the conditions proved unfavorable. Such discretion did much to establish his unique record, unblemished by a single rout, a failure to achieve his objective in battle, or an unsuccessful attack on a citadel. The true meaning of valor was exemplified by such accomplishments of his. In contrast, while your present strategy of swift assault may sound valiant, is it in accord with the genuine spirit of heroism? I doubt it. Surely you remember how your father used to express his admiration for Ieyasu, enemy though he was, as a formidable leader with judiciousness and stature far beyond his age. Your underestimating Ieyasu is in disregard of your father's illustrious military reputation.

"If Ieyasu were the only one involved, our best effort would be more than sufficient to pulverize him, a minor contender no matter how competent and versatile. But this time we are up against Nobunaga as well. We are outnumbered three or even four to one by his legions, which are not exactly lacking in stalwart fighters. Moreover, Nobunaga is a man of uncommon cunning known to spring devilish tricks on unwary adversaries. It is foolhardy to engage him solely by force of arms. He has erected double and triple fences reinforced by abatis along his entire front, not in an attitude of offense, but in one of firm defense. While it does betray his fear of our capabilities, you cannot deny the overwhelming inconvenience that it imposes upon us. To add to their numerical superiority, they enjoy all the advantages of a fortified encampment. Since an offensive force twice the size of the defense would barely strike a balance of power under these circumstances, it takes no genius to predict the outcome of our charge with a quarter of their strength. I beg you, my lord, please revise your plan so as to outmaneuver Nobunaga and Ieyasu. This is when we should be playing the stealthy game of hide-and-seek, a prize military secret of our clan.

"I apologize for volunteering my opinion before my seniors, Generals Baba and Yamagata, but I trust that the urgent nature of the matter at hand overrides protocol. Since our side will not benefit from a battle at this point, I recommend an immediate decampment and return to Kō-shū. Craven enough to hide behind fortification, the enemy has not the wit to sally forth after us; though of course, to be ready for the unlikely event of their pursuit, we can leave some rear guard units lying in wait or take any number of other measures to rub salt into the enemy nose. As our adversaries strike camp in disappointment, we will reverse our course and attack their rear. Should they make an about-face to fight, we will withdraw again. After several such elusive maneuvers, the other side, encumbered by its large size on unaccustomed terrain, will no doubt show fatigue sooner than our men, who can function more effectively in small numbers and on familiar ground. Indeed, our advantages easily double and triple their disadvantages. In the event that this kind of operation leads the enemy to make a rash mass advance, it will be a chance for us to lure them into an unfamiliar locality, thereby setting them up for the kill. We could even take the heads of both Nobunaga and Ieyasu together. Would you not agree that this scheme will tip the scale in our favor, transforming our handicaps into the very means of victory? I hope your lordship will adopt a prudent policy and avoid all unnecessary risks. Don't let your bravery prove your undoing. I beg you, sire, to reconsider and abandon your plan of attack at this time. I respectfully remonstrate."

Naitō made his plea eloquently, presenting his mature insight with artless candor and heroic fortitude, his head unbowed and his principles uncompromised before a man in power. Few could help but exclaim inwardly, "Well said, General!"

[6]

Baba, prostrate on the floor in deference to Katsuyori, quickly endorsed Naitō's plea with his own: "I am in complete agreement with General Naitō. I beseech you, sire, to accept his recommendation." Without a word, Yamagata also bowed deeply to express the same entreaty.

His mounting displeasure already visible, Katsuyori

nonetheless found it difficult to override the joint dissent of his three senior generals. In exasperation he glanced at Chōkan, who instantly grasped the message. The shrewd old man swaggeringly leaned his shoulders forward, cast a disdainful look around the assembly, and spoke:

"I cannot quite understand General Naitō's unsolicited counsel. First, I would have expected him to be aware of the battlefield taboo against making demoralizing remarks about the enemy's forte. Yet, to my regret, he was unsparing in his praise of our foes. The Oda soldiers may be great in number, but they are already intimidated by the reputation of our invincible army. Why should we fear a herd of cowering men? The only strong contender is the small Tokugawa force, which will pose no serious threat to us in any event, no matter how desperate and fierce their struggle. It is utterly unbecoming of General Naitō, who has proven his valor beyond dispute time and again, to suddenly counsel extreme caution, thoroughly alarmed by the enemy's numerical superiority. Not only do I object to his apprehension, but I even deplore the blemish he is bringing upon his own good name. A battle is never decided by the numbers. If we withdraw all the way home without crossing swords with the enemy, we will all be safe and sound, I grant you. But what would such an action do to our reputation? We have always sneered at enemies who were intimidated into a retreat by the mere sight of our mighty force. The Oda and Tokugawa troops certainly won't overlook this golden opportunity to repay us in kind, jeering, hooting, rattling their quivers, and clapping their hands in ridicule. While it may sound ideal to evade a battle and keep our army intact, the obvious consequences are just the opposite. Such a move will merely downgrade our prestige, tarnish the glorious name universally recognized since the days of Lord Shingen, and drastically reduce the number of warriors eager to serve under our banners.

"Now, a more crucial implication: The insurgent Okudaira not only will go unpunished, but will emerge a winner in effect. That may lead to an even greater crisis, if the other vassals in the Mikawa and Enshū border areas are encouraged to shed their fear of our retaliation and follow the Okudaira's example, switching their allegiance on the heels of our withdrawal. Is it not the poorest of strategies to defeat oneself without fighting and to self-inflict damage without losing a single soldier in the battlefield? Of course, I need not remind you that such dishonorable behavior as showing one's back to the enemy goes against the grain of our dauntless lord. Even if General Naitō's proposal were feasible, the disgrace of it would be more than our lord could bear. There is no need for further discussion, is there? I can't think of any alternative but for all of you to go forth to battle at our lord's command, fully prepared to lay down your lives in Nagashino Field. What say you, Atobe-dono? I can see no other choice. All of you must agree with me. Even if by chance you are of a different mind, the samurai code dictates that the vassal's duty is to obey his lord regardless." Chōkan's false loyalty gushed forth in unabashed arrogance, rhetorical flourish twisting logic and reason.

[7]

Following Chōkan's lead, the equally toadyish Atobe slid forward to kowtow before Katsuyori. "I believe the esteemed elder Chōkan is absolutely right."

Somewhat heartened by their obsequious support, Katsuyori's face brightened in approval. He surveyed the assembly, secretly hoping no one else would object.

Quickly taking the full measure of the situation, General Baba offered his opinion in a reverential tone:

"Old Chōkan and Atobe-dono seem to make a great deal of sense in what they say. Yet I would hesitate to call it perfect. Since General Naitō's assessment of our strategic position is totally accurate, we must defer impetuous actions if we hold loyalty to our lord and our clan supreme. Were we to foolishly charge the enemy with the blind courage of a mad tiger, we would certainly lose the battle and, I am sorry to say, gain absolutely nothing for our effort. Withdrawal may be a temporary disgrace, but who can say that it takes no courage to endure disgrace? Would you find more honor in inviting a chaotic rout and a decisive defeat? The ultimate victory belongs to the man of foresight who safeguards his own interests. My lord, please heed our advice for now and lead our army homeward.

"If we were to return from a long campaign without attempting to display our valor or take spoils, it would only serve to make our enemy gleeful and our own men disgruntled. I would not blame you for rejecting such a prospect. But I have an idea which would enable us to prove our valor and collect some trophies from this campaign as well. Before we make our orderly departure, suppose we storm Nagashino Castle in a swift assault and take Sadamasa's head to exemplify the exacting retribution for treason against the House of Takeda? The prestige of our name would be more than adequately upheld by sacking of a castle, modest as it is, and by the due punishment of the traitor. It would be rather gratifying to foil Nobunaga's relief mission and render useless Ieyasu's reliance on a massive reinforcement. I think we can readily take the castle, no matter how well guarded it is. During our skirmishes, I was able to estimate the number of their firearms at no more than five hundred. If we stage a coordinated charge from all four sides, the garrison would no doubt make full use of their firepower. Even if each of their shots found a live target, our maximum loss would be a mere five hundred. As our troops continue their onward rush over the fallen comrades, the enemy would counter-attack, perhaps claiming another five hundred. Nothing, however, could stop our valiant warriors from gaining the parapets. In the face of such a devastating onslaught, what choice has the garrison but to surrender or perish, even if the defenders were demon-gods incarnate? At the cost of one thousand casualties, we would retain our dignity and outwit both Nobunaga and Ieyasu. To be honest, this is not exactly my favorite plan of operation, but it would make our withdrawal more palatable than a defeat as the result of some ill-considered offensive."

Baba had expostulated well. Noted veteran general that he was, his judicious advice lacked neither in appeal to his young lord's combative ardor nor in tactical consideration of the need to sustain morale and self-esteem by keeping the inevitable losses to a minimum. It was all to no avail, however, for the intractably willful Katsuyori was not in the habit of yielding to anyone or countermanding his own orders.

Reading inacquiescence on Katsuyori's face, Chōkan interloped again, his self-importance bolstered by certain inside knowledge:

"General Baba's advice may sound reasonable, but it is actually quite hard to swallow. Why sacrifice a thousand of our own men only to withdraw, leaving the main enemy force untouched? Why not battle our real adversaries, Nobunaga and Ieyasu? It is obvious which is the more heroic alternative. General Naitō and others are busy bewailing our lack of advantage, but we have already set a secret strategy in motion. I am not at liberty to divulge its details, but I assure you that you will not fail to appreciate it when the time comes. Our lord's desire to wage a decisive war is not motivated by reckless belligerence." Chōkan, arguing testily, was dull-witted enough to believe that Nobunaga's trusted commander Sakuma had promised to betray his master out of a personal grudge. He never considered the possibility that Sakuma might be setting a ruse for the Takeda.

Nodding his assurance Katsuyori added confidently, "Listen well, Baba and Naitō. As Chōkan explained, I am not so witless as to enjoy losing my own men by mounting a harebrained charge against formidable enemies. I order an attack secure in the knowledge that the secret plan now under way will immensely enhance our chances of victory. If we move with one accord, even ten thousand enemy forces can be mowed down like so many blades of grass. There's no need to be afraid of their numbers. As the ancient Chinese saying goes, 'No tiger's lair ventured, no tiger cub gained.' Now, we can do without this senseless bickering."

[8]

Since the days of Shingen, the Kōshū Four—Baba, Yamagata, Kōsaka, and Naitō—had unfailingly demonstrated their battlefield prowess and had accumulated numerous testimonials to prove it. The most trusted among the Takeda vassals, they had always been privy to top secret decision-making at the tactical conference which was held each winter in order to formulate the following year's military objectives. Shingen had even accorded them the privilege of expressing their critical opinions on every maneuver involved in the confidential plans. Suddenly reversing this tradition, their young lord and Chōkan appeared to be harboring an exclusive secret.

"If the plan demanded strictest security, why didn't the lord call a private meeting to inform at least the three of us present on this campaign? Did he fear that we might not keep his secret? I don't exactly resent him, but I deplore his lack of confidence. What have we done to incur his disfavor? How have we come to deserve such distrust? On the other hand, who is Chōkan after all? We all know he was banished by Lord Shingen, but bought his way back into the new lord's service with a severed head he was lucky enough to pick up during a peasant uprising in Kōshū! Does the lord consider us inferior to this fellow? To think that he excludes us from his confidence yet so freely extends it to Chōkan!" Sharing the same bitter thought, Naitō and Yamagata sat silent, arms folded and heads lowered.

Baba, however, resolved to continue to speak his mind at this critical point in the young lord's life. Out of his desire to minimize tactical errors, he proposed a third alternative, similarly designed to prevent a rash aggressive move and to expedite withdrawal:

"I suggest that we capture Nagashino Castle directly and set up your command post within. Most of our forces ought to be stationed on the high ground behind the castle to make full use of the topographical advantage. In the meantime, Generals Naitō and Yamagata and I shall lead our own units across the river to keep the enemy in check. If we try to evade actual combat, but at the same time show that we are ready to hold our positions at any cost, it will be only a matter of time before the opposition shows signs of strain. They have a long and arduous supply line and will have experienced a prolonged encampment in mountainous terrain quite unlike their native plains. Known to be an impetuous sort, Nobunaga is not likely to keep his spirit up for long. When he succumbs to tedium, we will surprise him with a night raid or a dawn assault. Discretion is indispensable in a battle against a numerically superior opponent. If you feel disinclined to accept General Naitō's earlier advice or my own first suggestion, I beseech you at least to adopt this plan, though it is admittedly far from the best."

"General Baba seems to be the victim of a peculiar obsession," countered Chōkan with the persistence of a fox. "How do you expect Nobunaga, praised as a superb tactician by none other than General Naitō and yourself, to sit still at the mercy of our clever maneuvers? What if he decides to annihilate your three thousand troops camped right under his nose?"

"In that case, old Chōkan," said Baba unperturbed, "I would have no choice but do my best to fight back."

"My point exactly!" pounced Chōkan with a treacherous smile. "If you are to fight at all, you might just as well fight at your lord's command. Since it is all the same, wouldn't it be more sensible for you to obey the lord rather than making know-it-all objections?" Intent upon currying favor, the glib-tongued Chōkan, pandering to Katsuyori's whim and fancy, summarily thwarted the veteran generals' efforts.

The entire assembly fell into a chilled silence. Not only the three generals, but the other loyal vassals were also reacting in various manners: some silently lamented the fact that their lord failed to see the reason and merit in the well-conceived and well-presented suggestions; others were furious at the prattling Chōkan, who was single-handedly misleading the lord; some had closed their eyes in glum anguish; some glared at Chōkan with their brows raised in rage.

The awkward spell continued until Atobe made a motion: "In view of the serious disagreement among you, it seems best to call a recess. All of you ought to retire and deliberate more thoroughly in private."

Having no recourse, the counselors filed out. Before reluctantly leaving his lord, Baba repeated, "I implore you, sire, to reconsider."

[9]

Anxious though he was to have his own way, Katsuyori was beginning to vacillate in the face of the opposition from the foremost warrior-counselors that the House of Takeda had to offer. In this quandary he turned to Atobe, who had remained behind. "I want to give battle, but all my counselors are against the idea. This war council was fruitless because of our differences. Do you have any suggestions?"

A weak-willed opportunist, Atobe had no intention of dissuading his lord. Assuming an air of sagacity, he proceeded to say exactly what Katsuyori wanted to hear:

"Once you have decided to give battle, sire, no vassal should be allowed to question that decision. If your father were still with us, none of them would dare to venture an opinion. Young as you are, you have shown your own generals more deference than they are due, which has given rise to their presumption. As the late lord himself often told us, numbers do not decide the outcome of a battle. If you issue an order, they cannot oppose you. If any of them dare, you can easily stifle them with a written oath, as prescribed by the house tradition, that you shall stand firm on your decision regardless of remonstrations and appeals. Even the humblest footsoldiers, not to mention Baba and Yamagata, are well acquainted with the established rule that once sworn upon the flag of Lord Minamoto-no-Hachiman-Tarō Yoshiie and the Shieldless Armor handed down from your ancestor, Lord Yoshimitsu, an oath shall not be breached even if mountains split asunder and oceans turn dry. Your oath will put an end to all dissension."

Having momentarily wavered between reason and emotion, the young and inexperienced leader was now reconfirmed in his willfulness. With a complacent smile on his face, he nodded and said, "Summon back Baba and the others promptly."

When the group had reassembled, Katsuyori tartly informed them, "Since the war council failed to arrive at a resolution, I have, upon careful consideration, made it for you. We shall give battle. Make your preparations without further ado. That's an order."

Naitō and Yamagata had been clinging to a shred of hope that Katsuyori might still be moved to change his mind. They along with Baba and the other commanders were all plunged into despair by their lord's announcement, though it was not totally unexpected. The ordinarily taciturn Yamagata stepped forward briskly, no longer able to hold his silence.

"Has my lord taken leave of his senses?" he thundered. "Did he not comprehend the counsel of Naitō and Baba? No, my lord, you could not have failed to understand, but you still insist on having your own way. Do you mean to dismiss as utterly worthless the elders whom Lord Shingen left behind expressly to assist you? Humble and unworthy though we may be, it would be a grave mistake for you to ignore the practical counsel of seasoned warriors whose battlefield experience has yielded many a new tactic over the years. Admonition always grates upon the ear, as medicine is bitter to the taste. Not even the late Lord Shingen was above rejecting advice occasionally, but once proven wrong, he was quick to mend his ways. That is how he earned the well-deserved reputation of not taking a single serious misstep in his life. At my age I still believe that a lack of self-command, which may give the impression of strength, is nothing but a sign of weakness. If one listens only to pleasant words and feeds only on sweet food, the dire consequences are probably beyond measure. The kind of man who urges his lord to persist in a wrong decision enjoys his favor, but he is the ultimate bane of his lord's welfare. Beware of such a man's advice. Who counseled you to give battle at this time? I suspect either a sycophant or an idiot with the tactical insight of an infant. I hereby challenge him to a debate. If I lose, I shall surrender my head to him; if I prove him wrong, I shall not let him leave here alive, for in misguiding you he is much the same as a traitor working for the enemy. My lord, you must not give battle. You must not on any account."

"Silence, Yamagata! Speak no more! I refuse to listen," exploded Katsuyori, his face aflame and his eyes blazing. "Here and now, upon our sacred flag and armor, I pledge my decision to wage war. Not another word of objection from any of you. I have made my oath! If we lose, so be it. My late father used to assure you that battles were not won or lost by numbers. Furthermore, we fight under the divine protection of the god of Suwa Shrine and the war god Hachiman. Barring the unlikely waning of their divine grace and power, the House of Takeda could not possibly lose such a crucial battle. Cast aside your doubts, and prepare the troops to move at my command."

At the sight of their leader's expression, maniacal and seeming to threaten to halve any dissenter with a flash of the sword, the assembly shuddered.

[10]

Shocked into silence by his lord's shameful display of temper, Yamagata hung his head for a long time. At last, his deep voice supressed, his impassioned face blanched by grief, and his fierce eyes giving way to tears, he said, "Now that the lord has spoken thus, what more can we say? Our lives are dedicated to his service; regardless of right or wrong, we shall obey his command to fight any enemy to the best of our abilities. I trust Generals Baba and Naitō have made the same decision. What do the rest of you say?" Yamagata turned to sweep his eyes over his colleagues, spattering hot teardrops across the scarlet sleeves of his suit of armor.

Baba and Naitō were also tearful, frozen in dejected silence for some time before responding.

"As General Yamagata says, we will never hesitate to

give our lives. Seeing that the lord has sworn on the Flag and the Armor, we have no choice. Whatever Nobunaga and Ieyasu may be, they are not made of stone or iron. We must resolve to carry out our lord's wishes—to wield our swords as long as their blades last, to fire our guns until their barrels burst, and to press onward ready to fall dead in the river bed if need be. No more time for councils and debates. Posterity will sit in judgment over us—whether Old Chōkan was justified in calling us cowards, and whether or not our counsel against war was actually motivated by our reluctance to die. By the way, Old Chōkan and Atobe-dono, you have been rather eager to send our lord off to battle, but what do you intend to do if we lose? I wonder if you will have the nerve to flee before the enemy and show your disgraced faces to our people minding Kōshū in our absence after losing the war that you personally insisted on starting. We are the ones who opposed your idea, but we do not dream of getting out alive to face the colleagues of ours who took no part in this campaign." The two expressed their shared feelings, speaking alternate sentences.

Everyone then retired to begin combat preparations. Five companies of eight hundred men each under Baba and five other leaders headed for the enemy sector commanded by Hideyoshi, Sakuma, and Akechi; Naitō and six more with their forty-six hundred proceeded toward Gamō Ujisato's camp; Yamagata, Atobe, five others, and some forty-five hundred troops set out to face a Tokugawa wing. Katsuyori himself advanced between the forward and the rear contingents into Pure Well Field to bear down on Ieyasu's command position. All thirteen units made their bold, imprudent approach toward the Oda-Tokugawa lines, which had been cautiously entrenched behind impromptu fortifications.

[11]

The next day, May 20, the Takeda commanders took an inspection tour of the area soon to be the battlefield. Already resigned to a fight to the death, they were concerned only with forestalling tactical blunders and thus safeguarding their honor. A party including Baba and Naitō rode along the bank of the Iwashiro River to survey the conditions of the ground, the grade of slopes, the breadth of roads, and to make note of significant landmarks such as a grove or a tall, solitary tree. They shared one wish—to leave behind a name honored for its owner's valor even as his body fell into decay unmourned. At the small hamlet of Pure Well Field they dismounted and took a brief rest on their campstools. They had all lived through countless battles, gasping amid the acrid clouds of gunpowder fumes and drenched in the vermilion showers of fresh blood. Knowing that tomorrow they would at last fulfill their appointment in the judgment hall of the nether world, they today were in no mood to enjoy the fragrance of the young leaves that adorned the sky with their proud green or the birds twittering cheerily above the clouds. Although the place at which they stopped commanded a pleasing view, none of them so much as mentioned the scenery.

"Will tomorrow find my body lying in that yonder bamboo grove? Am I to seek my permanent abode in the shade of this old tree, which has been kind enough to spread its silky green-boughed canopy?" Tacitly sharing such ominous visions, none uttered a word to shatter a stillness so deep that the butterflies might have deemed it safe to alight on the armor of the bewhiskered samurai.

Long-time comrades at arms, Naitō and Baba had once stood side by side on a battleground, unruffled by spears dancing like the silver-tipped pampas grass in the autumn field and arrows showering down like rain and hail all around them. "Here's a riddle for you," one had said. "However hard you make it, I promise I won't need any more time to solve it than I need to fell that enemy warrior over there," replied the other, enjoying the little game in the thick of battle. In the present crisis, each remained his usual self, the one cool-headed, the other open-hearted.

"What do you think, General Baba?" said Naitō cheerfully. "The fifth month is already half over. The blossoms are gone, but their scent is still drifting through the treetops. The sky is not all that bright, but neither is it cloudy. The air is warm, even without a strong sun. If we were peasants free of care, armor, and helmet, we could sprawl on a bed of grass with a tree root for our pillow, comfortably loosen the collars of our humble cotton kimonos, and enjoy an innocent nap. Is it for want of meritorious karma from previous lives that we are deprived of even the simplest pleasure of enjoying the quiet music played by the wind upon the pine trees? From spring, when willows burgeon new leaves, through winter, when snow mantles the landscape, we spend all our time handling bows, arrows, guns, shields, swords, and halberds. We never have the time or inclination to appreciate flowers and the moon, except when we happen to realize that a scarlet-braided suit of armor is named "cherry blossom" or when we see the cream-tinted color of a "moon-coat" horse. If we ever do notice them, it is usually during a lone scouting mission along a mountain path. But how can we really enjoy the white cloud of blossoms cloaking the mountainside if we must suspect the enemy lurking in the shadows of the trees and tall grass? (How our hearts used to jump, mistaking the smoke from a farmer's field fires for human figures!) And the bright moon on a frosty autumn night only reinforces our tragic resolve—when we see it over a helmet visor above the sooty smoke of torches or while we keep a tense vigil against surprise attacks from a formidable enemy.

"I do not mean to bemoan the sad lot of the samurai, who must turn his back to the moon and flowers, but in this ephemeral world how can I help feeling sorry for myself, an aged warrior who has never known as much peace as a bird singing above the clouds on a blissful early summer day such as this. In my youth my sole concern was not to fall behind others, and my middle years were dedicated to aiding the late lord in his attempt to unify the country. Now toward the end of my life, the truculent new lord forces me into a hopeless battle. I hope you won't laugh when I say this, but somehow my entire past seems to be passing before my eyes, as though in admonition for all the wrongs that can be committed in the human life-span of twenty thousand days. It has been a long, long dream since the time when I struggled into my first suit of armor until this very day when my helmet strap is about to break. More than ever I envy the humble lot of woodcutters and mountain men. How I regret that I was born a samurai, to squander a whole lifetime fretting and gloating over vain glory! You are more learned than I, General Baba. How do *you* feel about this?" Naitō ended his monologue on a somber note.

"Your feelings are shared by all of us, I believe," replied Baba, the same sorrow clouding his face. "Just as the last bright light is reflected off the eastern mountains at sunset, so is our past projected in our mind's eye at the approach of our last day on earth. No one can blame you for your heartfelt lament, General Naitō, for all but a few among us must feel exactly the same way. But there is no use voicing regrets now. How sorry I am that fortune has deserted the House of Takeda and that our loyalty has proved inadequate to forestall tomorrow's battle. I too regret our futile life, bereft as it is of the freedom enjoyed by birds riding the clouds or the tranquillity accorded butterflies wafting serenely upon the wind. Alas, such is Heaven's ordination. Today we may envy woodcutters and mountain dwellers, but isn't it also true that we were lucky enough to encounter a brilliant lord, one who led us to discover the glory of being men and warriors? We aspired to follow him over hundreds of miles in pursuit of exploits and honor, forsaking salvation, defying death, and gladly shedding the sweat of blood to serve him. The bones within our flesh and the fire in our blood have allowed us no idle life. How could we be content to emulate birds and butterflies?

"Think of it, General Naitō. Have we not found our share of pleasure in the way of the samurai? It is true of any other way, but pleasure means nothing more than self-satisfaction, or a smile that brightens your face unawares. If you have experienced such a smile even once in the pursuit of a particular way, you ought to be glad to dedicate your life to it. What I myself find most shameful and regrettable is for a human being to end his life without ever having committed himself to any way, and consequently without ever having smiled such a genuine smile. Putting aside a life of idle ease, which is beneath our consideration, hasn't each of us arrived at his own understanding of the way of the samurai by now? If only in just payment for the precious smile that we have been fortunate to attain, we are obliged to give our lives to the sword and the spear, forgoing the luxury of envying birds, woodcutters, and mountain men. I am certain that you did not mean it that way, General Naitō, but some ill-wishers might take your statement as an expression of resentment toward the lord. At this point we can do nothing but regret our own failure to protect him from his own mistake. We are as trivial as specks of dust floating between the boundless earth and the vast sky. Of what possible consequences are our opinions? Let us laugh, General Naitō, let us laugh it all off and look forward to racing our steeds side by side, competing to be the first to gain the iron gate of Hell!"

"You are right, General," said the ungrudging Naitō, joining in Baba's sonorous laughter. "I did resent the fact that our lord refused to heed our sincere counsel, only to accept the unctuous words of Chōkan. Perhaps a case of spring fever, but those careless remarks may very well be my last slip of the tongue. Ha, ha, ha! Oh, well. Even if the foxy Chōkan and his cronies catch me in my indiscretion and slander me, their clever tongues shall wag to little avail this time in my permanent absence! Let's not even mention them. Then again, it depresses me to think that having failed to impress our loyal intentions upon the young lord, we have no happy report to bring to Lord Shingen in the nether world. I must admit that my own injudicious rebuke of Chōkan at the last year's war council prompted his clique to intensify their animosity. For that incautious provocation, which was directly responsible for thwarting your loyal efforts, I would like to extend my sincerest apologies to all of you in our last brief moment together. With your kind forgiveness I shall be able to go to my death with a clear conscience." Naitō bowed his head before each of his colleagues in turn with the innocence of an uncorrupt soul.

Yamagata, who had been silent, rose from his campstool and gestured for Naitō to stop. "You owe us no apologies, General," he protested. "None of us here blame or resent you. Fate itself has brought this upon us. Is it not so, General Baba?"

"I can see how General Naitō took to heart my remark that we had only ourselves to blame," said Baba, nodding in agreement. "It is quite estimable of you to reproach yourself for having antagonized Chōkan, but there is no point to self-reproach now. Who among us could criticize you? We are all bosom friends who have owed our survival each to the other through many battles. Errors of judgment are forgiven and forgotten among us. All the more reason why you ought to know better than to extend formal apologies to your comrades for an incident which was not entirely your fault.

"In any event, to get back to tomorrow's battle, all of you must have already resolved to fight to the death. I do not intend to be the last, either. Perhaps the time has come for the House of Takeda to fall, if the devious advice of sycophants has become official policy, while our opinions are ignored. No matter how hard we rack our brains to perfect a strategy or how desperately we fight, there is no possible way for us to score a victory. Under similar circumstances some warriors are known to have eluded death to bide their time, but I could never bear to witness the downfall of our clan. I would rather die a valiant samurai's death. Such being the case, this is the last day I can share with my comrades, shaking hands and engaging in genial conversation.

"Maybe we are lucky to have been born in a time of disorder and unrest. We have been blessed with a comradeship well tempered by life-and-death situations amid flashing swords and roaring guns; and we have come to know each other so well. I wish we could throw a farewell party in honor of the karmic mystery that has ordained us not only to live side by side in this life, but also to journey into the next with our armored shoulders abreast. I only regret that the time and the place preclude such a gala affair. But look! Here is the spring that must have given this hamlet its name; it is all but begging us to dip from it. Why don't we toast with its clear water instead of saké to bid our final farewell and seal our pledge to travel as one to see our late lord? What say you, my colleagues?"

"You read our minds, General Baba!" Naitō and Yamagata exclaimed, breaking their somber silence. "All of us have read each other's minds. Among warriors braving common perils, there is but one resolution to be shared. At such a gathering, pure water is far more appropriate than saké to toast our immaculate hearts."

As Naitō and Yamagata fought to suppress their tears, the other commanders bowed their heads in silent lament. An alert attendant of Baba's fetched the water in a cedar pail. Using the dipper he carried in his waistband, Baba took the first sip and then silently handed the dipper to Naitō, who in turn passed it to Yamagata.

When it had completed the round of all present, Baba lifted himself to his full height and exclaimed, "How refreshing! This pure cold water coursing down my throat extinguished the smoldering fire of worldly desires. I feel as though my body is made of ice-clear bones and muscles, containing not a single thing in this world to distract my mind or hold my heart in bondage—a state of true purity. Tomorrow I shall demonstrate a fitting end for a Kōshū samurai. Until my bones are rasped down to quivering threads and my battle cries spray the red mist of hot blood, I shall not stop wreaking havoc and terrorizing Ieyasu and Nobunaga. Ah, what a delightful thought!"

Gazing at the distant enemy encampment, Baba smiled a valiant smile so inspired and inspiring that it rendered his wrinkles nearly imperceptible. His comrades followed suit, rising and turning their eyes toward the enemy lines.

"I won't be far behind, General Baba. Since this world holds nothing dear to me, I look forward to regaling the late lord with reports of the daring feats I fully intend to perform tomorrow." Naitō burst into a spirited laugh that would surely have chilled his enemy if any happened to overhear it.

"How amusing! Nor shall I die empty-handed. I shall demonstrate my steel-hard spirit to my dying breath," declared Yamagata, the Demon. His words sent chills down the spines of his comrades, who could all but see his fiery eruption in the coming battle.

The warriors gazed at one another, their surging emotion bespoken by the plaintive smile touching but one cheek and their grim resolution emanating in the sharp glint of their eyes, until the deathly silence was abruptly shattered by an outburst of weeping as uninhabited as a baby's tantrum. Whirling around instantly, Naitō demanded, "Who weeps so loudly? How odd! Not any of us here. Ah, Sanada, behind you! See the rustling bamboo bush beneath the magnolia blossoms: Someone seems to be lurking there. Go investigate."

Gripping a commander's fan in one hand, Sanada approached the thicket and challenged, "Who's there?"

A man rose from among the shrubs and strode into the center of the group; he then sat down on the ground undaunted by their collective gaze. "There is no cause for alarm. Some of you may not know me by sight because I have been in General Kōsaka's command for many years. I was stationed at the Kaizu checkpoint by Lake Biwa, except when I was engaged in intelligence activities in Echigo.* Let me introduce myself. I'm Kasai Dairoku Takahide, now serving in the division commanded by my uncle, Kasai Takatoshi, who is here among you," the man concluded, raising a sanguine face framed by a lacquer-black beard and as red as a jujube.

Baba, Yamagata, and those who knew Dairoku returned smiling greetings, but Naitō, who had only made his acquaintance recently, and others who had never met him before still appeared perplexed.

Sanada stepped up to Dairoku and sat down beside him on the grass. "Pleased to meet you. I am Sanada Masateru, a brother of Nobutsuna, whom you probably know. So you are Old Kasai's nephew, who, I was told in confidence,

---

*The domain of Uesugi Kenshin (see the entry for Uesugi Kenshin in the Selected Allusions, p. 259).

has been on a secret mission in the northern region. I am honored to make your acquaintance." The rest of the group then took turns introducing themselves to Dairoku, and all settled down on the grass.

"Well, Kasai-dono, I believe you were weeping in the thicket a moment ago. What made you cry so?"

Even before Sanada had finished speaking, the elder Kasai glared at his nephew, anger flooding his aged face, bony and angular as a rocky mountain stripped of surface soil. "Look here, Dairoku! What's come over you? I never thought you were such a fool. It was bad enough to find you, a low-ranking samurai, lurking on the fringes of such a high-echelon gathering, but even worse you had the audacity to squall so shamelessly. Even General Naitō seems to find it hard to understand. Now, answer Sanada's question. . . . Oh, blast it! Are you crying again? I can't bear the sight of those fat teardrops rolling down your red face. Speak! Explain yourself! You! Dairoku! Have you gone insane? Have you lost your wits? I hate to say it, but might not those be tears of cowardice in the face of imminent battle? If you can't answer my charge, get away from here this instant. I refuse to look upon that dastardly, craven, sniveling face of yours. Get up and begone! Today of all days when this old uncle of yours has but a few hours left to live, spare me a senseless disgrace the likes of which I have never known in all of my long life. You raving lunatic! If you refuse to get up by yourself . . ." The old man seized Dairoku by the scruff of his collar, straining to pull him to his feet.

"Wait, uncle, please calm yourself," began Dairoku in a tearful voice, brushing off the elder's hands. "I am neither cowed nor deranged. I am still the same old Dairoku. If I'm a fool, nothing can be done about that, since that is how I was born. Anyway, *I* should be the one to ask your honors, 'Have you lost your minds?' I find it deplorable that you should be asking *me* that question. Since Sanada-dono kindly requested my explanation, I shall sum up my feelings, useless as that may be. My mind is so muddled by grief that I may offend such an illustrious company, but still I must speak my piece.

"In the dawn mist this morning I left our camp alone to survey the enemy positions and to explore the ground we will cover tomorrow. I scouted the entire area on foot until sunrise and returned to the camp only to be told that my uncle had gone on a survey tour with your honors. Since I would lose nothing by retraversing the same route, I followed your track all the way here. Being of humble rank—barely on speaking terms with your honors—I considered it wise to retire behind the tree until you were done, rather than intruding recklessly. But even from that distance I was able to sense an atmosphere which greatly alarmed me. Then some of your words drifted within my earshot. How distressed I was when I finally fathomed that you were intent upon dying tomorrow! 'I'm too late!' I lamented. 'Never mind my inferior rank and experience. Had I arrived here sooner, before their minds were made up, I could have leaped out before the generals and done my desperate best to present my humble opinion and try to reverse their resolution. What a shame! Does my delay spell calamity for my lord, a stroke of luck for our enemy? Has my chance for altering the course of events passed forever? Will tomorrow see the able leaders, the backbone and spirit of all the Kōshū samurai, the limbs and fangs of our lord, fall at the enemy's hand in an act of futile heroism?'

"Such a thought froze my heart and spread dark clouds over my mind's eye, obliterating any glimmer of hope in our path ahead. I do not mean to sound like a querulous woman or child, but I cannot help wishing General Kōsaka were here to dissuade you. Young and humble though I am, I take this liberty to express my bewilderment. I simply cannot understand why you have set your hearts so zealously upon death to the exclusion of all alternatives. I agree that the already unfortunate state of affairs seems daily to take a turn for the worse. Bewitched by the devil and by the sweet flattery of Chōkan and Atobe, the lord refuses to listen to the advice of his loyal counselors. So you have abandoned all hope, choosing death rather than surviving to witness the fall of our clan. But why stop there? Why not reassess the situation? Yes, I heard what had transpired at the last war council—how the agonizing remonstrances of the three senior generals were flatly rejected, while Chōkan and Atobe gained influence with their toadying. In your despondency you must have committed yourselves to the Buddhist motto decorating many of our banners, 'Forsake the corrupt world and aspire to the Pure Land.' Not only do I find it hard to deprecate you, but I even sympathize with your honors. Nonetheless, this is the very time when a warrior must be strong. Anguish is not to be shunned by a samurai. He honors his covenant with his master not merely through this life but beyond death, even if he must turn into a fighting demon to serve his lord. How sad, though inevitable, that you of unfailing loyalty should be so bent on deserting this world.

"You doubtless need no reminding, but it was in 1569, I believe, that Lord Shingen launched an attack against the Hōjō family in Odawara. After a great deluge we came upon a river so swollen that it was all but impossible to ford the torrent. A certain Hajikano waded into the water to measure its depth and then urged his two hundred men across the river. 'I claim the honor of being the first! Follow me, men. Head your horse upstream, ride off the saddle, and give him rein to swim. Footsoldiers, interlace your spear shafts and arms to form a chain. Wade in groups,' he shouted, rushing his mount into the water.

Swirling waves washed over his horse's back, the tassels of his breastplate danced on the river surface, and only the pennant carried high on his back was visible amidst the breaking waters. A gallant feat it was! Thereupon Lord Shingen said to an aide, so I was later told, 'Hajikano is a valorous warrior, yet I cannot love him for his aggressive competitiveness. By a *shōgi** spear emblazoned on his pennant, he seems to indicate his determination to move ever onward, but I think it is senseless.' Some of you must have been there to hear it for yourselves. Had the lord cared nothing about Hajikano, he would have ignored him. His remark, though, was constructive criticism. Isn't it lesson enough for us to review what he said in the light of his own conduct? I may be committing the folly of preaching to Buddha, but please hear me out. While the late lord renounced even Hajikano's reckless move forward as senseless, you commanders, especially Generals Baba, Naitō, Yamagata, the hope and bulwark of Kōshū, have no better idea than to charge the enemy lines seeking your certain death. Whether or not fate has turned against the House of Takeda, I am anguished beyond words. Upon losing all of you, the foundations and pillars of Kōshū, what will become of the young lord? I cannot believe you are past caring, so what drove you to the drastic decision? The more I think of it, the more excruciating my agony. Can you blame me for crying? Or for wondering how you manage to restrain yourselves from crying?

"Is there none among you who would retract your decision and try instead to survive as long as possible for the sake of the lord? Not a one? Oh, Hachiman and the god of Suwa, how unreliable you are! Have you forsaken the Takeda clan of the impeccable lineage? Loyal as these commanders are, they need only a spark of divine inspira-

―――――――――
*Japanese chess; its spear piece can move only forward.

tion to light the darkness in their hearts and resurrect the valiant warriors in them! What a shame! Here are dreaded heroes who would strike terror into a demon's breast, now petrified like so many dead men. I have often heard that the pale shroud of doom stalks a man nearing his death, but until now I never realized how true it was. How eerie to behold with my own eyes someone whose shadow is fading fast. Has the sun fallen from the sky? Isn't this still the same world in which blossoms bear fruit and man's wishes are fulfilled? I beseech you, commanders, rally back to life!"

Dairoku had delivered his plea lustily, his tear-washed eyes blazing. Nevertheless, the score of Kōshū veteran commanders, all but strong enough to conquer demons, remained speechless and immobile, like weathered statues of legendary heroes immersed in unfathomable thoughts, their eyes closed, their heads hung low and breaths bated.

"Has my entreaty been lost on you?" cried out Dairoku again as he leaned forward, glaring fiercely and gnashing his teeth in desperation. "Is there no one willing to respond, to reaffirm the world so summarily renounced? What a pity your stout hearts only abet this unyielding silence! Is there not even one live soul among you, one solitary spirit loyal to life? Have you found flaws in my reasoning? Where is your well-known candor, General Naitō? Do you disagree with me, General Baba, Sanada-dono, Tsuchiya-dono? Anyone? I cannot believe, uncle, that you do not agree with me. How can you all be so unfeeling, when I am writhing in anguish right before your very eyes?"

Dairoku's frantic cries rose in vain. The shadows of clouds sailed tranquilly across the sultry summer field, transforming the luster of armor into a somber, forlorn, leaden gray.

Finally at the end of his patience, Dairoku pulled himself up on his knees and, unmindful of protocol, shuffled closer to Baba. "Do you still intend to die? Will you not live,

General Baba?" he demanded in a voice trembling with rage, shaking Baba by the shoulders.

Easily disengaging Dairoku's hands, Baba got to his feet and embraced him. "How wonderful that the House of Takeda is still blessed with one such as you!" exclaimed the general in his rugged voice. "Who can fault your sound argument! Nevertheless, our time has come. We are old, it is time for us to die, and this is a worthy occasion for it. If it were merely a matter of personal preference, we might be influenced by your pleas. But we cannot defy the time, the circumstances, the event, and fate itself. Please try to understand why we choose death. It is because we are in no position to do as you ask. I am not distorting logic, may the god of Kōshū and Hachiman be my witness! Please watch me, spirit of Lord Shingen! This fate is far beyond our control. Perhaps you have much yet to learn, Dairoku-dono. In any event, *you* must live. I beg you simply to consider the emotions driving the rest of us, who have only our lives left to give in our lord's service. Who would not prefer to live to see his lord prosper in glory? As ill luck would have it, we have been forced to our drastic resolve in the slim hope that our deaths might later prompt our lord to mend his ways, if only out of pity for our sincere effort. Since we accept this as our fate, we deem it beyond right or wrong. We are neither ashamed to be accused of misjudgment nor cheered by vindication. That is all there is to it. Today I have met a man of spirit, but I am powerless to respond to his impassioned plea. Leaving us no time for a heart-to-heart talk, death will come tomorrow to separate us eternally. A misfortune of having been born into chaotic times—how I regret it! Please don't misunderstand me, but I hope you will manage to survive and observe the consequences of tomorrow's battle. I rely upon you to be a living witness. I do implore you, Dairoku-dono. This will probably be the last time we see each other, for

I shall go to my death no matter what." His eyes widened with determination, Baba firmly clasped Dairoku's hand and stared into his bearded face.

Unable to find words in the face of the old warrior's immeasurable anguish, which clearly overrode any possibility for reversal of his stand, Dairoku fastened his unblinking eyes upon Baba's face. One deathbound in the twilight of his years and the other adhering to life in his prime—the downturned and the uplifted eyes of two dauntless men conducted a boundless and wordless discourse transcending the realm of life and death.

The spell was abruptly broken by the piercing cries of a cuckoo bird flitting past overhead, unseen in the drifting clouds. Immediately regaining his composure, Baba swung his eyes up, sprinkling a few icy teardrops over the flaming face of Dairoku.

[12]

The wind deepens the melancholy of a hamlet under falling plum blossoms, while it enhances the peace of a house beside dancing willow branches. The silent spring rain makes the fisherman knit his brows, while it delights the farmer. Likewise, this day's sun found the Oda camp in an atmosphere diametrically opposed to that in the Takeda's. Imposing in appearance, albeit with dread apprehension beneath the surface, the massive Oda force sported a forest of banners bearing the insignias of the brigades arrayed under them. Animated neighing of horses from the distance added to the exhilaration at the Oda command post. The exacting leadership of Nobunaga, true to his nickname, General Vigilant, was aptly supplemented by Ieyasu's resourceful discretion. The common fear of the reputedly invincible Kōshū army, moreover, galvanized the ranks into a determined mass—a reassuring omen of victory.

Nevertheless, successive scout reports confirmed that the positions of the Takeda legions were all but impregnable. Oda commanders paled at this alarming discovery, and a nonplussed Nobunaga sent for Ieyasu.

At the emergency war council Nobunaga went over the intelligence reports. "Does anyone have a suggestion? Shibata, Takigawa, Sakuma, Hideyoshi?" Nobunaga called on each of his commanders, resting his expectant gaze upon one after another, but none broke the silence. Noticing an eager expression on the face of Sakai Tadatsugu, who was seated at the far end of the group, Nobunaga, his ire subsiding, beckoned him, "You must be the reknowned Sakai in the service of Lord Ieyasu. Come closer, right over here. Now, Tadatsugu, tell me what you make of the enemy's disposition." As if already certain of Tadatsugu's reply, Nobunaga had changed impatient tone to a confident, leisurely one.

Striding forward, Tadatsugu bowed and enunciated his opinion:

"I venture to disagree with your scout, in view of my own reconnaissance and the observations of my undercover agents. Our adversary has but half our strength; furthermore, he has recklessly blocked his rear with a great river, by his own choice! Now that he has fallen headlong into your lordship's trap, our victory is as good as guaranteed. My prediction will no more miss the mark than a hammer would fail to hit a target as large as the earth itself."

"How true, how true!" exclaimed Nobunaga, beaming. "What is seen by a cowardly eye and reported by a cowardly mouth never merits our consideration. Now that you, the bravest warrior in the coastal region, have reached this conclusion, our victory is all but won. My mind's eye can already see us scattering the Takeda forces, taking possession of Kōshū, and pushing on to conquer the entire eastern and northern regions."

With a jubilant smile Nobunaga lifted a handy saké cup, swallowed its contents, and handed the cup to Tadatsugu, saying, "Drink from this and pass it to my heir Nobutada over there. No need to decline for the sake of formality. I am hoping that a touch of your unequaled valor may be transfused into my son."

Honored with such an accolade, Tadatsugu drained the cup, hesitantly offered it to Nobutada, and prostrated himself before him.

"You, Tadatsugu, are not a rough, ill-bred warrior whose only virtue is prowess in battle," began Nobunaga again with an approving smile. "I have been told that you are quite a dancer, particularly proud of what you call the 'shrimp-catching dance.' I want you to show it to us. Lift the morale of our commanders—they must be as anxious as I am to see it." Though genially given, Nobunaga's command left no room for evasion.

"Of all things, the shrimp-catching dance! I am quite confounded by your request. However, since you have already found me out, I cannot very well plead a lack of dancing ability. Despite the shame and embarrassment I feel before the critical eyes of someone like your lordship, who is accustomed to the sophisticated style of the capital, I have no choice but to comply."

Tadatsugu slid back a few paces and rose to commence his dance.

> Soundless and unhurried flows the water under the spring sunlight, clear to the bottom of the brook. Little shrimp playing among the river weeds, little shrimp teasing the water moss, in a brook along the paddy fields. Quiet observation reveals, oh, what a precocious shrimp! Bedecked snugly in heaven-endowed armor, crowned with a natural helmet like a dragon's head, spreading its two short barbels into a

V-shaped crest, and flourishing two long whiskers like spears and halberds—oh, what a precocious shrimp!

Funny little shrimp, let me catch you! A tall man wades into the brook, where sunlight flickers upon the shallow water. Stooping down, he watches, motionless. As the ripples die down, the shrimp resumes his play among the weeds, brushing against the moss, secure and unsuspecting. With a lightning flash of his hands, the man lunges, but misses the shrimp. The hands pursue, and again it skims away. He stalks in a circle; it flees in an easy glide. Oh, what a close call! The man withdraws his hands to wait for the waves to subside.

Again a pompous little warrior garbed in red armor wields his whisker-halberd. Another one over there. Another right here. Another, another, another, there, there, there. In mockery or rage, the protuberant eyes glare upward in a proud show of force. Casually undertaken, this trifling task is now impossible to quit. The hopeful giant rounds his eyes, alert as a cormorant, and spreads his hand wide as a palm leaf. He aims; his quarry eludes. He gives chase; it takes to flight. Pounce, slip. Here, there. In his impatient struggle, the elbow-deep water surges over his shoulder, and splashing waves break upon his back. Still, only the slippery feel at his fingertips, and no catch.

A colossus whose head would loom above a field of corn, whose arms could lift a stone mortar with no strain, stands erect, his dignity undiminished by the elusive little shrimp. The blossom-scented breeze pokes fun at his ruffled sidelocks, and a lark trills across the sky as if tattling on someone. How embarrassing to be found soaking wet on a sunny day! He curses his ill luck, but without recourse, he returns home. In the light of the pine twig fire, he weaves a fishnet with a makeshift knitting needle. Vowing not to fail again, he attaches it to a willow hoop atop a bamboo pole. He rests his head upon his elbow, pleasantly dreaming of catching the shrimp with his new net in the morning.

A spring dawn brightens the sky, against which a flock of crows, cawing cheerily, etches a vivid contrast. With the net on his shoulder, the man retraces his dew-drenched steps to the brook. The little shrimp sporting among the weeds, the little shrimp tickling the water moss, having the time of his life, secure and unsuspecting. This time you shall not escape. You shall not be forgiven. The man cautiously steals closer, his net at the ready. He springs and captures a handful of shrimp with ease. Oh, what fun! He scoops again; another three or four. Swish, and four, five more. Five or six now. Caught unawares, the shrimp raise a clamor of consternation and protest, but they are as powerless in the net as butterflies on the spider's web. They leap, dance, flounder, and squirm, only to the amusement of their captor. The splendor of their helmets and armor, the flourish of their spears and halberds—alas, nothing but yesterday's dream!

From the initial slow movements of a commander's fan, Tadatsugu had broken into a fast and furious dance brandishing a long halberd in place of a fishnet. At his humorously realistic gestures, the entire assemblage roared with laughter, beating on their quivers, clapping their hands, and causing a commotion for some time.

"How amusing! A most appropriate dance for the occasion!" blustered a jubilant Nobunaga. "Listen Tadatsugu and the rest of you. Katsuyori is indeed a shrimp, is he not? Do you not agree, Lord Ieyasu? He is swaggering his whiskers now, but it won't be long before he ends up in our net. Ha, ha, ha! He is a shrimp, a little shrimp. What a delightful conceit!"

"Right you are, Lord Nobunaga," echoed Ieyasu, beaming. "That little shrimp boasts his reputation, wiggling his spear and halberd, but he is only wallowing in self-importance. Some of our men may be in awe of the Kōshū army, but Shingen's days are all in the past. Nothing can be the same under Katsuyori. Our total victory is all but accomplished. My only wish for tomorrow is that each of you commanders may catch as many Kōshū shrimp as the next man."

"Well, now. Come tomorrow, the Kōshū men shall taste our blows." Sharing the same hope, everyone present squared his shoulders and raised his brows in eager anticipation.

Having personally surveyed the enemy deployment earlier, Tadatsugu had devised an offensive strategy based on his observation. Finding this an opportune moment to seek official sanction for it, he sidled up to his lord and whispered the plan. "A very interesting idea," Ieyasu replied. "This is no time to hesitate. Submit your suggestion to Lord Nobunaga."

Delighted by the encouragement, Tadatsugu turned to Nobunaga. "I beg the Commander General's indulgence for a moment. The odds are overwhelmingly with us in the upcoming battle now that we have secured a topographical advantage against an enemy force less than half the size of our own to begin with. Still, it would be desirable to defeat him most expeditiously. At the risk of being presumptuous I venture to submit a plan for your consideration in the belief that to withhold knowledge under the present circumstances would constitute an act of disloyalty. Despite the forward encampment of Katsuyori and some of his ablest generals, their main body is probably located somewhere to the rear of Nagashino. If we strike at the enemy trunk, his limbs and leaves will not be able to withstand the shock. Suppose we dispatch a detachment of a few companies tonight? If they ford the Yoshi River and cross Matsuyama Pass in the darkness, they can climb Hawk's Nest Hill and Kuma Hill undetected. Then if they set fire to the outposts and camps in Nagashino and push on to Norimoto Village to cut off the enemy's rear and capture their supplies, the Takeda army will be thrown into panic. When our main forces sally forth in a coordinated offensive, Katsuyori will have no alternative but to beat a hasty retreat in the face of our whirlwind assault. Since I am well acquainted with the lay of the land, I humbly request permission to lead one of these detachments." With his forehead pressed to the floor, Tadatsugu awaited Nobunaga's approval, of which he was quite certain.

To the warrior's complete surprise, however, Nobunaga stiffened his expression and thundered, "Silence, Tadatsugu! Stop talking. How you wag your useless tongue! I thought you were a man of wisdom and tact. How dare you presume to make such an inane suggestion! You may be accustomed to commanding a mere four or five hundred men, or at most a couple of thousand, but you are probably ignorant of the grand-scale strategy involved in pitting two great armies against each other. Don't spread incautious ideas to mislead the troops! Your plan might work in a skirmish between small units, but not here. Our opponents are seasoned troops of Kōshū, and our side represents the combined strength of my Owari-Mino and Lord Ieyasu's Enshū-Mikawa forces. It is foolish of you to recommend a petty trick as if we were dealing with mere bandits and outlaws. A grown man ought to be ashamed of resorting to effeminate wiles and childish pranks. This sort of petty maneuver cannot serve a great army any more than a sickle can fell a large tree. I am not interested in listening to useless suggestions. Return to your place."

Tadatsugu retreated to his original seat, red-faced in disappointment and humiliation.

Thus the war council ended. Ieyasu returned to his post, as did the other commanders.

Before long a personal attendant of Nobunaga's delivered a secret summons to Tadatsugu. Baffled but compliant, he accompanied the messenger back to the Oda headquarters.

"Come closer, Tadatsugu," called a smiling Nobunaga in a conspiratorial whisper, belying his angry mood of a few hours before. Laughing, he offered dried abalone to the warrior. "Don't resent my harsh treatment of a while ago, Tadatsugu. Your suggestion is the best plan of action I have heard so far; there's no doubt about it. But if I had instantly approved your plan at the general council meeting, there would have been no telling where and how the plan might leak out to the enemy. That is why I pretended to disparage you. Don't give it another thought."

Struck dumb again by Nobunaga's unpredictable behavior, Tadatsugu prostrated himself to indicate his gratitude.

"Look, Tadatsugu," continued Nobunaga with a note of satisfaction. "This is my favorite bit, a type used by *ninja** for their horses. Take it. It's yours." Nobunaga then summoned retainers who had been standing by. As they filed in, he issued his instructions: "Kanamori shall be in command. Satō, Aoyama, and Katō shall serve as his tactical staff. I give you four thousand troops and five hundred guns to reinforce Tadatsugu's unit. Get ready to move out and cripple the enemy from the rear. I am counting on you to succeed."

Charged with this grave mission, the Oda commanders were in high spirits. "General Sakai, please don't hesitate to give the orders. Our common objective is to accomplish this task and please our lord. Let us dispense with formalities so we can fight as one." "I agree," responded Tada-

---

*Professional undercover agents.

tsugu, returning their bow. "Let us endeavor to do our best."

"I intend to borrow a few regiments of our own, with Lord Ieyasu's permission," Tadatsugu explained to Nobunaga. "Fortunately, a storm seems to be brewing. We can strike the enemy's rear tonight under cover of clouds and fog. If the storm proves severe, so much the better. When you sight columns of smoke rising behind Nagashino tomorrow, you can assume that we have succeeded in destroying the Takeda encampments on both Hawk's Nest and Kuma hills. I promise to reduce their fortifications to ashes at Crone's Bosom, Inner Mountain, and Lord's Chamber as well, and to strike terror into Katsuyori before you engage him in a major confrontation. Rest assured—I have a number of guides, including the old man Okudaira, who could lead the way blindfolded, so we are sure to reach Hawk's Nest Hill before dawn. Since our success will be the key to your victory tomorrow, I shall stake my life on this mission if I must turn into a demon to accomplish it. I hope, sire, that you will enjoy the ignoble sight of Katsuyori rushing about helter-skelter like a chicken burned out of its roost. Well, time is flying, and there is so much yet to be done. I must take my leave now." Concluding his speech, Tadatsugu bowed deeply.

"How valiant! I am delighted. I do indeed look forward to witnessing Katsuyori's fumbling tomorrow. After it's all over, I will describe it to you. Then we can have a good laugh together." Nodding his head, Nobunaga ended the meeting with hearty laughter.

[13]

Back at his own camp, Tadatsugu completed his preparations. He was impatiently awaiting nightfall when he noticed one of his footsoldiers escorting someone he took to be a stranger toward the camp. Presently he beheld before him a young boy in dashing attire, his silky blueblack hair gallantly held in place with a steel-ribbed headband of white linen. With a fond look of recognition playing on his pale face, the boy carefully placed his halberd on the ground and kneeled to take a bow in the proper samurai manner. Initially beguiled by his unfamiliar appearance and mature demeanor, Tadatsugu at last recognized Kotarō, the orphaned son of his late friend Yanagi Sadaharu, a boy whom he loved like his own younger brother. He started up from the campstool.

"Kotarō! What a surprise! What on earth are you doing here? I thought you were back at Hamamatsu in Enshū. When did you join this campaign? I had no idea. Well, come sit on this fur rug. You must be careful not to catch a chill while you're convalescing. I want you to take good care of yourself."

Tadatsugu returned to his campstool only after handing a nearby fur to Kotarō. Leaning forward and peering into the boy's face, he mused, "I haven't seen you since our last meeting in the spring, but I heard that your health was improving almost by the day. It may be just my imagination, but your face is much fuller, which delights me. Still, you were born delicate of constitution, so I want you to take every precaution. Ever since you became big enough to ride a horse, I've dreamed of spending one whole day riding side by side with you, hunting rabbit or pheasant. Alas, in these turbulent times it has remained only a hope to this day. Seldom, for that matter, can we even have a hearty talk together. But at every critical moment, whether in war or in peace, my mind always races toward you: I settle this matter in such and such a way and survive this crisis thus and so; when this or that problem is disposed of, I shall tell Kotarō all about; he compliments me on what I have done and flashes a smile of approval. As I can all but hear your voice and see your smile, fierce courage mysteriously wells up in me. A flame of embarrassment sears me just to think that you might frown in disappointment and disapproval if I failed to conduct myself judiciously in some affair. The prospect of such unbearable humiliation has always driven me to do my desperate best, for your image is etched in my heart even in a moment of life or death.

"Today I was entrusted with a task which would provide me an excellent opportunity to make a name for myself. I was already rejoicing in advance, picturing the imminent pleasure of seeing you after the battle and describing all my exploits for your amusement. It's not that I fight solely for such a private reason, but I must admit that you're the prime inspiration for my zeal. I want you to take care of yourself, for you're more precious to me than all the treasures in the world; you give me a life beside my own that embraces mine, and courage beside my own that sparks even greater courage in me. I'd be wretched without you! That's why I can't exactly say that I relish seeing your frail body in combat dress. There, you see, it's beginning to rain. It's been threatening all afternoon, but the clouds must have given way at last. Such light clothes may be appropriate for a seasoned warrior on a night raid or a dawn assault, but they're not for you in this chilly wind. A true samurai is provident enough to care for himself, undergoing moxa treatment even when his body is in perfect condition. You, on the other hand, are already in precarious health—all the more reason why you ought to do your utmost to take better care of yourself with a view to becoming a fine samurai. I don't expect our lord to send you into the shower of arrows and bullets, the forest of clanging swords and spears. With due respect to the lord's kind consideration, for the sake of your own future, and lastly in recognition of my own foolish yet sincere concern, please be careful what you eat, drink, and wear, even at the cost of incurring sneers from your friends and colleagues. There'll probably be a respite after the battle, so I'll look forward to spending a quiet day with you then. I'll have my old servant cook chicken stew and prepare some raw fish. We can toast with top-grade saké, converse over tea and salted beans, and reflect upon the martial feats that I shall have witnessed during the battle. Today, unfortunately, I must attend to some urgent business. Since I don't have enough time left to talk now, I can only hope that our next meeting will take place soon." The stalwart samurai spoke in a tone of sincerity and tenderness.

Kotarō sat still, staring at Tadatsugu. His eyes, grieving, were as luminous as stars on a frosty night. At last he shook his head grimly and spoke:

"What a heartless thing to say! How long do you intend to regard me as less than a man? Seeing me in this outfit, you admitted I looked like a seasoned warrior ready to embark on a night ride or a dawn assault. Why can't you commend me for it? I wish you could find it in your heart to say, 'Splendid, Kotarō! You have decided to tread the blood-soaked battleground with your own feet. Your determination does you credit. Most admirable!' I didn't come to your field camp merely out of idle longing for your company. It was a solemn resolve that drove me here. I am deeply grateful for your counsel on prudent care of my health, but I can't help regretting that you consider such counsel necessary at all, when I fully expect to die a man's death in combat. Of course it is not you, but my own useless self, that I resent so vehemently. Your advice pierces my heart all the more painfully because it stems from such tender concern for me—I hope you can see that. You said that you'd been unaware of my assignment in this campaign, but there's good reason for that. I came here of my own accord pretending to be a supply-wagon attendant, for I am neither under orders to accompany the lord nor assigned to anyone's command. Not even my colleagues know I'm here, much less Lord Ieyasu. If you care about me as much as you profess to, please listen to me and grant my request, if only out of pity.

"Ever since the Kōshū army crossed the border to strike into Enshū, all but threatening Hamamatsu, I have looked forward to accompanying the lord to the battlefield. I can shoot at least an arrow or two at the enemy, raise battle cries to cheer our soldiers on, and stand as a living shield against the Takeda archers. I wanted a chance to strip the dreaded Takeda of its semi-divine reputation with my own hand, but all to no avail. Thinking that the lord had spared me active duty because of my supposed ill health, I missed no opportunity to assure him of my readiness. 'My illness has quite abated of late,' I reported, 'and I have regained much of my weight and strength. With a horse that Sakai-dono gave me, I have trained until I can now jump a stream four or five yards wide without trouble. I do not mean to boast, but I have also greatly improved in swordsmanship, making it harder for anyone to beat me.' To my disappointment, the lord invariably smiled and told me to attend to my health. In the meantime Lord Nobunaga advanced his standard to join forces with our lord in punishing Katsuyori. All the others, from my peers down to those even younger than I, have been called to arms. How do you think I feel, watching them as they happily brace up for battle, checking their swords and cheerily twanging their bowstrings to savor the reverberation? My repeated pleas met only with words of comfort: 'This is not the last of battles. Be patient and nurse yourself.' Frail as I may be, I am no longer ailing. What a shame that the lord continues to treat me like a sick boy! In the face of his considerate yet disheartening reply, I had no choice but to swallow my tears and remain behind. Even the penniless younger sons of samurai families who lacked even the armor to cover their backs rushed off to make their names in this momentous battle; not one stayed behind to share my lament. 'Yonder is where the battle takes place,' my heart cried out as I sat immobile watching clouds sailing slowly but steadily in the very direction. Oh, how my heart churned, writhed, and thrashed in frustration! Sleepless and out of sorts, I often kicked off the covers at night and sprang up in spite of myself. I don't think you could blame me for that.

"What battle was it that claimed my father's life? Whose hand delivered the malicious blow? When and at whose hand did our lord suffer humiliation? It sears my heart to think that my mortal enemy, the one who killed my father and humiliated my lord, is none other than that rugged-boned bumpkin from Kōshū! My sworn enemy, whom I hate with an unequivocal vengeance, has come forth as if calling for all to hear, 'My head for sale!' Rising to his challenge, our lord is about to fight to a bitter finish, not pausing for a crack in the sword or a chip on the blade, until all our enemies are cut down and devastated. If I am eliminated from such an opportune encounter, how can I rest in peace, squandering my days and nights in a meaningless, mundane way? Is that any way to live? Just imagine yourself in my lamentable position, and you'll know what I mean. What would you do in my place? . . . Thank you, your tears are your answer. I am doubly grateful for your unfailing kind regard for me, and I feel greatly comforted in my hour of desperation. At the risk of incurring my lord's displeasure, I have resolved to take my place in this campaign; seeing your tears of sympathy, I presume you would do the same.

"To reflect upon my ill luck at being born so frail as to waste half of each year in treatment, I am forced to conclude that I can expect nothing but disgrace in the future. No doubt in reward for my father's humble services, the lord has been more than generous with the useless vassal I am. I have tried to decline his favors on the ground that I do not deserve to profit from my father's accomplishments, but he won't hear of it and still keeps me on a stipend. If I die in vain from illness without being able to repay his patronage in worthy service, I would be a stipend thief in effect. I may be no match for women and children in strength and less skilled than a scarecrow in archery, but full well do I know the meaning of shame. I would not think of feasting on my lord's generosity only to die in a warm bed savoring the aroma of steaming herbs. If I am going to die anyway, I want to vindicate my useless life with a meaningful death. Why should I cling to a body that is destined to be claimed by illness sooner or later? Rather than rotting to death after frantic rounds of acupuncture, moxa treatment, and medication, I'll take pleasure in casting myself upon the tip of a sword or spear. If I am lucky, my thirsty sword will drink some hot blood to fuel my dash to the nether world. Death in combat rather than from illness; death by choice rather than by natural causes. To repay even a fraction of my moral debt to my father and my lord, I must try to peel even a bit of skin and pull one hair off my archenemy so that after I am gone, people will know my spirit was not as frail as my body. I only pray that penalty for insubordination would not catch up with me in the other world.

"One dark, moonless night I paid my last visit to my father's tomb; and to my only sister, who is in the service of Lady Tokugawa, I bade a secret farewell, not confiding in her, so as to spare her tears of grief. After putting my affairs in order, I rushed here alone without my attendants. How disappointed I was when you told me merely to take care of myself! Please don't treat me as if I were still the child who used to laugh over trifles and indulge in guileless amusement. I have used all my mental resources—meager as they may be—in reaching my decision as a man. Can't you accept me as such? Judging from the agitation and commotion in this camp, as well as your reference to the preoccupied state of your own mind, I must assume that your unit, if not others, is ready to attack tonight. You cannot possibly be heartless enough to deny me: please take me along with you! I may accomplish less than others, but I swear I won't bring dishonor upon your name, not even if my bones are rasped into powder. All our reknowned commanders have been kind to me in memory of my late father, but you are the only one I can beg to take me to battle without the lord's permission. Please! Why don't you answer? Do you disapprove? Are you trying to spare my life out of pity? If so, I would resent that your affection for me should be so superficial. Or is it that you have too much affection? I am sorry about that, too. Not for a moment, of course, do I believe you are fearful of the lord's censure. But why are you silent? Why don't you open your eyes, my esteemed brother?" In his mounting anxiety, Kotarō drew nearer and nudged Tadatsugu with sheepish gentleness which belied his initial bravado.

For his part Tadatsugu was being racked by painful thoughts. "Should I help my beloved Kotarō fulfill his wish to give his life? I couldn't bear the thought. But should I thwart his aspiration? No, I couldn't bring myself to do that, either. What should I do? How can I answer him when neither alternative is bearable?" Caught in an agonizing dilemma between emotion and samurai honor, Tadatsugu could find no easy answer. His eyes averted, he clutched Kotarō tightly and blurted out, "Forgive me, Kotarō. Please forgive me. I was inconsiderate in speaking to you the way I did. I am truly sorry. Even before this state of emergency arose, I hadn't seen you for nearly one hundred days, despite my constant concern for you. Never did I dream that you have grown thus into a full-fledged samurai. I beg your forgiveness for my thoughtlessness, Kotarō. Oh, no! I did it again. Please take no offense, for I shall correct myself and henceforth duly address you by your adult name, Muneharu. It seems so pretentious and unnatural, though. The form of address doesn't matter between us, does it? . . . Good. Then let me continue to call you by your childhood name. Now, Kotarō, until this very moment I had no idea how much you had matured. Not that you have suddenly lost the smile that crinkles the corners of your eyes or the timbre of voice that is so familiar to me, but you have ripened into a man with a new glimmer in your eyes and an extra depth to your voice. Your late father must be overjoyed to see you from the world beyond. I have been an elder brother to you all but in name, and today you have made me a proud man. You have filled my heart with more happiness than if you had been honored for an exceptional deed of valor. I thank you for what you have made of yourself. Guardian of Samurai Marishiten, be my witness! I rejoice not for selfish reasons or out of my personal feelings for you. Rather, I rejoice from the bottom of my heart in the name of samurai honor, which prizes moral fortitude over physical safety and calls forth a smile in the presence of tears."

Tadatsugu paused to shift his gaze from heaven down to Kotarō. As though the gloom in his heart had cast its shadow upon his voice, his tone sank pensively.

"Nevertheless, Kotarō, please do me a favor and reconsider. An impetuous rush to death is not the honorable choice. I can understand your preference to bury your frail body in the dust of the battleground. No one can call you right or wrong for this. But I can't altogether condone anyone's decision to throw his life away in defiance of his lord's wishes. If I take you along on my mission, I can more than atone for my offense toward the lord with meritorious service in action. But I hate to send you to death at this stage in your life. Think of the reason why the lord wishes you to remain behind. I can't believe he considers you infirm and unfit to serve. You are the only male heir of a loyal vassal who gave his life in exceptional service, and you are still very young and not exactly in robust health. Obviously the lord wishes to save you for a later time. Why else has he kept you on a generous stipend and exempted you from this campaign? If you truly appreciate his profound kindness, you should look patiently toward a future time when you can offer him the full measure of your devotion, and you ought to regard your body as something more than your own possession to dispose of lightly. Despite my love and respect for you, I can't assure you that your resolve is the best and bravest by any standard. Perhaps you have yet to mature in your judgment. Look, Kotarō, seeing you in such anguish pains me. I would much rather cajole your expression into one of delight by blindly applauding your decision, but for your sake I must overcome my preference and risk the pain of displeasing you. Even if my words sound harsh, please ponder on what I say.

"Our present adversary is your mortal enemy Katsuyori, your health is not good, and all your colleagues are on active duty. I can hardly blame you for arriving at your drastic resolve, but hasn't it occurred to you that suicide for personal reasons is an act of ingratitude toward your lord? How do you suppose your father would feel to meet you in the nether world so prematurely? No doubt he'd blame me, lamenting, 'How unreliable Tadatsugu proved to be! Why didn't he try to help my son attain adulthood, if necessary supplementing the boy's want of wisdom with mature discretion?' I wouldn't mind being called unreliable, but you'd end up being an unfilial son, you know. Granted, your motive is steadfast loyalty toward your lord, which doesn't of course run counter to your filial duty to preserve your father's good name. Nevertheless, which is the correct choice for a man aspiring to be a true samurai —loyalty and filial duty achieved through premature death, or the same achieved through perseverance in the face of life's anguish? Don't you detect a subtle difference in quality and moral significance? You're bright enough to have grasped my reasoning already.

"I may seem unable to stop harping on the same point, but it's only due to my sincere concern and a fear of failure to do my duty. You've been driven to desperation by shame and resentment for your ill health, but as our lord once said, self-punishing training would lead to no great martial achievement unless accompanied by simultaneous effort to be lenient with oneself. If you deal less harshly with yourself without abandoning your commendable determination, you can mature into a stalwart warrior and valuable vassal, to the immense satisfaction of your father, not to mention mine. What a waste to throw your life away in such haste! As the saying goes, 'Indiscretion leads not to success, and impatience is unprofitable.' Since you can die anytime, your headlong rush to death smacks of a petty sulk. I would never lie to you or knowingly lead you astray, any more than our lord would neglect the orphaned son of his loyal vassal. Please be grateful to the lord and trust in my sincerity. You won't regret it. . . . Kotarō! Don't look so sullen. Do you think I would recommend anything harmful to you? Won't you compromise and accept my advice? Please rescind your decision gracefully. . . . No? You look unrelenting. How unreasonable and headstrong you are! I'm bowing my head to plead with you. When the time comes for you to offer your life for the lord, I won't let you die alone. I'll ride shoulder to shoulder beside you through the mountain of swords and forest of steel straight unto death. You know only too well how I feel. I resent your overeagerness to die in a battle which is already ours to win. Please trust in my judgment." Tadatsugu thus tried to rein Kotarō in with a verbal rope woven of duty and love.

"You must stop such cowardly talk," said Kotarō, squaring himself into a taut posture and impatient as a young hawk fluttering wildly to be airborne. "I listen to no senseless lecture. Do you think any amount of advice can make me reverse my sworn resolution? If I should break my oath because of a mercenary calculation of profits and losses rather than because of the moral right or wrong, how could I ever answer to my own conscience? Regardless of the intrinsic value of your advice, I am mortified by it. You assure me that one can die any time, but is it really so? I don't mean to refute your kind words, but I am convinced that this battle affords my only chance. Not just any day would do for dying. One who fails to die on an ideal occasion lives to suffer pangs of regret and disgrace worse than the death itself. If you oblige me by acceding to my wishes, I will be forever grateful for your supreme expression of affection. Why can't you grant me this one request?" Kotarō flushed slightly from the heat of emotion.

Still unyielding, the warrior scowled in dissent. "You're being insensible! Young or otherwise, you ought to have better discernment. Think it over again."

"No, I shall never change my mind. Please take me along."

"Do you refuse to listen?" Tadatsugu demanded.

"Do you refuse to assign me to your command?" countered Kotarō with a note of recrimination.

"You're being much too obstinate," deplored one.

"You've never been so cold-hearted," bewailed the other.

A young warrior driven by a desperate determination, and a seasoned veteran with foresight born of experience striving to stop a needless sacrifice—neither was willing to yield or compromise.

Time was pressing hard upon Tadatsugu. "Under normal circumstances I would spare no time or word in persuading Kotarō to change his mind," he thought, "but today on the eve of a momentous mission, I don't have the advantage of that leisure. Any minute now I must lead my detachment out of the camp to venture across the rugged Matsuyama Pass. If I allow him to accompany me, I'll be putting him through the ordeal of climbing over hidden rocks and roots along a precipitous path throughout the pitch-black night. When such a task would sorely try the endurance of even a robust man of experience and training, Kotarō's delicate body would never be able to withstand it no matter how fierce his determination. Besides, this is the fifth month, the rainy season. Tonight's dark sky bodes torrential rain. If he has to scale cliffs using wet vines for as long as eight hours, there's no telling what would become of him, even before we reach the enemy camp on Hawk's Nest Hill. No, I can't let him join my troops."

"A million more words of entreaty will not make me consent," declared Tadatsugu. "It's not that your absence from this battle spells disaster for our side, or that your furious fighting promises to tip the balance of battle in our favor. When our victory is so clearly assured, is it not an utter waste to cast away your life? You're no longer young enough to think the samurai's sole objective is hasty death, although your illogical attitude makes me feel you are still callow after all. Think about it. There's no use in frantically trying to coax me—I'm not going to give in. I don't mean to sound cruel, but neither do I insist on defending myself against your allegations of cruelty. If you ever regarded me as your elder brother, heed me now. I have no other choice."

Kotarō, whose eyes had been riveted on Tadatsugu's face, said in a voice quivering with agitation, "Are you really speaking from your heart? Or are you lecturing me for the sake of expediency? Since I recall that what you taught me earlier was quite the opposite, I can hardly understand how you expect me now to accept your sudden advice that I preserve my life. I am not calling it cruel, but I suspect that your exceeding love may be causing you to try to mollify me, even by twisting truth. And that you should think me so faithless as to readily abandon my resolution! 'A flying arrow draws a straight line in space, and an inspired man wends his course undistracted through life. It is merely a matter of destiny whether the arrowhead will shatter upon the target, or a man's life should be sacrificed to his ambition. Once inspired by righteous wrath, a man must be ashamed to stop in his tracks, unable even to die.' Isn't that what you told me some time ago, when you had an old minstrel monk from the capital entertain us with tales of yore? I was deeply impressed by that remark of yours with regard to the men who failed in their attempt to overthrow the Heike clan in the Shishigatani Conspiracy of 1177. As if it were yesterday, I distinctly remember the expression you wore on your face that night. Have you forgotten? After coming this far, why should I reconsider even after hearing your advice? Past or future, to die or to live, this life, later lives—these are now past my care or consideration. Is there any harm if you let me have my way? If you remain adamant, there is nothing I can do. I have only myself to blame for my frail constitution, which is undoubtedly what is compelling you to deny my request. Do you wonder what will become of me? You will see soon enough. Be that as it may, I thought you loved me for myself, not as a five-foot helmet rack or armor stand. But are you now striving to preserve my body even if it means invalidating my entire existence? No, I can't believe that. Is it really so wrong for you to let me die if I so choose? Take me along!"

At this point, thumping footfalls announced the arrival of a bullnecked man with short hair and dark face, his huge eyes glistening in the shadowy twilight.

"Oh, Nagura-dono. How are the troops?" asked Tadatsugu, turning toward him.

Rudely eyeing Kotarō, Nagura growled impatiently, "Every company is ready. Kanamori and the others have already left their position and are stealthily advancing toward the mountainside. In accordance with your plan, I'm going to join the Oda detachment. This intermittent rain makes conditions ideal; it's just the time for you to make your move. So, I'll see you tomorrow." With a bow, Nagura departed.

Having heard every word, Kotarō bristled even more eagerly for action, while Tadatsugu was hurried by the pressing need to decide what to do about the youth. Equally frustrated and chafed, each became impatient with the other and heated in his speech.

"You're still being insensible, Kotarō! Would I wear out my tongue trying to dissuade you if it were not impossible for me to take you along? There's no way I can oblige you."

"You're heartless! How much of a burden would I be?"

"Young as you are, you ought to be better able to divine another's feelings. Must you torture me like this?"

"Do you mean to dismiss my resolve so lightly?"

"Permission cannot be granted."

"I implore you!"

One refusing to consent, the other refusing to obey—as the battle of wills continued, the rain resumed and the sun set. In the ensuing darkness there arrived a man whose bearing betrayed him to be Nagura. "What are you waiting for, General Sakai? Aren't you acting a little lackadaisical for one who's the commander of this entire operation? You are well known for keeping your cool in any crisis, but this dawdling is approaching indolence, don't you think?" Finishing his speech, Nagura stalked out as if urging Tadatsugu to follow him instead of making a reply.

"Yes, I intend to set out immediately," said Tadatsugu, leaving his campstool. Jerking his armor belt tighter, he turned toward Kotarō. "No more time for discussion. I want you to follow my advice."

No sooner did his forceful voice die than Kotarō countered, "No, I can't. Please grant my only and final request on earth."

His youthful intransigence had an implacable force of its own. The disheartened Tadatsugu looked toward heaven, speechless, but the next moment he seized Kotarō in his left arm, an eagle snatching a small bird, and flung him over his shoulder. Grabbing Kotarō's halberd off the ground with his right hand, Tadatsugu dashed out through the torrential rain toward Tominaga's camp in the distance.

"Tominaga-dono, do me a favor," panted Tadatsugu. "This young man insists on making his debut in the battlefield. Please attach him to your company, for initiation, but not for actual combat. He's bent on dying, but don't let him die in a battle which is all but won. He's the son of Yanagi Sadaharu. Watch over him."

"Son of Yanagi, eh? I understand. I won't let him die —leave him to me," bawled Tominaga in a voice like a cracked temple bell, showing the instant comprehension of a seasoned samurai accustomed to communicating with his eyes.

When Tadatsugu set him down on the ground, Kotarō at last realized why he had been brought there. With a tender smile, Tadatsugu regarded the disgruntled youth and said, "All I can do is to assign you to this company. Tomorrow, get to know the enemy at first hand. There's no rush to die. Remember what I said. Just don't be careless or overeager." He squeezed Kotarō's hands firmly, let them go, and bolted out, leaving behind only a "Farewell."

A few yards away he took a backward glance. The downpour had tapered off to a drizzle, and Kotarō was distinctly visible against the flickering torchfires in the misty distance. Probably forestalling the youth's attempt to run after Tadatsugu, Tominaga's tall figure stood behind him, his hands on Kotarō's shoulders.

"Take good care of him!" Tadatsugu involuntarily enjoined.

"Don't worry," replied Tominaga.

"I'll be depending on you."

"No need to harp on it. Second thoughts are unbecoming," scolded the answering voice, dissolving into friendly laughter that reverberated against the black sky.

[14]

The opposition was in full force against the Takeda's modest numbers. They had taken to the higher ground, taxing the Takeda with an uphill fight. They were entrenched behind solid fortifications, forcing the Takeda to cross a wide-open field fully exposed. They were united in their will to fight, while the Takeda ranks were plagued by dissension. Every maneuver had been executed with precision, to which the Takeda, without countermeasures of their own, fell easy prey. As if these factors were not enough to carry the tide of battle, the Takeda lost their supplies in a surprise raid, which also dislodged them from their chosen positions.

Since the battle was now being fought by individual warriors spread over the terrain, no single man could accomplish stupendous feats to redress the balance. Slight of build yet acclaimed for his pluck, Yamagata set upon the enemy undeterred by no less than twenty bullet wounds; he finally succumbed to the twenty-first hit, which entered his saddlebow and coursed through his waist. Pierced by an arrow as he was guarding the rear of Katsuyori's retreat, Naitō yielded his head to a Tokugawa captain. Baba led his seven hundred troops through nine engagements, protecting his lord with competent maneuvers until his command dwindled to a mere eighty. At last, leaning on his plover-hooked spear, he stood on a rise watching his lord's standard emblazoned with the character for "great" disappear into the northeast. "My lord must have crossed Monkey Ridge by now. There's nothing to keep me here," he decided. Loudly announcing his identity to the enemy warriors, Baba fought to his heart's content and finally took his own life in a lordly manner. With the Sanada brothers and numerous other valiant commanders already fallen, the Takeda army broke away and straggled toward Hōrai Temple.

Although resigned to certain defeat, Dairoku had not expected a debacle of such extent. Bitterly chagrined yet powerless to stem the tide, he intended at least to ensure his lord's safe retreat. Falling in with a like-minded comrade, he returned to a low-lying piece of land set off from the road and stood his ground using a sparsely branched, thick-trunked old pine for his shield. "Come on, foes! So long as my arrows last, I shall teach you the meaning of pain!" His rapidly fired missiles leveled like so many *shōgi* pieces a handful of Mikawa warriors among the swarm that had advanced in pursuit. No sooner did some alarmed foot-soldiers shout warnings than another handful succumbed to the exacting arrows shot into the pack, sending waves of shock and rage through it. Veteran warriors Tamon and Hachisuka dashed forward with their great swords upraised, jeering and chastising their ranks, "Don't panic! Disgraceful! Push right through! Never mind a few samurai on the run shooting arrows from the wayside. Strike them down and tear ahead!"

"I'll shoot the front one; you take care of the other," Dairoku called out to his comrade, releasing his bowstring with a sharp report. Hachisuka dropped with a scream, his chest pierced by Dairoku's missile. Just as Tamon, startled by the scream, looked back, an arrow whizzed past his face, chipping the back of his helmet. Doubly enraged by his narrow escape, he swooped forward like a bird and swung his sword one-handed at the archer, who had tossed his bow aside and taken a backward step to snatch another weapon. The great blade stretched across the distance to hack off the archer's right arm. The swordsman wasted no time in turning his furious and now confident blow toward the remaining enemy. Falling one step back, Dairoku, his eyes limpid, his face flaming like a crystalline autumn stream, drew himself up to his full height and glared at the assailant. The lacquer-black beard, the firmly drawn straight mouth, the towering stature, and the heroic bearing—Dairoku emanated the commanding air of a general. A priceless catch! He's all mine! Tamon eagerly lunged at Dairoku, thrusting his sword and giving a sharp cry. Without drawing his own sword, Dairoku dodged the blows with light, easy footwork until he tripped Tamon with a powerful sidelong sweep of his thick bow. After forcing the fallen man down to the ground with a few rapid raps of the bow, Dairoku left him alive—as if to say he deserved worthier antagonists than he found there—and sped away northward.

[15]

Until yesterday he had boasted of his military might, surrounded by a horde of intrepid commanders and paladins. Today, alas, all that became a dream of the past. Now his retinue consisted only of a few footsoldiers and a handful of warriors, including Hajikano and the elder Kasai. Gnashing the invisible fangs of bitter regret, Katsuyori, disconsolate, was on his way to Hōrai Temple. The weather was warm, and the battle had raged overlong. Both the lord and his vassals were suffering from exhaustion, their weary bodies no longer matching their gallant spirits. In moments of despair Katsuyori more than once thought of returning to the battleground, there to die in combat. But he was forced to dissuade himself in consideration of his vassals' loyal effort to save him. The intermittent breeze carried the unintelligible clamor of the pursuing Mikawa men, alarming and disheartening Katsuyori all the more. He used to take pride in his flag bearing the character for "great," as though it housed the war god himself, but now he was as much ashamed before it as he was exasperated by the unbearable disgrace of showing the cantle of his saddle to the lowliest of enemy ranks for the first time in his life. "If only Nature or some worthy opponents see fit to obstruct my path now, I'd gladly make them an offer of my life," Katsuyori thought, seething in impotent rage and longing for a valorous death. He rode his charger at an unhurried pace, stretching up on the stirrups now and then to scan the scene around him. His haunted eyes, in which a smoldering blaze was threatening to flare up, scrutinized the arrow-strewn riverbed, banks, ridges, and valleys bathed in the afternoon sunlight.

Whether or not he failed to surmise Katsuyori's state of mind, Hajikano turned around and approached him. "I would like you to urge your horse to move faster. The rear guard unit some distance behind us consists of but fifty odd men. If a large enemy force should overtake them, they would have a hard time holding them off," he advised, as tactless as he was skilled in martial arts.

"Silence, Hajikano," thundered Katsuyori, venting his pent-up emotions. "You insolent fool! What if the enemy overtakes us? Do you expect me to retreat at a gallop? I am well aware that the rear guard is undermanned. I know not what the likes of Nobunaga would do under such circumstances, but I for one would not think of riding at any pace other than a jog trot, no matter how urgent our withdrawal. You gallop when fortune rides with you. Now that my luck has run out, I intend to leave at my leisure, taunting the enemy. What do you mean, telling me to withdraw in such haste? Shame on you for all your excellent field record! If I am to die at the enemy's hand, so be it. At least my last show of courage will bring respect upon my corpse. After the full day's hard riding, my mount is nearly exhausted. Can't you see how heavy his steps are? Beast as he is, he has served me to the utmost of his strength. Is it humane to whip him on mercilessly to his death? I don't find life desirable enough to sacrifice my own mount in hasty retreat, only to invite contempt and derision upon myself. Don't waste your breath."

Hajikano fell silent in the face of Katsuyori's intemperate outburst, hurled against a man in favor of a horse. The mature Kasai, however, interceded with a reassuring smile in his placid old eyes. "How right you are, my lord! Your charger has been on the verge of collapse from exhaustion. My own young steed ought to bear up much better. I dare say that it is rather incautious of you to be on a nearly incapacitated mount. Please exchange horses with me, lest you be caught ill-prepared for action, quite aside from your humane concern for the animal."

"Well said, Kasai! For your loyal advice, I shall give you my horse and borrow yours," Katsuyori consented in good humor. He then instructed a warrior, "Since you are young, Tsuchiya, let Kasai have your mount lest he lose his."

Swinging off his horse, Kasai waited for Katsuyori to mount it before climbing upon the saddle vacated by his lord. Meanwhile, a score of Mikawa horsemen apparently fell upon the rear guard. Perhaps the distant clashes of steel mingled with battle cries hastened Kasai's resolution. "Let me take my leave now, sire. With this none too young life of mine, I shall help secure your withdrawal." As soon as he had finished the sentence, he took a deep bow upon the saddle, turned his horse southward, and spurred him on, heedless of his colleagues' shouts to restrain him.

Straight into the midst of a hot engagement between some fifty Mikawa warriors and thirty Kōshū rear guards galloped Kasai, his speartip glinting and his aged voice calling, "Move aside, comrades! Hand over any foe unworthy of your effort. One of me is enough to dispose of them all." Encouraged by his spirited cheer, Aoki, who had been protecting the rear guard commander, halved an onrushing opponent like a bamboo stalk, cleaving another from armpit to shoulder with a sidelong return swing. "Kasai-dono, thanks for coming to our aid! Just watch— I'll take care of these in no time," Aoki shouted as he claimed more enemies, new vigor surging into his tired body. Their morale immensely uplifted, the Kōshū men took to the offensive with a vengeance, at last pushing back the Mikawa force almost a dozen yards. The rear guard, whose mission was simply to expedite their lord's withdrawal, collected the survivors and made an orderly retreat toward Hōrai Temple. Already sworn to death, however, Kasai fearlessly gave chase without breaking his momentum. Only when the widening distance proved his pursuit futile did he stop at a tiny roadside shrine, set in a sparse grove of young cedar trees. Beside it flowed a small stream which probably served as the shrine's ablution basin. Seeking a drink to soothe his parched throat, he reached the stream to find its water clear all the way to the bottom.

"Thank heaven for this!" Cautiously glancing in all directions, he dismounted. He led his mount downstream and let him drink first, stroking the animal's mane with his left hand. "Oh, how exhausted you must be! You look as if you have but little time left to enjoy this life. An inevitable fate for the lord's charger, but please don't resent it," the old man murmured to the poor beast—or to himself—sighing at the sight of his lord's favorite horse, which had developed shadowy hollows beneath his eyes in a single day. After another careful look around, he laid his spear on the ground and smiled as he felt the finger-numbing cold water. In the absence of a dipper, he scooped the water into his palms and rinsed his mouth out a few times.

Just then the sound of approaching footsteps arose. No sooner did his trained ears catch the stir in the air than Kasai spit out the water and snatched up his spear. A split second later, a sharp cry and a spear struck at him. The assailant did not announce his name, but he appeared to be a man of impressive standing. Whirling round on his heel and brushing the spear aside in one movement, Kasai assumed an alert fighting stance, showing no disdain for this tall, formidable enemy warrior clad in brilliant armor. For some moments the two were fixed in a silent glowering match. Perhaps in youthful impatience the younger man issued a battle cry and thrust his spear, the bamboo-shaped tip of which flashed a lightning glint barely short of Kasai's nose. Not to be outdone, the masterly elder attempted to wrest the enemy weapon away with his own. It was a fierce contest between two spears, one long-bladed and the other with a point shaped like a bamboo leaf. One would parry the other's thrust; the other would fend off the former's drive. The equally consummate skill of the two contestants struck an interminable balance, intertwining a pair of steel serpents in space. Though his spirit was valiant and his eyes clear, advanced age and fatigue took a heavy toll on the older man's limbs. Gradually his spear dropped to a defensive low angle, and he was forced to continue parrying and backstepping until he stood under a short tree. When the butt of his spear was caught in the tree's low-hanging boughs, Kasai suddenly found his own midsection vulnerable to attack. The enemy speartip nearly bit into his unprotected flank, but not a moment too soon a ferocious growl shook the forest. The silvery flash of an enormous sword projected the image of a samurai falling in a jet of blood. Onto the vacated space loomed the crimson face of a giant, his long beard fluttering in the wind.

"It's you, Dairoku!"

"Right, uncle."

An exclamation and a forward step later, each was drawn to the other by the emotional impact of another unexpected encounter in this world, though within such a short time of the last one.

Clasping Dairoku's hand the elder sat down on a flat rock nearby and remarked, smiling wryly, "I was about to quit this world, but thanks to you I must suffer this precious life of mine a little longer. I wouldn't have minded letting that worthy adversary do the honors, though. How luckless of him!"

"At such a critical moment, I had no choice but to cut him down without so much as a glance at his live face. I am sorry for the cruelty of it." Dairoku forced a slight smile as he regarded his victim's corpse. "At any rate, what will you do now, uncle? You seem to have escaped serious injury. Won't you come with me to rejoin our lord? It's foolish to engage in a useless fight—rather thoughtless to offer your head to a nameless foe, as you tried to do. Let's be on our way. . . . Do you have a better idea? Why don't you come along?" Far from oblivious of his uncle's pledge at the hamlet of Pure Well Field, Dairoku assumed an easy tone in his effort to prevent a needless death when the battle was, by and large, over.

But the elder Kasai showed no sign of conceding. "Leave an old man to his own devices; no need for a young fellow to lend him youthful wisdom. Save your breath, Dairoku. Do you expect me to follow Chōkan's example? You fool!

Why don't you urge me to emulate Generals Baba and Naitō instead? A young man whose glib tongue betrays a lack of moral fortitude earns no one's trust. Today's battle has proven a disastrous defeat for us, not that it was unanticipated. How could I possibly set foot upon the Kōshū soil again, safe and sound, uninjured as I am? No, I'll make my stand here, but for a purpose. If I can stop even a soldier or two, it will help ensure my lord's safe withdrawal. If I can die the way I was about to, I'll have my wish and the enemy can claim due credit. How can that be called useless or thoughtless? To my lord I offered my own fresher mount, and I've returned to this spot on his tired horse. Why should I renege now? Don't worry about me. I have only to die, but I shall not fail death. What worries me is that you might fail life. After expounding your brazen opinion in the presence of our illustrious commanders at the spring, Dairoku, I hope you're not going to fail life. Would you like me to leave you my ancient wisdom as a farewell gift to supplement your own lack of it? What was it that you said, about rejoining our lord? Merely to trail after him? What an ignoramus! That's exactly what I mean by failing life. You must realize your own shame upon having lost a battle. One who clings to life unabashed by a loss of mission has done nothing but fail life.

"Much as I had foreseen it, I can hardly bear this defeat —the hardest-fought battle in the history of our clan and an unprecedented blot on the Takeda name. Now that those braggarts from the plains have netted the greatest windfall victory of their lives, they will doubtless gloat with redoubled arrogance, loudly predicting the imminent downfall of the Takeda. How vexing that we are powerless to check their vainglory! With their bravado adding double and triple insult, our morale will sink as much as theirs will soar. Oh, the shame of it! Dairoku, are you still content merely to follow in the trail of your lord? The mighty reputation of the Takeda clan, painstakingly built upon a foundation of perpetual training and discipline, has just crumbled in a day, doomed to permanent extinction unless some immediate measure is taken. Those of us on our way to death are an altogether different matter, but I don't believe those who choose to remain in this world can claim a lack of plans to redress the situation. You don't intend to live and do nothing, do you, Dairoku? No, not my own nephew, a nephew of the man who has enjoyed a close friendship with Generals Baba and Yamagata! You can't possibly fail life. You must have some plans up your sleeve. Why, then, did you pretend to trail after the lord like such a fool? Do you rate your own uncle beneath your confidence? Well, I will no more fail death than you will life; I'm no craven soul who'll retreat on the heels of Chōkan and Atobe. It must have been around six this morning when General Baba was observing the troop movements of both sides from a vantage point——"

In the middle of the old warrior's reminiscence, a handful of soldiers appeared out of nowhere, brandishing their swords. "Vermin!" roared Dairoku, swiftly cropping three of them with his great blade, while his uncle speared one.

Leaning on the shaft of his weapon as it impaled the victim's throat, the elder continued, ". . . that he asked, 'Who is that samurai in our ranks fighting under a white banner with the cross-cornered rhombus emblem? I don't recognize him, but he's obviously quite a fighter.' 'I am proud to report that it is my own nephew Dairoku,' I answered elatedly. 'Since the bamboo hat is already known as my own crest, I gave him permission to use the rhombic well for himself.'* 'Your nephew indeed! His fierce fighting

---

*"Kasai" is written with two Chinese characters, one meaning "bamboo hat" (*kasa* 笠), the other "well," "spring" (*i* 井).

confirms what he said to us yesterday. He pledged to survive, but I am now confident that he will not fail life. You are fortunate to have such a fine nephew,' said the general, smiling. How do you feel, Dairoku, to hear this now? At the time, the expression 'fail life' struck me like a thunderbolt; for a moment the shock rendered me deaf to the battle cries and the roar of guns. You are my own nephew, but I must admit your fine character has independently earned my respect. What will you do now? Not live to fail life, I hope. One man's strength may be limited, but his will can attain heaven. A heroic warrior aspiring to accomplish a mission in this life should not be beguiled by a juvenile, asinine notion such as predestination. If your destiny is already predetermined, overturn it. If it's yet to be sealed, let your own hand shape it. This may not apply when you're on the verge of death, but you have neither heaven to fear nor a man to obstruct your vital will. You must agree that a great warrior's way of life is to fight to a finish. Much to our regret we conceded victory to the likes of Nobunaga, and the Takeda army, which had never failed to play by its own rules and safeguard its honor through the fiercest of battles under the late lord, withdrew today impotent and dispirited. You insist on surviving in spite of it all. Will you live merely for the sake of living? You of all people, so confident of your ability to endure the bitterest shame suffered by the House of Takeda, you could not possibly fail life. I can't believe you'd swallow our defeat and still hold your head high, utterly lost to shame. How can you keep on living unless you plan to reverse the outcome of this battle or to erase both the victory and the defeat? But, Dairoku, you are young and low-ranking, and you have yet to distinguish yourself in the lord's eyes. Saving the clan in the aftermath of this war is obviously far beyond your power, so you must have suggested to follow the lord entirely on my account. Don't be concerned about me. I won't fail death; just don't you fail life. Looking back now, how portentous was General Baba's farewell wish that you survive to live well!

"Alas, I hear men and horses heading this way. This time there are more than a score of them—it looks like a company of at least one hundred. You, who elected to live, must leave at once. Look! The lord's charger didn't stray far; he's grazing his way back toward us on the other bank. It almost seems as if he could differentiate the enemy's approach from our own. With him I'll be happy to end my life upon an enemy blade. I've said all there is to say. Farewell, Dairoku, and live well!"

The old man rose swiftly, braced the butt of his spear on the ground, and swung across the stream on its shaft. Overtaking the shying horse, he mounted it and walked the animal unhurriedly toward Dairoku, his amazing agility despite old age and exhaustion attesting to his lifelong experience and training. The noble resolution to proceed on his steady course toward death seemed to suffuse his profile with a chilling portent of heroism in the face of doom.

Gripping a great sword, Dairoku silently watched his uncle ride past. Presently he raised a determined voice and called after him, "Uncle, I understand you perfectly. I shall not fail life. I promise to live out my days meaningfully. Please watch me from the observation tower that they say soars up in Hell. I shall not rest until I have nullified the outcome of today's battle. I wish you a valiant death in combat, uncle. Now that I must guard myself against even a scratch, I have no alternative but to leave you to your fate. Forgive me, uncle. Fare thee well!"

In the echo of the parting words, one raced away toward a side road as unflatteringly as water seeking its own level, and the other plunged, a single rock hurled into the onrushing tide of enemy forces. The briefest instant interspacing dream and reality marked their long separation, until the advent of the bodhisattva Miroku.

[16]

Tominaga, who had taken charge of Kotarō at Tadatsugu's request, was an unassuming samurai. In his artless sincerity he tried to soothe and mollify the youth.

"You'd be better off restraining your eager pursuit of glory and settling for careful observation of the battle this time around. As the saying goes, 'No great feat can be accomplished in one step, any more than an acolyte can become an abbot overnight.' You grow into a warrior gradually, accumulating knowledge through observation. As a rule, even your physical condition improves as your mental maturity grows. Don't hasten your own death; rather, love and cherish yourself, for there's no telling what exceptional glory you may be capable of attaining in your long future life."

The well-meaning admonition did not fail to penetrate the listener's ear, nor did Tadatsugu's thoughtfulness in leaving him under Tominaga's care go unnoticed. Yet the more keenly he felt the kindness of others, the more vehemently Kotarō hated himself for appearing to be such a feckless, vulnerable figure. Despite all his effort to suppress his emotions and resign himself to the genuine kindness of others, the flames of furor in his heart gave him no rest, just as the embers of a bonfire burst back to life, even under stamping feet, with each blast of mountain wind. Soon he began to feel that Tominaga's advice was nothing but the trivial prattle of a foolish mediocrity who had no insight into his character, and that he would forfeit his integrity if he heeded it.

"Let people call me an ingrate. Dying is no crime. I'll slip away through Tominaga's blind spot and fight at my own will. General Sakai has long gone out of my reach. This is totally counter to my original plan, but I have no time to lose. It must be possible for one man to make a dash into the Kōshū line. What have I to fear when my body and my life are already lost causes? Shall I run for it now, this instant?"

More than once, Kotarō contemplated such precipitous action, but he could not elude the wary eyes of Tominaga. Besides, he was somewhat hesitant to frustrate the well-intentioned efforts of others, and so he deferred his escape plan for the night. Around dawn, however, the colors and drumbeats of the two great armies began to converge. Horses tossed their manes with animated neighing and men swaggered about with arched shoulders and furious glares. Soon swords and spears were flashing like bolts of lightning, and the thunderclaps of guns were rending the air. An irresistible urge overcame Kotarō's last shred of self-restraint when a perfect opportunity presented itself in the heat of battle. Now totally oblivious of his obligations toward Tominaga and even of his own regard for Tadatsugu, Kotarō raced away from Tominaga's unit in search of the enemy.

Tominaga had been keeping a vigilant watch over Kotarō, fully aware of his impetuous craving for death. However, partly misled by the boy's seeming compliance with his advice, he had let down his guard as his unit became engulfed in battle and remained entirely unaware of Kotarō's disappearance. By the time the fighting slackened and Tominaga remembered his charge, there was no trace of Kotarō. "Damn it all," he thought. "It was not an official assignment, but I can't sit idly by after failing another's trust. I must do something, but I'm not at liberty to leave my post in search of the boy right now. What should I do?" For lack of a better alternative, he finally dispatched a dozen men on Kotarō's trail, but none found even a shadow of him. The battle was abating in one sector after another, and Tominaga's hope that the boy might appear among the returning soldiers rapidly faded. Helpless and increasingly exasperated, he waited, chafing and fretting, too restive to sit or stand. He hoped against hope that the most trusted searcher, who was still unaccounted for, might return bearing good news. Two hours passed, then four. At last the man reported back. Impatiently beckoning him closer, Tominaga questioned him.

"Upon receiving your order, I searched everywhere from the mountainside to the river banks, determined to find him. I saw no one even remotely resembling him. But loath to return empty-handed, I combed some distant villages just on a slim hope. Near the road leading off Araumi Square toward Yatsukaho, there was a giant old chinquapin tree spreading thick branches. In its dark shade I spotted a short halberd. I rushed over, only to find Master Kotarō, his body bearing the mark of one fatal stroke delivered by some unknown swordsman. Grieved and enraged though I was, I had been too late to catch the perpetrator and could do nothing but to bring back the young man's head and his halberd. Discoloration had already set in, but the beauty of his features and the familiar halberd left no room for misidentification. The only odd thing is that his topknot is missing. Look for yourself."

When the man had finished his dismal report, he proceeded to untie the sleeve torn off a combat jacket in which he had wrapped the severed head. Already chocking with emotion at the sight of Kotarō's halberd, Tominaga averted his face. "How can I ever apologize to General Sakai? Damn my carelessness! Now what should I do?" he cried, springing to his feet.

[17]

The battle of Nagashino was over. The Oda-Tokugawa

victory became an established fact, and the legendary fame of the Takeda was, like a broken icicle, shattered beyond repair. For a while, Ieyasu was kept busy by a visit to the Oda domain and an attack on Futamata Castle in Enshū. Toward the end of the sixth month, he found time to spend a few days to relax in his own castle.

The supreme pleasure of summer is the caress of a cool breeze after a bath. Clad casually in a light linen kimono, Ieyasu was on the veranda of his quarters in the company of a handful of ladies-in-waiting, waiting for the moon to rise over a miniature hill in the garden.

"Sire, General Sakai has been in the front room for some time, wishing to make a petition. What is your pleasure?" inquired a page twelve or thirteen years old, no doubt a son of some renowned vassal who had died in war.

"What? Tadatsugu, at this hour of the night? Well, no need to arrange an official audience; send him in," Ieyasu instructed offhandedly.

Soon after the women had discreetly retired, Tadatsugu followed the page into the room and prostrated himself at the far end.

"Tadatsugu. Make yourself comfortable, as I'm dressed quite casually. Come up here for the nice breeze." The genial invitation was conveyed with a broad smile. Always affable, the lord appeared in exceptional good humor this evening.

"A propitious occasion for making my request!" Elated, Tadatsugu expressed his gratitude: "I must apologize for seeking your audience at this late hour. I am grateful for your gracious permission and for your most kind words."

"What's on your mind?"

"Begging your pardon, I would like to speak frankly, even at the risk of incurring a reprimand for my impertinence. It concerns Yanagi Kotarō. For his unauthorized participation in the battle and his death in combat, the blame was placed not upon myself but upon Tominaga. Knowing that you have already passed judgment on the matter, I cannot help but feel profoundly guilty for having acted contrary to your wishes. I know I deserve reproach for making such a brazen request now, but I can no longer hold back. My petition pertains to none other than Kasai Dairoku, who was captured when he attempted to assassinate Lord Nobunaga at the party celebrating our Nagashino victory. Since Kasai had somehow smuggled himself into General Akechi Mitsuhide's command in order to gain that access, even the innocent General Akechi became an unwitting target of Lord Nobunaga's wrath. To alleviate the volatile situation, your lordship volunteered to take custody of Kasai. You told Lord Nobunaga that your retainer Naruse, who once lived in Kōshū long enough to know practically every samurai there, would be just the man to question this prisoner, that Lord Nobunaga could execute him later by upside-down crucifixion or quartering by oxen, but that you wanted him to be turned over to you so that you could extract a full confession from him.

"Since the man was handed over to you, however, he has undergone only a few interrogations, each of which was deadlocked by his stubborn silence. Without resuming the questioning, you have treated him leniently, quartering him comfortably, though under guard, in Hōkō Temple outside the castle compound. Kasai has been repeatedly urged not only through Naruse but once even by your lordship in person to give up his revenge and serve the House of Tokugawa instead, but he has been obstinate in his refusal. Quite admirable of that bearded man, I must say. Your mind is of course not for me to fathom, but I presume that you will eventually dispose of him unless he pledges his loyalty to you. I cannot believe you would set him free no matter how much you admire him. The alternatives seem to be limited: either to grant him a graceful death here, or to send him back to Lord Nobunaga for a brutal execution. Could you leave his disposal to me? In place of all the rewards I might earn for my future services and in exchange for the testimonials I have already received from you, I beg you to grant him this one request.

"In the past few days, a respite in my schedule allowed me to visit Kotarō's grave and to have a pleasant talk with Naruse. When our conversation happened to touch upon the circumstances of Kasai Dairoku's capture, the fact that he had been caught wearing two short swords in addition to the regular sword aroused my curiosity. I prevailed upon Naruse to let me take a look at the belongings that had been left in his keeping for investigative purposes. The long sword and one of the short ones were obviously a set, both excellent blades in plain black sheaths bearing no signature of the swordsmith. The other short sword, however, was an unusual item made to fastidious taste—a saliently grained unlacquered sheath and a sandalwood hilt—uncommon, yet disturbingly familiar to me. While I was examining them, it suddenly occurred to me that incredible as it seemed, it was the very sword that Kotarō had once shown me. At the time, I had pointed out to him that it was tastefully fashioned but that the hilt lacked slip-proof designs to ensure a firm grip. Most likely in response to my advice, Kotarō reported at our subsequent meeting that he was rather proud of the new carving done on his sword—deep herringbone notches on the hilt and raised wood grain in the midsection of the sheath. Beholding the unmistakable herringbone pattern and the grain of the cedar sheath, I concluded that Kasai had slain Kotarō and taken this eye-catching sword for his own use. In a fit of unbearable anger and anguish, I took a hasty leave of Naruse and went home to deliberate. A private act of revenge is, of course, out of the question. I do not mean to second-guess an official sentence, but Kasai's execution seems a foregone conclusion now. I hereby request that his custody and disposal be granted to me. Your permission will be received with immeasurable gratitude, not only by myself, but by Kotarō and his father in the nether world as well. I have come in the night like this so as not to commit the indiscretion of making such a private request in public at court."

With a slight frown on his face, Ieyasu replied, "I can well understand your reason for making this request. If it were anyone else, I would just let it pass, but you of all people ought to know better than to put me in such a difficult position. Before I could let you have your way with that rogue, Nobunaga and Akechi would no doubt assert their prior claim. No, Tadatsugu, permission cannot be granted. You may have Kotarō's small sword instead. I shall instruct Naruse to release it tomorrow. Be content with what I *can* do for you." Well-grounded in logic and delivered without harshness, the words of his lord circumvented any rebuttal.

Yet Tadatsugu remained unappeased. "With Kotarō's mortal enemy all but within my grasp," he thought, "how could I leave him in peace? Such betrayal of his faith in me would put me to shame, I who used to behave toward him as if I were his elder brother! I can't stop at my lord's first rejection; I must pursue this matter until he grants me a free hand, either to kill the paroled prisoner in a fight or to put him to the sword right where he sits. . . ." Tadatsugu tried to speak again, but precious time had been lost in a few moments' hesitation.

"Well, Tadatsugu, I do not think you intend to be unreasonable," Ieyasu pressed on in a low voice, peering at him with piercing eyes. At a loss for words, Tadatsugu hesitated again, only to be dismissed in a tone of finality. "Permission denied. The matter is closed."

Tadatsugu might as well have been facing a cliff one thousand feet high without a single handhold.

[18]

The night was still. In the dense bamboo grove of the garden of Hōkō Temple, fireflies flickered feebly. The moon had not yet risen to cast a graceful spell over the scene, but the faint glow of the starry sky over dark treetops struck a rather engaging scene for a man in captivity.

"Ever since I failed in my attempt after the battle of Nagashino, I've been in detention here. Their hospitality has been quite generous. I've nothing to complain about, except for their occasional pestering for my total surrender. How irksome of Ieyasu to resort to psychological manipulation, attempting to turn me into his own hunting dog tethered to a yoke of duty and obligation! I shall never surrender my loyalty to him. Sooner or later he's obliged to grant me suicide or to execute me, so what is he waiting for? This is so exasperating! Not that I'm overanxious to die even now. Show me a slightest chance for escape and I'll flee to Takatenjin Castle in Enshū, if not all the way back to Kōshū, and put up a memorable fight. My treatment here may be casual, but the outside is tightly secured day and night by vigilant guards. Lacking a pair of wings on my back and a weapon in my hand, I'm virtually helpless. If I died in my escape attempt, barely out of the temple compound and under the undistinguished swords of nameless footsoldiers, I'd surely suffer disparagement and a charge of improvidence even in death. If I were recaptured alive, I could never live down the disgraceful reputation as a coward shamelessly clinging to life. I must make no attempt unless there's absolute surety of success. If fate ordains my death at the enemy's hand, so be it—there's no use arguing. Since my aspiration is not directed toward the Western Pure Land, I shall face north to bid a quiet farewell to my home province and end my life by seppuku. In the meantime, I can take advantage of my detention in this temple and spend my remaining days chanting sutras so as to offset the agonies of Asura tormenting the late lord and all the war dead—my uncle, Generals Baba, Yamagata, Naitō, and the others—and help expedite the release of their unavenged souls."

Six times daily Dairoku prayed and chanted sutras. Today again he finished reading aloud the Parable Chapter of the Lotus Sutra with the sentence, "To all those able to believe and comprehend, you should preach the Lotus Sutra of the wonderful law."

Just as he was bowing deeply to the sutra, which he had replaced upon a small desk, an acolyte appeared. "Tominaga-dono and a lady are here from the castle to relieve your tedium. He has brought some saké and refreshments, so the repast will be served soon. Please greet your visitors."

"Oh? . . . Ah! Ieyasu must have at last given up the idea of ever winning me over. As a prelude to my impending death by whatever means he chooses, he must have decided to demonstrate his graciousness by treating me to some refreshments delivered by a messenger of consolation. Now that I'm ready to accept my sentence, I shall avail myself of my visitor's hospitality and unburden myself by divulging something that I've kept to myself until now. It's quite sporting of Ieyasu to send along a woman as well. Does he mean for her to enhance the flavor of the saké with a dance? No sophisticated prince of the Heike clan, I wouldn't know what to do if I met the fairest of women on the night before my death. What a laugh!" Dairoku waited, unruffled, chuckling softly to himself.

Before long, Tominaga, trodding heavily, was brought in by a monk. Not exceptionally tall, the rugged samurai was solid of build, with wide shoulders. As if square jaws and a squat nose were not enough to define the unmitigated ugliness of his dark face, a scar extended from his right eye into the brow, obviously a souvenir of some battle. Far from impressive in his appearance, he seemed a redoubtable warrior nonetheless. He was followed by a woman about twenty-five years of age, fair and genteel. Before Dairoku had time to take a more careful look at her, the man dropped down close to him and the woman settled by a lamp some distance away. After the exchange of formalities, Tominaga, commiserating with Dairoku on his ill luck, said, "Such is the samurai's fortune that some day might find me in your place, a captive guest of the House of Takeda."

Soon a train of acolytes set individual trays of saké and snacks before them. Tominaga tasted the first cupful of saké and offered the large drinking vessel to Dairoku. "Now, Kasai-dono, please drink as much as you like. It will do you good to dispel the weariness of inactive days with some saké. It will cheer my heart to see you enjoying yourself. I shall do my best to keep you company."

"I, Tamae, am in the service of Lady Tokugawa," the woman introduced herself. "As you can see, Tominaga-dono is a rugged man of arms, poorly skilled in the finer art of flattery. But his candor and rectitude are quite unrivaled even among our clansmen, and I think you will find him a fit companion for conversation. Please relax and feel free to reminisce about your exploits in wars, both recent and long past. I would like to hear some interesting stories to commemorate this occasion." She seemed anxious to raise Dairoku's spirits and relieve the dreary monotony of captivity. Her speech was crisp and distinct, rather unexpected from such coral lips.

Dairoku, who had listened with a slight smile, now drained the large vessel. "Since you are kind enough to offer, I shall be happy to drink my fill. I am quite fond of saké, as a matter of fact, and, if I may say so, I have a hero and fair lady for company. What more can a man ask? By the way, Tominaga-dono, Miss Tamae, why don't you inform me of the official decision that must have been reached in my case? It becomes neither of you to pretend ignorance. There is no harm in your telling me, for I have been resigned to the ultimate prospect far too long to lose my nerve or appetite over the confirmation that I face summary decapitation. No, you cannot hide it, for I have already guessed that my fate was sealed today. Why else are you here now if not to regale me on my last night on earth? Why don't you tell me frankly that I am to be executed on the morrow or that I have been granted the privilege of honorable suicide? Not only will I remain unruffled by the news, but I even promise to enjoy the drink all the better for it. Now I can get the last burden off my chest. Can you honestly say that I have guessed wrong? Pray, be candid and tell me."

"You are free to guess anything, but we have no such knowledge. Why would we withhold such information? Please have some more to drink."

Tossing down another cupful, Dairoku sat rubbing his beard for a while. "How long do you intend to keep it from me? There is really no need. . . ." All at once he broke into a smile. "Tominaga-dono, you must find me more than a bit funny. I was foolish to insist on knowing my exact fate when my death was simply a matter of time anyway. Ha, ha, ha, ha! Now I am convinced more than ever that tomorrow my eyes will gaze for the last time upon this world—the world which has nothing to hold me and where I have no wife or children to leave behind. This evening I stand on this shore that marks the end of a brief dream; tomorrow night will find me taking my first step on the other shore. Looking back on this night then, perhaps I would be amused by a vision of this scene hovering above the cloud, or is it water, that separates life and death —this scene of our little gathering at which we, enemies in this world, share a jug of saké and a lamplight for the night. May I have some more? Ah, thank you. How delectable! It feels as though my teeth are beginning to swim in my mouth. This must be the famous saké of Chita. Sharing the shade of a tree and a drink of river water together supposedly attests that the participants are linked by a common tie of karma from their former existences. Our lives must have crossed somewhere in another time that we should meet here thus—of all people, the three of us who, on opposing sides, might have glared at and reviled one another on the battlefield. Strangely enough, I feel close to you both." Dairoku reflected pensively, his sentiment visible in his face.

"You are quite right," responded Tominaga, betraying none of his own emotions. "Until this evening you and I were antagonists, neither of us to be forgiven or left unchallenged by the other. Hereafter, I might again deem you my sworn enemy to be harshly dealt with. Be that as it may, we are not facing each other with swords in hand, for the moment at least. Now to change the subject, what did you mean by 'get the last burden off your chest?' If you have something to confess, you can confide in me, one who is subject to the same vicissitudes of the samurai's life. I am not saying that you are to die tomorrow, mind you, but I would like to help if there is anything I can do for you. This is your chance to unload whatever burden you may be carrying in your heart. I am particularly anxious to hear all about your adventures in the last battle and to learn how you came to make an attempt on Lord Nobunaga's life. The final outcome of the battle was decided fair and square through the formal match of strategy and military strength waged between the two armies. Yet you disguised yourself as a footsoldier in General Akechi's command and set upon Lord Nobunaga with a deadly sword during our victory celebration. Judging from your demeanor since the arrest and from my own personal observation this evening, I cannot believe you are a man of disreputable character. Why did a warrior of your caliber resort to such a dastardly means, one unfit even for outlaw samurai and bandits? Granted, in this war-torn age of ours, no act of duplicity or foul play goes unattempted. Still, assuming a false identity to lurk in a man's vulnerable flank in order to spring a surprise attack is to act worse than a viper crawling stealthily up to a victim to strike with its fangs. Dastardly, contemptible, the ultimate in perfidy! Isn't such behavior condemned as unmanly or ignoble in Kōshū? It absolutely defied my comprehension. Please enlighten me on this, too." Tominaga, ending his comment in a severely accusatory tone, waited for an answer, staring intently with hardening eyes.

Utterly unperturbed by the charges of personal dastardliness and perfidy, Dairoku had maintained his composure, but in the end countered Tominaga with arched brows:

"This is more than I can tolerate. Do you intend to denigrate my homeland? It is foolish of you to imply that a disgrace is not considered disgraceful in Kōshū. Where on earth could you find a land where man's sense of right and wrong is exactly reversed, any more than you could discover a country where people's hair grow on their heels? Call me dastardly and ignoble if you like, but don't slander the entire domain of Kōshū based on your opinion of me alone. I do not claim that my own action was the most honorable of all. Since each man is limited by the range of his own potential, what is so wrong with serving one's lord to the best of one's abilities? Dastardly or asinine, it matters little. So long as one's motive is honorable, another man's opinion of right and wrong or good and evil is no more material than a feather or a speck of dust over a blazing fire.

"To begin with, the battle of Nagashino ended in an unspeakable defeat for our side. Victory and defeat may be heaven-ordained, but ours was such a crushing blow, so hard to accept. We sent our veteran commanders and valiant warriors to their deaths and suffered the first rout since the founding of the House. How humiliating! Our adversary was none other than that windbag Nobunaga, who would no doubt gloat over an inflated account of his victory. The sun and moon gracing our sacred treasure flag have lost their radiance, and the glory of the heroic Yoshimitsu's lineage has crumbled. The more I reflect upon the cataclysmic blunder in the single battle that annihilated all the marks of distinction that had been painstakingly built during Lord Shingen's lifetime, the more deeply I feel, even now, the grinding pain of bitter rage. At first I wanted to die just as much as I wanted to live; had it been possible at all to split my heart asunder, I would have sent the two halves flying in opposite directions. You can imagine my anguish under such circumstances, can't you? When the battle was half over, I stood in a field suffused with the smell of blood steamed by the sun and stirred by the silent wafts of the lukewarm breeze. As I turned to scan the far distance, my tired eyes were seared by the sight of bright enemy colors flying intact beyond the battleground littered with fallen bodies. Full aware as I was that I, a mere soldier of the losing army, was powerless to do anything, how could I remain impassive at such a moment, unless I were a clay figurine or a wooden statue?

"This might sound like self-justification, but one finds friends among foes, and strangers among fellow warriors. Since your remark struck a responsive chord in my heart, I would like to consider you a friend among my enemies. Please pour me another drink. A pleasant discourse in the face of impending death—quite a suitable occasion for drinking. Ha, ha, ha! Please don't dismiss me as someone trying to drown his sorrows. You call my conduct dastardly? Yes, it was paltry. You label my conduct disgraceful? Yes, indeed, it was. Nonetheless, 'dastardly' and 'disgraceful' are mere words born of wagging human tongues. I refuse to lend an ear to such unworthy sounds. Worldly judgment cannot match the strength even of a cobweb when it comes to restraining a man's feet. Fully anticipating criticism and censure, I tried to do exactly what I wanted to do. I failed, and the result is this—my plight, my present status, your remark. . . . Ha, ha, ha! Well-nigh a good laughing matter, this is! Just think of it. A survivor of the Kōshū army devastated by the defeat, how could I, a young and low-ranking soldier, hope to assist my lord and rebuild our army until Nobunaga and Ieyasu are forced back where they had been during Lord Shingen's reign? I had to admit to myself that I lacked the genius indispensable for devising a momentous plan that could reverse the tide of fortune. I was able to take pride in nothing better than my humble ambition and fool's courage. Fortunately, however, I was not lacking in strength and spirit.

" 'Suppose I keep moving forward instead of returning home—could I then perhaps stem the tide and recapture our lost luck? True, the victor and loser are already distinctly marked. Nobunaga has plainly stolen the show at Nagashino; we have lifted the siege of the castle, and leaving countless dead behind, the Kōshū survivors have withdrawn. Nevertheless, unless I alter the outcome of the battle before it becomes public knowledge, the future of the House will be beset with all kinds of trouble. Once Asura captures the sun, all distinctions between black and white in this world will be instantly obliterated. I'll stretch forth my arm to squeeze the life out of Nobunaga, wiping both his victory and our defeat off the record. Before they can chop me into little pieces, I'll savor the taste of many an enemy sword. Quite a report to astound my uncle with at our encounter in Hell, isn't it? . . .' That is what I thought, at any rate. Just the same, Tominaga-dono, there may be such a thing as fate after all. Not only did I let Nobunaga practically slip through my fingers at the last minute, but I ended up getting myself captured because of a freak accident: my sword broke right below the guard, making it impossible for me to go down fighting or to be killed in fair fight. I am ashamed to be alive today, being entertained by you."

Concluding his discourse, Dairoku returned the empty vessel to Tominaga. After taking a few sips, the latter filled it again for Dairoku.

"Now I have a fairly good idea as to your motive," Tominaga said, his face still a wooden mask devoid of expression. "Next, I would like to learn how you smuggled yourself into General Akechi's command. You must have found nothing but your enemies overrunning the territory from the river banks to the forest. How did you manage to go south when the Oda-Tokugawa forces were sweeping northward? You must have killed a few who tried to challenge your identity on the way. Tell us about them."

"Well, I feel foolish talking on and on about myself, but I won't be here tomorrow anyway. Since you asked, and since there happens to be something that I intended to tell someone when I receive my death sentence, I might as well tell it to you. Let me see. . . . It was after I separated from my uncle, who was pledged to die. In lone contemplation of the battleground, I resolved, as I already explained, to steal into the Oda camp. But the cowardly plainsmen must have been reluctant to venture beyond their fences, for none was to be found. I was frustrated in my plan to come upon a few of them, ascertain which unit they belonged to, and take their insignia for my disguise. Rather unsure of my way, I trudged along a path between the mountains, intent upon reaching the Oda command post after skirting around the back of the Tokugawa positions. At the foothill east of Araumi Field—I am not well acquainted with the local place names. . . . You say it might have been the road to Yatsukaho? In any case, I was turning at a crossroad when a young samurai leaped at me from behind a large tree, shouting, 'Don't show your back!' Smartly dressed and wielding a halberd, he bore down furiously upon me. After a few clashes, I knocked the halberd out of the none-too-powerful grip of my young foe. Far from discouraged, he drew his sword and resumed his attack. What a nuisance! With no hankering for a fight at the moment, I tried to leave him alone and get on my way, but he kept persistently at my heels. I was forced to turn and strike the sword out of his hand, but next he came at me with open arms to grapple. Such an admirable boy I could not very well put to the sword summarily, so I dropped my weapon and wrestled with him. Of course, it took me hardly any effort to pin him down. To my surprise, he stabbed at me with an astonishingly swift flick of his shorter sword. If my eyes had been a fraction less alert, my throat would have been pierced. I narrowly dodged his thrust, but you can see this scar across the left side of my neck—a vestige of my careless moment. . . . What did I do next? Well, in my alarm I seized his hand, held it under my left foot to force his fist open, wrenched the little sword out of his grip, kicked it off to a distance, and——"

Cutting him off in mid-sentence, a voice cried out as sharp as the rock-rending shrill of a pheasant starting up from a field. "That little sword is right here! You must remember this sandalwood hilt and this unpainted sheath." The woman seated by the lamp drew a small sword out of her bosom and hurled the empty sheath at Dairoku. The next instant she was before him, holding fast at his forehead a blade glistening like a wet serpent. Her swift move had taken Dairoku by complete surprise, but he stared back unflinching and silent.

With one knee on the floor, the woman was trembling with impatience to the ends of her rich, fragrant hair.

Undaunted by the bright lamplight, she fully exposed her dewy eyes and fair face, which had the color of a pear blossom at dawn. "You must recognize this blade. It bears the rancor of my young brother, who died at your hand. Your exploit, which you have so proudly described to me in your own words, is at the same time my grudge against you. I am none other than Tamae, the only sister of Yanagi Kotarō Muneharu. I will not leave my brother's mortal enemy in peace. I have come here tonight to make you a present of this sword. Will you end your own life with it? Otherwise, I have no choice but to smear it with the blood from your neck. Even a woman's arm can be charged with the full force of human will. Shall I bring death upon you, or do you elect to kill yourself? Make your choice promptly and give me your answer."

"Take my words with you as a memento of this world, Dairoku," followed Tominaga, poised with one foot forward, ready to draw his sword in a flash. "I was dishonored when you snuffed out the life of Yanagi Kotarō, who had been entrusted to me by Sakai Tadatsugu. I have come here resolved to lay down my life at the risk of incurring my lord's wrath. I won't let you escape alive. You played right into our hands, describing the death of Yanagi. Indeed, your confession marked the end of the devil's own luck for you. You have no hope of prolonging your life anyway; are you willing to yield it to us, or shall we take it from you? Sakai has been frustrated in his attempt to gain custody of you, and Miss Tamae is inconsolable over the extinction of her lineage. Caught between the two, I am moved by the sight of rage and grief—one over the loss of her own flesh and blood, and the other over his failure in his moral obligation to protect an orphan left in his care. I am moved to the point of wishing to tear you apart and disembowel myself afterward in apology to my lord, even though I harbor no personal hatred for you. Once the small sword proved beyond doubt that you were the cruel killer of the young and innocent Kotarō, there is no way I can let you sit here so securely. You also have Miss Tamae to contend with. You might as well give up any hope of living through this night. Will you die at your own hand, or shall I put you to my sword? If you are contemplating resistance, I'll be happy to cut you up for easier serving. Captive as you may be, I am not one to murder an unarmed man. If you are reluctant to go to your death with good grace, I can lend you this combat sword. Try to live if you so decide, but only over my dead body. Well? Are you afraid? Answer me!"

Starting to his feet, Tominaga kicked a sword lying beside him toward Dairoku, quickly loosening the blade catch of his own. Dairoku had no time to dodge the heavy sword sent flying squarely at his face. His left arm shot up to intercept it, and the sword was in his firm grip. Once she confirmed that Dairoku was armed, Tamae gave full vent to the wrath that she had been keeping under restraint until this moment. Time to avenge my brother! She attacked, and Dairoku parried with the point of his sheath. The sparrow-hawk tackling the great heron was light of foot but ferocious of heart, gaining step after step with each relentless swing. Immutable as a boulder, Dairoku remained seated on the floor in dealing with her blows. The sharp blade charged with her single wish cleaved the edge of Dairoku's shoulder. He let the steel just bite into his flesh, then caught her wrist in his iron grip. Pulled down to the floor by his enormous strength, she found her sword arm helplessly pinned under his knee, a snow-white lotus blossom writhing beneath the cartwheel of a green leaf. Instantly, Tominaga roared like a wild bull, his immense sword whistling straight toward Dairoku's neck.

"Hold it!" Dairoku's bellowing voice rocked the building as he clanged his assailant's sword to a dead stop with the hilt of his own. "Look at me! You hothead! Does a Mikawa samurai find honor in the reckless killing of an unresisting man? Listen, Tominaga, if you are so terrified of Kasai Dairoku here, listen with your sword ready. If you attack me so unreasonably again, I'll crush this woman under my knee. Can you afford to take that chance? Withdraw your sword! You refuse? Then shall I press her to death? Which is it going to be? Ha, ha, ha, ha! Oh, well, Tominaga-dono, I am not a man to plan a temporary escape from the tiger's mouth using a woman as hostage; I am just telling you not to act impetuously. I won't hide or run. What would you lose by hearing me out? If I die in the middle of my story, how will you learn what happened to your beloved Kotarō? Am I anxious to continue the story for my own benefit? No, it is only in behalf of the dead boy that I want you to listen. You, too, Miss Tamae, calm yourself and listen for a while longer."

Noting Tominaga's acquiescence, Dairoku helped Tamae back into her seat. "Please be patient," he continued, unflustered by the two sets of wary eyes and the pair of drawn swords. "After our sedate drinking, your entertaining sword dance seems to have brought on a warm flush all over me. A lovely feeling indeed! As pleasant as if I were free, breathing the outside air once again after all these days of captivity. Well, let me accept another drink. Lucky for me you didn't kick the trays over. Ha, ha, ha! Thank you."

Dairoku poured himself another cupful, downed it casually, and resumed his monologue:

As I was saying, I had the young warrior in my restraining grasp. I had already stripped him of all weapons, and he had no strength to speak of. Since one of my arms was more than enough to subdue his flailing and squirming, I took my time in drawing my stiletto to cut off his head.

Just as the blade was about to touch his throat, I had a close look at this foe of mine. His face, flushed and moist from excitement, was as pure and fair as a glistening white jewel. His tightly pulled petals of lips were flaming red, his soft eyebrows blue-black, and his rage-widened eyes shimmering with gentle dew. A beautiful young boy, too delicate to be handled by rough hands. Except for our differences in allegiance, there was no real grudge standing between us. It would be a grave shame, I thought, to shorten the life of such innocent beauty with my own hand. While it was admirable of him to have braved into the battlefield when he seemed fragile enough to be a female, he even had the courage to set upon a rugged warrior. What an adorable boy, already showing such promise of valor! What would be the harm if I let him live? How can I put a cruel blade to his snow white skin?

Staying my thrust, I said, "Well, young man, in admiration of the bravery you've shown despite your tender age, I'll give you back the life that I hold in my palm. I won't kill you, so concede your inadequacy and come at me no more. I say this because I hate a useless killing of someone with a long life ahead of him. Since I promise never to mention our encounter in claiming credit for my feats, I'll neither tell you my name nor ask you for yours. Let's go our separate ways, and that will be the end of it. I have never set eyes upon you, and you have never seen me."

Then I meant to tell him that he was free to go wherever he pleased, but a sober realization dawned on me: I'm planning to smuggle myself into the Oda camp to assassinate Nobunaga. Suppose this young man belongs to the Oda command? He might prove to be the death of me yet. What a pity the way of Asura is such that I must break my promise right here and now, in eliminating the only witness who could later stymie my plan. With my stiletto still poised over him, I said, "Before I let you leave, tell me whether you are with the Oda army or the Tokugawa."

He answered me, and oh, how he answered me! I still feel a thrill just to remember it. Unafraid in such a desperate moment, the young warrior shouted loud and clear, "Stop talking nonsense! If you want to stab me, stab me. Slash me if you like. When you already have me pinned down, what is holding you back? I would much rather lose my head than live at the charity of my enemy. I did my best, but I have been overpowered. Now I make you a present of my life so that you can take credit for it. Who would want to play such a cowardly game, pretending we'd never met? How can a man live in such shame before heaven and earth! And how dare you insult me by declining to know my name! As a souvenir to take with me on my last journey, I condescend to mark your name. Identify yourself, you crimson face! Stab me quickly. Kill me! But listen well: I hereby announce that Kotarō Muneharu, the only son of the renowned Mikawa warrior Yanagi Sadaharu, dies in combat this day this month."

He cried fiercely and closed his eyes in heroic surrender. So valiant, so laudable! His show of courage was so winsome, in fact, I couldn't help smiling to myself. And his self-introduction demanded my response in kind.

"Spoken like a brave man!" I commended him. "If you must know, I'll tell you. My name is Kasai Dairoku Takahide, merely one of the humblest among the Kōshū ranks. Now you know who I am, but I shall not kill you. I was thrilled to hear what you just said. A fine man you are going to be! If we happen to meet again when you are grown, we can have another match to see whether I end up giving you my head or taking yours. Farewell for now; count your years well in training until you grow a beard like mine. I wish you luck. If I survive in the meantime, it will be a pleasure to hear occasional bits of news about you. Otherwise, it might be even more pleasurable to watch you from the nether world, I suppose. Well, if someone should stumble upon us now, we'd be in trouble. I'll proceed on my way, so quickly, go wherever you wish." To prove my sincerity, I tried to help him to his feet.

The boy opened his resolute eyes and stared into my face, brushing off my helping hands. "Your tender words remind me of someone who tried to dissuade me from going to battle. You shattered the heart of Asura within me, and I no longer feel you are part of my sworn enemy. But, once we crossed our weapons, which by definition are blind to human sentiments, the rule allows for no arbitrary mercy or ready acceptance of such. You live if I am slain; if I am spared, I cannot leave you alive. We may both die, but not survive together. I am chagrined to think that you consider a Mikawa man low enough to crawl for life even at a time like this. I have already chosen death, so allow me a proper and swift one, rather than trying to force a life of disgrace on me. I was beaten in a fair fight, and death is the only honor I have left. In exchange for making you a gift of my head, which is to turn to ashes in any case, I can safeguard the dignity of my ancestral name. Besides, in death I will find the satisfaction of fulfilling my heart's desire. Why should I make a cowardly choice of life over death? If you insist on freeing me, I swear I'll come after you and challenge you again. Please take my head this instant. If I am to die at the enemy's hand at all, I am glad it is by a man such as you. I have left some relations behind, but my only wish is that you let the word filter back to Mikawa that one Yanagi Kotarō died in combat. There is nothing more to hold me here. Please take my head."

Lacking the time to assuage the boy's intractable conviction, I didn't argue with him. Without a word I pulled him up, pushed him away, and sprinted south. Picking up the halberd, he shouted, "Where do you think you're going, Kasai Dairoku? What's the use of running off in that direction? You can never get out of my sight." Like a flying bird, he pursued me, still obviously intent upon fighting. The minute I looked back at him, he yelled, "Do you think I'll let my enemy slip out of my sight alive? Be a man and fight!" Knowing full well that he was no match for me, he made a lunge charged with the certainty of death. I was reluctant to kill a boy whom I had once decided to spare, and after some perfunctory parrying I pulled back to leave. He followed and again swung at me. Some more feinting and parrying, and I stepped back. Panting and gasping, the boy still persisted. Unable to cut him down in cold blood, I tried to leave, but he held me back. Time was fast slipping away, to my disadvantage, and I was extremely distressed. Just then three soldiers— low-ranking men from the plains, judging by their garish armor—happened by.

"Hey, Kōshū man on the run! Let us carve you into so many slices!" Bawling boisterously, they fell upon me in a body, their spears and swords glinting. Too late to run or get clear of Kotarō, I made a fast defensive stand in front of a tree. Up against so many assailants, my senses and limbs were all but overtaxed, even without the trouble of trying to avoid injury to the young man, who held the lead position in the assault and fought with more ardor than all the rest. My concern for his safety severely restrained my movements; my arms and will refused to work in unison, more than once subjecting me to untold danger. While I was barely holding my own, I found a chance to slash at an opponent with one sidelong sweep of my sword. Within a split second, though, my target moved back, and smack into the vacated space stepped Kotarō. No sooner did my heart freeze in horror than my sword in its momentum slashed deeply into his body. Oh, damn it! I killed the wrong man! No more need to contain myself, I thought. I instantly launched into a violent offensive, dispatching two on the spot and finishing off one on the run. Blood dripping from my sword, I returned to the original spot to find a pitiful sight. It wrenched my heart to behold the small form lying lifeless on the ground on account of my blunder, a boy endowed with the beauty of heart as well as of countenance, whose life I had fully intended to save. Had he been a little less scrupulous, he would have accepted quarter and enjoyed a long life. But he chose to deny himself another spring, faithful to the polished core of the samurai spirit rather than to take disgraceful advantage of an enemy's mercy. Estimable conduct belying his tender age!

Once, after the battle of Mikata-ga-hara three years ago, I heard General Yamagata remark, "The Mikawa men are the best-trained and most well-disciplined troops west of Edo. They are our foes but I must admit that they conduct themselves admirably." Remembering that comment, I earnestly envied the Mikawa warriors their good fortune in having such brave, gracious young boys for sons, brothers, and friends. If only those certain individuals in our clan had half the sense of honor this boy demonstrated, this battle would not have been such a fiasco. To think that the slick-tongued cowards mishandled the critical situation to bring all this upon us! Ah, the shame!

It makes me wonder what ruthless mind invented the differentiation such as friend and foe. All friends are not necessarily friendly, any more than all foes are detestable. Yet the inexorable command issued in accordance with that elusive differentiation deprives a man's mind of freedom, just as solid ice encases mountains and fields, allowing trees and grass not the slightest movement. If it is called a friend, even the wisteria vine which saps pine trees of their life fluid is spared, while the arrow must be pointed at a graceful cedar bird pecking at precious ivy berries if he is designated a foe. What a woeful rule! Solely because the label "foe" bound this boy and me like an unbreakable chain, one of us adamantly rejected life and rushed to his death, while the other tried to save him, only to fail in the end. Is this what is meant by the saying "No one can escape the law of karma"? It was useless to lament and too late to regret, but how I wished we had won the battle so that I could send his body back to his home with due honor, along with a detailed report of his valiant death as a samurai! Under the circumstances, unfortunately, such was out of the question. After all, I myself was a summer insect about to leap into a peril more deadly than fire. Yet how could I leave his body in the field where the wind and rain would bleach his bones? I couldn't bear the thought of consigning him to the ground unmarked, but what could I do? I lingered there, unable to decide. When at last an idea came, I picked up his smaller sword and thrust it in my waist band. Then I cut off his topknot and wrapped it in a sleeve of his combat jacket. I set out on my way carrying the little packet securely in my bosom. Before smuggling myself into the enemy camp disguised with the sleeve insignia taken from the plainsmen I had slain, I scribbled a note on the boy's sleeve recording his name and describing his end so that in the event of my death, someone examining my body would surely discover what became of Yanagi Kotarō Muneharu. Well, I then made my way into the Akechi command, and the rest is already an official record. When I was brought here as a captive, I could have immediately carried out the boy's last wish to let the news of his death reach someone in Mikawa, but I decided to wait until my death sentence was passed, for fear that my revelation might be construed as an ingratiating gesture.

Dairoku brought his story up to the present without pause.

"Not even suspecting that the two of you came here to avenge Kotarō tonight, I started telling you about him in the belief that my end was imminent. To my surprise, Miss Tamae proved to be the sister of the boy I had killed. You already have his sword, but please take a look at this. Here is the lock of his hair I have been carrying, wrapped in his own sleeve."

The item that Dairoku produced was unmistakable. At the sight of the familiar sleeve, Tamae dissolved in grief, giving way to silent sobs.

Unmindful of her weeping, Dairoku mused, "Now I have said all there is to say, and I can die without regrets. Now that my death is inevitable, it might be more fitting for me to tender my head to you tonight. Is it fate that I should die not in the Oda camp but in Mikawa and not by official execution but by giving my life to you—Heaven's dispensation to have the retribution fit the sin? Rather ingenious! Well, it is time I put an end to it all. Ah, don't be alarmed. Ha, ha, ha! The saké is all gone, and I might as well return to the original void which fills this drinking vessel. With no regret binding me to this world, I shall join, by virtue of my sutra chanting, an existence as infinite as the bright dawn sky. A couple of short steel pieces called sword and blade are about to halve and quarter the ephemeral body of mine. Why should I resist? Miss Tamae, go ahead and kill me. Avenge your young brother. I will gladly accept your blade, for I see no sense in raising my hand against a lady. I'll let you kill me as I sit. Hurry, put your sword to me."

Dairoku craned his neck in staid composure, but Tamae, having learned the truth, was speechless in her vacillation.

"Why are you faltering now?" Tominaga urged impatiently. "Lend no ear to an unconfirmed story. What is this hesitation before the mortal enemy of your young brother?"

Her emotion inflamed once again by Tominaga's bellows, Tamae sprung to her feet in spite of herself, calling out, "Slayer of my brother!" Her enlarged eyes stared down at her foe, seated just below the gleaming tip of her short sword held upside-down, ready to plunge.

The hulking mound of a man sat calm and still, his eyes slightly upcast in an attitude of expectancy. His crimson face was as fresh and serene as a baby's. His tightly drawn mouth was firm yet unspiteful; his clear eyes and unclouded forehead radiated the purity of his heart. A magnificent growth of beard covered his cheeks and his jaws, harboring an almost imperceptible smile. A splendid picture of masculinity he was.

"There's nothing about him that I can hate," thought Tamae. "Perhaps he truly did look upon his young foe, my Kotarō, with tender fondness." Momentarily dazed, she suddenly felt the lamplight grow dazzlingly bright. Unwittingly she staggered back a few paces and let her weapon fall.

"For shame, Miss Tamae! Have you taken fright in spite of what I told you? I stand by you; kill him without fear," Tominaga prompted.

Tamae sat down. "It's very ungracious of you to ask if I have taken fright," she observed pensively. "I may be a woman, but I am not one to lose courage in avenging her brother. It is just that I have lost my hatred of Kasai-dono. In truth, the goodness of his heart makes him all but impossible to hate. I cannot bring myself to take his life for Kotarō's. Rather than being resentful, my brother in the nether world is probably very grateful to Kasai-dono for keeping his promise. If our lord wants to take his life, I intend to plead for clemency on his behalf. The official sentence is yet to be passed, and I no longer contemplate a private revenge. To my deepest grief, my young brother died in combat to fulfill his heart's desire. It is a grievous blow to the Yanagi family, but man's life and death are not his own making. They are perhaps machinations of an omnipotent deity and therefore far beyond the conjecture of a humble human mind. Is it mysterious divine dispensation, predestination, or what is commonly called the law of cause and effect? I am but a creature more evanescent than a dewdrop, and I can do no more than sense some vague shadow hovering above the heads of others. This extrasensory sensation chills me to my marrow and bathes my eyes in tears of some nameless emotion, neither grief, regret, nor resentment. Ah, among the mortals standing helpless under this ominous cloud called Providence, among humans who can communicate formless thoughts in words and voiceless feelings through their eyes, I wonder if such things as hate and resentment can really exist. Rest assured, Kasai-dono, I have already abandoned the idea of killing you. I would be most grateful if you feel pity for my poor brother and say prayers for the repose of his soul on occasions when you recite sutras."

"How heedless of you, Miss Tamae! How like a woman!" howled Tominaga, barely able to hold his breath to the end of her tearful speech. "Where is your sense of moral responsibility toward your slain brother? False mercy is a useless thing. You are all too readily taken in by your enemy's honeyed lies. Your weak-kneed behavior does not become a sister of Kotarō Muneharu. How scandalous! How disgraceful, disgusting! Stand aside! You may be willing to forgive this bearded face, but I refuse to do so. Upon my honor, I cannot let him be. I shall not stop until I present General Sakai with your head, Dairoku, swinging upside-down by that overlong beard of yours held firmly in my own hand. Now stand up and fight!" Tominaga leaped up and stamped his feet.

Dairoku glared back. "What a crass, bullheaded cad! I would have let Miss Tamae kill me, but even that because I believed my execution was set for tomorrow. Now that I know otherwise from what she just said, I fully intend to live as long as I can. Why should I yield my life to the likes of you? When the actual party in this vendetta has forgiven me, do you still mean to busy yourself with killing me just to clear your conscience before a friend? I don't particularly hate you, but I can't back down in the face of your challenge, can I? If you want my head, go ahead and make your bid for glory. Just be careful you don't wind up proving the sharpness of this sword that you have so honorably provided me with." Unsheathing the blade in a flash, Dairoku rose on one knee.

"Damn you!" Tominaga barked, driving his sword down with enough force to split a mountain.

It was too late for Tamae to intercede. Two redoubtable warriors already crossing swords, relentless and unyielding, their blades glinting as radiant as frost on bamboo leaves in the windy dawn—there was no room for her to edge between them. While she watched in helpless horror, there arose the clang of weapons and the thud of footsteps of men approaching the room. Letting in sudden beams of bright light, the wooden doors clattered open one after another, yielding some thirty armored guards. At the head of the throng was Sakai Tadatsugu, distinctly identifiable under the torchlight held high in his hand.

"This is an outrage! Stop it, Tominaga. You too, Kasai Dairoku, hold your sword. Men, pull them apart!"

At his command, the men tackled the pair in a heap. Dairoku withdrew his sword unresisting, but Tominaga was implacable. "Get out of my way, men. Stand aside, Sakai, and just watch. I won't stop until I see his blood." Tadatsugu caught hold of the growling Tominaga's arms, restraining him forcefully. "Come to your senses, Tominaga! Who asked you to kill Kasai? An attempt of personal revenge upon a prisoner in official custody is an affront to our lord." Even as Tadatsugu was chiding Tominaga, a number of guards, including Tamon, who was in charge of this guard unit, piled upon Tominaga and managed to remove his sword. Forcibly subdued, Tominaga sat down with a thud and glared indignantly at Dairoku, gnashing his teeth.

[19]

The abbot's chamber was becalmed by a faint scent of burning aloeswood incense and tranquil flickers of the lamplight. Inside sat Dairoku, Tadatsugu, Tominaga, and Tamae, relishing the properly prepared tea served by the white-browed abbot. In direct contrast to the mood of less than two hours earlier, their speech was congenial.

"Now that we are opening our hearts to one another, Dairoku, I will be quite frank with you," said Tadatsugu, a smile flooding his face. Ever since I learned that you had killed Kotarō, I could not bear the thought of you sitting safe and sound within my reach; I even pleaded privately with my lord to let me have you. The compassionate lord refused, however, to grant permission, most displeased with my request for the right to dispose of his prisoner. But even then I was unable to give you up entirely. I asked this old abbot to send me a daily report of your activities and to send a special messenger to me should anything untoward happen. My primary motive was to catch you as you tried to escape so that I could avail myself of the opportunity to avenge Kotarō. Thanks to my precaution, I was informed as soon as Tominaga and a lady called on you this evening. Since Tominaga was involved with the Kotarō incident, it was not hard to divine his motive, and I was almost certain that the lady was Miss Tamae. Quite alarmed by a prospect of trouble, I rushed over here at once.

"When I arrived at this temple, I learned everything, so I no longer bear the slightest grudge against you, just as Miss Tamae admitted herself. On the contrary, I feel quite close to you now. Tominaga has also abandoned all thoughts of harming you. Putting your official status aside, there is no one in this room who doesn't consider you a friend. So, Kasai-dono, will you compromise yourself a bit and become a Mikawa subject so that you can share a long friendship with us not only in private but with official sanction as well? Our master commands only a modest domain and even more limited political power, but he is mellow of heart and broad of mind, considerate enough never to resort to force in dealing with his subordinates, and a discerning judge of character. All in all, he is a master one can serve with bright hope for the future. Since his entire domain scarcely fills your palm, it is probably impossible to offer a stipend attractive enough to entice you. But I dare to hope that you find a deserving object of your devotion in our master, whose character, disposition, profound regard for his retainers, and steadfast allegiance to the way of the samurai must be all but public knowledge by now.

"A man must live equally well through prosperity, decline, adversity, and peril, but under a master of no quality, he is but a prize painting to a blind man, a flute to a deaf man, something to be discarded or, worse yet, to be toyed with into destruction, with no one to appreciate the rich glow of his heart or to give him a chance to strike up a pure note. Who can but regret such a fate? If you consent to become a Mikawa subject, we hope to do our humble best to enjoy a long, genuine friendship with you and to stride through this chaotic world hand in hand, jubilantly exchanging cheers, helping and competing in friendly rivalry. Doesn't the idea appeal to you? I may be inane, but I am never malevolent. As you can see, Tominaga is also as open and straight as a split bamboo stalk. We, the Mikawa comrades, have lived in harmony and friendship all these years, regardless of the differences in our abilities and experiences, for there is not a single scheming sycophant among us. If you join our clan, all of us, not to mention our lord himself, will be overjoyed to gain a good comrade. Will you accept my invitation? I cannot call it judicious of you, with all your admirable qualities, to persist in the fruitless fate of a tree buried in a desolate valley. I would regret that very much."

Dairoku laughed resoundingly when Tadatsugu had finished his logical and emotional appeal. "I appreciate your concern," he said. "However, if I were to take your advice, you would have done your lord no more service than reinforcing a great mountain with a handful of soil, but what would it mean in terms of my service to my own lord? I am fully aware of what is or is not to my own benefit, but personal interests concern me less than an itch or a pain that might assail me in a dream. I cannot accept your offer. If granted death, I am prepared to die, even tomorrow. Otherwise I shall cling tenaciously to life, waiting for a chance to escape and make my way back to Kōshū. I might even come face to face with your lord Ieyasu in the battlefield some day. If such a time does come, Tominaga-dono, I shall be glad to finish the fight that was interrupted today. General Sakai would not play the worrisome old woman to stop us again, I trust."

Dairoku burst into spirited laughter.

[20]

Some time later, when Katsuyori came out of Kōshū again to defend Takatenjin Castle in Enshū, Kasai Dairoku, still unexecuted, somehow learned of the campaign and escaped from Hōkō Temple, injuring many guards in the process. Taken by surprise, people expressed their dismay at Ieyasu's handling of the prisoner. After some deliberation, Ieyasu said with a smile, "Well, it's no matter. The Kōshū lads are soon to be my limbs in any case." At that, he reverted to his old self.

❖ Selected Allusions

AKECHI MITSUHIDE (1526–82): one of Nobunaga's vassals; he eventually staged a coup d'état and drove Nobunaga to death, only to outlive him for a few days.

ASURA: the fighting spirits of the dead warriors inhabiting one of the Six Spheres of the Buddhist cosmology.

GAMŌ UJISATO (1556–95): a samurai who served Nobunaga and Hideyoshi successively, eventually to command a large fief. He is said to have sent a mission to the Vatican, but this is as yet unproven.

HACHIMAN: the Japanese god of war; his origins are uncertain.

HASHIBA HIDEYOSHI (1536–98): later known as Toyotomi, one of Nobunaga's field commanders at the time of this story. After Nobunaga's death, he seized power and united much of Japan.

JŌHA (Satomura Jōha, 1524–1602): noted poet in Nobunaga's retinue; later served Hideyoshi as cultural advisor.

MARISHITEN (Skt., Marīci): a goddess worshiped as the guardian of samurai.

MATSUDAIRA NOBUYASU (1559–79): Ieyasu's eldest son and a fierce field commander. He was married to one of Nobunaga's daughters, who later trumped up a false charge of his conspiring with Katsuyori against Nobunaga, which resulted in a death-by-suicide sentence for Nobuyasu and his mother.

MINAMOTO-NO-HACHIMAN-TARŌ YOSHIIE (1039?–1106): Katsuyori's grand clan ancestor and a reknowned hero, worshiped almost as a divinity by the warriors who descended from him. Generally known as Minamoto-no-Yoshiie, he was given the name Hachiman-Tarō at his coming-of-age ceremony at the Iwashimizu-Hachiman Shrine, Kyoto.

MIROKU (Skt., Maitreya): a bodhisattva, the Future Buddha who is predicted to manifest himself to save mankind at a time exactly 5 billion 670 million years after the historical Buddha, Shakyamuni of India, entered Nirvana (died).

NOBUKATSU (Oda Nobukatsu, 1558–1630): Nobunaga's second son; an army commander. He survived his father and commanded a 50,000-*koku* fief under Ieyasu.

NOBUTADA (Oda Nobutada, 1557–82): Nobunaga's eldest son, an army commander who would be responsible for defeating the Takeda and forcing Katsuyori to commit seppuku. He eventually died fighting in the aftermath of the Akechi uprising.

ODA NOBUNAGA (1534–82): warlord and senior ally of Ieyasu. He deposed the last Ashikaga shogun in 1573, destroyed the Takeda in 1582, and was on his way to unifying Japan when he died in fire surrounded by Akechi's army.

OKUDAIRA SADAMASA (1555–1615): garrison commander at Nagashino Castle. He rebelled against his newly imposed overlord, Takeda Katsuyori, and later served Ieyasu and was awarded one of Ieyasu's daughters as his wife.

SAKAI TADATSUGU (1527–96): hereditary vassal of Ieyasu's and one of the Tokugawa Four generals. He married Ieyasu's aunt.

SAKUMA NOBUMORI (d. 1582): vassal of Nobunaga's and planner of his "false traitor" plot.

SHIBATA (Shibata Katsuie, 1522–83): member of Nobunaga's war council. He married Nobunaga's sister, was eventually defeated by Hideyoshi's army, and died in the fall of his own castle.

SHINGEN (Takeda Shingen, 1521–73): warlord and father of Katsuyori. He is believed to have been undefeated in battle. He died of tuberculosis on a campaign in Mikawa before the battle in this story.

TAKEDA SHIRŌ KATSUYORI (1546–82): warlord, son of Shingen, and lord of fictional hero Dairoku in this story. (For a fuller treatment of Katsuyori, see Historical Notes on "The Bearded Samurai," p. 275.)

TAKIGAWA (Takigawa Kazumasu, dates unknown): vassal of Nobunaga's. He was later defeated by Ieyasu's army and surrendered. He ended his life as a lay monk.

TOKUGAWA IEYASU (1542–1616): warlord and ally of Nobunaga's, later founder and first shogun of the Tokugawa shogunate (1603–1867), which Rohan's family served until the Meiji Restoration.

TORII SUNE'EMON (d. 1575): Okudaira Sadamasa's messenger; crucified by the Takeda forces at the battle of Nagashino.

UESUGI KENSHIN (1530–78): Shingen's most renowned rival, lord of Echigo and Etchū provinces.

WESTERN PURE LAND: a Buddhist paradise presided over by the Amida Buddha of the West.

YOSHIMITSU (Minamoto-no-Yoshimitsu, 1045–1127): Minamoto-no-Yoshiie's younger brother and direct ancestor of Katsuyori.

AFTERWORD

As MENTIONED in the Introduction, one of the concepts with which a pagoda is identified is that of the universe, in which the ancient Buddha, symbolized by the moon, and the present Buddha, by the sun, exist side by side. In "The Five-Storied Pagoda," Jūbei is ordered to build the pagoda by a mysterious figure in a dream; after his faith passes the test of Nature, the pagoda launches the moon and swallows the sun. In Mahayana (greater vehicle) Buddhism, which has been dominant in Japan since the ninth century, salvation is not a goal attainable by a privileged few through rigorous physical and spiritual training, as in the Hinayana (lesser vehicle) branch. On the contrary, the universal salvation of Mahayana, in which Rohan firmly believed, cannot be achieved without the collective endeavor of the human race. Only by sacrificing his ear can Jūbei save his pagoda from the fate of the Tower of Babel. Both Jūbei and Genta must risk their lives and artist's honor in the storm to prove the power of art (human accomplishment) to recreate eternity. Satan in the Judeo-Christian tradition is a grand antithesis to God, an evil tempter bent on misleading souls away from the path of virtue. In marked contrast, the demons in Buddhism are guardians of the Law and chastisers of miscreants, and their mission is to shepherd erring mankind toward the collective way to universal salvation. Hence, it is the demons who personify the forces of nature that test human faith, while the Abbot Rōen embodies the humanly attainable Buddha-like perfection.

If the raison d'être of art is to enlighten and save mankind, as Rohan believed, art as a structured microcosm is superior to nature or even religion in its power to inspire and educate ordinary people. The effective use of literary art is exemplified by the Abbot's tale in "The Five-Storied Pagoda" and by Tae's story in "Encounter with a Skull." In Rohan's view, moreover, art is man's sublime achievement, for art is immortal. Art can be the best exemplar of collective accomplishment through the concerted effort of mankind: Jūbei's pagoda is not possible without the dedicated labor of his entire crew and the proud tradition kept alive through artisans of both past and future, as typified by Genta and Jūbei's young son, who is already building little pagodas. More importantly, even nonconcrete art is immortal because, for Rohan, artistic creation is not an idle fantasy in the static, conceptual, linear dimension, but a dynamic, self-perpetuating, omnipresent, vital cosmos that embraces time, space, self, others—all opposites and antitheses as well. It is not mere gothic touch or grandiloquent metaphor when a bleached skull and demons come to life and interact with humans in his works.

Jūbei's total confidence in his own ability is by no means the hubris of the Greek hero. It was Rohan's belief that what separates man from animal is ambition—ambition on the grandest scale and of the most sublime order, neither political nor personal. The supreme ambition of the Confucian scholar-gentleman *(kunshi)* was to become a sage, a man who perfected himself morally and spiritually to be harmonious with the absolute. But a sage would be considered worthless unless his knowledge and virtue contributed actively to the betterment of society. He had only his own inner values to rely on, for compromise and conformity to lesser or external values would jeopardize the salvation of all others. Thus, self-confidence and willpower were indispensable virtues in a person with aspiration and a sense of mission in Rohan's moral cosmos.

The conspicuous absence of villains in Rohan's works is regarded as a literary failing by some critics, but it is no surprise when viewed in the light of Rohan's moral optimism. If, as Confucianism affirms, human nature is basically good, man can never be totally evil, any more than a sage can turn into a megalomaniac. So when conflict and confrontation do occur in Rohan's stories, they arise not from the classic fight between Good and Evil over the possession of an eternal soul or a clash between two antagonists, but rather from an agonizing struggle of a soul trying to be a sage and still live among, and for, fellow men. Despite the pervading Buddhist ambience in his mystical visions, Rohan was an orthodox Confucian in his primary concern with man's life in the here and now of human society.

Profoundly influenced by the social- and moral-activist aspects of Confucianism in general, and by the action-oriented theory of Wang Yang-ming in particular, Rohan advocated that every person ought to aspire to the highest goal in his or her own field to the benefit of society at large. He found an ideal character type in his artist-artisan heroes—"real people with real work to perform" who "would be just as viable outside of the artificial world of fiction." The Neo-Confucians in Ming China (1368–1644) saw the fundamental characteristic of the universe as creativity, and they considered man as similarly creative in his essence. In this vein, Rohan's artisan, poet, or novelist heroes can become sages in their own respective ways by creating an artistic or literary work that is a self-contained organic universe.

Rohan had every reason to believe that his heroes, embodying lofty ideals, were realistic representations of the real world. Without creative energy, uncompromising dedication, and a grand vision far beyond conventional values, such as that championed by Jūbei and demonstrated by Rohan's real-life contemporaries, the Meiji Restoration would have had no chance to grace the pages of history, and Japan's modernization would have been much slower in coming and would have taken drastically different forms. The mainstream of modern Japanese literature to this day portrays predominantly negative or introverted views of the times through superfluous heroes and antiheroes—self-doubters, losers, escapists, self-absorbed dilettantes, misfits, and masochists. Rohan's activist heroes are unique literary creations, reflecting the constructive forces in Japanese personality and society that made Japan what it is—with all its strengths and weaknesses.

"Encounter with a Skull" not only echoes Buddhist views and the eerie atmosphere and rich allusions characteristic of the fourteenth-century Noh theater, but also mirrors the structure of the typical Noh ghost play. A traveler (the secondary character, or *waki*) meets a mysterious person in humble guise (protagonist in Act One, or *maejite*); solicited by an interested *waki*, the protagonist reveals her real or former identity as a person of noble birth (the protagonist in Act Two, or *atojite*) and recounts the anguish of her life on earth. In the Noh play, the *atojite* may continue to relive her moments of humiliation or frustration in eternal torment of regret, or else attain release by virtue of the *waki*'s prayers or by her own self-awakening, before vanishing from sight at the end. In "Encounter with a Skull," the protagonist's metamorphosis is more complex: she changes from a charming hostess to an attractive maiden, a desolated woman, a crazed sick beggar, a bleached skull, to an enlightened spirit. Born a cherished heiress, she spends a happy childhood. In her adolescence, she learns the pathos of life through the death of her father, and the sinfulness of human nature from storybooks. Her mother's last letter teaches her the meaninglessness of the flesh. When the noble suitor (whose love for the unseen lady can only be Platonic and spiritual) dies, he inspires true compassion (tears for unknown causes—for all suffering) in order to prepare her for a pilgrimage. And after her body is stripped of flesh by a degenerative disease, she attains a state of perfect contentment.

Since her spirit is already free of attachment, it is not a vengeful or tormented soul (as in most Noh plays), but an enlightened being on a bodhisattva mission, awaiting a receptive wayfarer in order to transmit visions of the other world. After his spiritual preparation by the ordeal of mountain climbing, the young Rohan of the story is purified in the bath. Protected from the harm of lust by women's clothes (or by shedding his male identity to be restored to the undifferentiated state of quintessential human being), he shares a Buddhist-Shinto vegetarian meal with a priestess (her freshly washed hair flows straight down rather than being piled high into the mundane coiffure). Now he is ready to learn the meaning of life and true compassion through vicarious suffering. At last his soul awakens to the mystery of the mind that makes it possible to communicate and empathize with all other minds beyond time and space, regardless of surface distinctions.

In Buddhism, suffering serves as a means to the attainment of salvation by causing a person to "forsake the sinful world and aspire toward the Pure Land." All who wish to be saved can be saved, but even Buddhas and bodhisattvas, potential Buddhas on the mission of universal salvation, cannot save an individual who is unwilling to be saved. The beautiful young girl's longing to join her dead mother is a first step toward her salvation, just as the rejected suitor's loathing of himself and his wish to depart from this world qualify him to be a guiding spirit. The girl who helped his enlightenment by teaching him sorrow and anguish is in turn guided by his phantom (this is the essence of Mahayana Buddhism, the doctrine of universal salvation attainable only through the mutual efforts of mankind). The spirit of the skull, which had lingered in this world in order to impart the gospel, is finally released as Rohan assumes the responsibility of propagating the message through his novel. Thus, in "Encounter with a Skull," Rohan affirms the power of literature as ardently as he does the power of concrete art, such as architecture, in "The Five-Storied Pagoda."

As for the mysterious disease that helps release the heroine's soul from the flesh, Rohan never identifies it by name. Consensus among Japanese scholars has diagnosed it as leprosy, which was traditionally believed hereditary as well as contagious until Rohan's time. Once at a party, Rohan was physically assaulted by an acquaintance who mistakenly thought that Tae had been modeled on his own sister, who was stricken with leprosy. Rohan's description of the beggar woman, nonetheless, would apply just as well to the symptoms of congenital syphilis. Emperor Wen's Chinese poem, "Elimination of Desires," also seems to sound an ominous warning about sexual contagion in this story. In any case, Tae's condition is a visible reminder of the lethal danger inherent in the illusion of physical beauty and indulgence in carnal pleasure. At the same time, such a disease provides a realistic cause for the mad scene, in the course of which a typical Noh play protagonist deranged by anguish would vanish into thin air. As attested by Noh plays, in which an unavenged or unsublimated soul forever agonizes in regret and resentment, death in itself does not guarantee the release of a soul from emotional attachment originating in the flesh. From this Buddhist tradition stems the necessity for a motif such as a degenerative disease that would rid the living body of its corporeal substance as a step toward enlightenment.

There is, furthermore, a metaphysical reason why the heroine cannot attain the ultimate goal of Buddhism in her own physical form. Recent years have witnessed some egalitarian attempts to redefine the Judeo-Christian God as "she" or "it." Even the most militant feminists, however, would be hard put to find a metaphysical or religio-symbolic justification for pressing for equal rights or non-sexist terminology for the Buddha. To summarize at the risk of over-simplification, the Buddha can be construed as an abstract cosmic principle that from time to time manifests itself as human-shaped beings representing its various aspects, such as function (Healing Buddha), cosmological element (Sun Buddha), space (Amida Buddha of the Western Pure Land), and time (Future Buddha). By virtue of the "buddha nature" believed to be innate in every sentient being, theoretically anyone can become a Buddha. Actually, the Indian prince (*c.* 556–485 B.C.) who came to be known as Gautama Buddha is the only historical person to have done so. (He is in fact the founder of Buddhism as a religion, but what concerns us here is the Buddhist ontology and cosmology predicating the infinite past.)

According to the Buddhist scriptures, all Buddhas are unequivocally male. This is not because the historical Buddha was a man, nor because women allegedly lack in virtue and determination. To begin with, how can one tell if and when someone attains Buddhahood? Christ failed to convince the Romans that he was the son of God, but in Buddha's case, no one can mistake him, for he is supposed to manifest the "Thirty-two Physical Signs of the Buddhahood." Iconography displays some of these signs: a curl of white hair on the forehead, pendant earlobes, hands long enough to reach below the knee, golden skin color, a prominent cranium. Some signs are olfactory (heavenly body odor) or auditory (musical voice). Unfortunately for women, one of the thirty-two describes the male anatomy. Inasmuch as a woman by definition is unable to manifest *all* of the Signs, she can never hope to be a Buddha—in her present body, that is.

In the *Lotus Sutra,* Gautama Buddha proves that women can indeed become Buddha. He summons the daughter of the Dragon King and preaches the Law to her in person. However, not only is she eight years old but, upon achieving enlightenment then and there, she instantly turns into a male, perfect with all the Thirty-two Signs. In "Encounter with a Skull," Tae as a grown human female cannot be expected to execute a spontaneous change of sexual identity. Her loss of human shape is Rohan's metaphor for metaphysical transformation.

In addition to his speculations on the battle of Nagashino in "The Bearded Samurai," Rohan poses a cogent question: What role might the various samurai attitudes toward death have played in this historical drama? The Takeda generals uphold the feudal view that even if the lord proves to be an unworthy lord, the vassal should still behave as an ideal vassal; and Kotarō acts out the common belief that the way of the samurai culminates in the manner of dying. Dairoku, on the other hand, seems to reflect (as evinced by Ieyasu's admiration for him) the pragmatic attitude of his real-life contemporaries such as Ieyasu and Nobunaga, who, after all, managed to survive and thrive in the power struggle by means of underhanded, if innovative, strategies.

Rohan presents the battle primarily as a conflict of personalities and moral principles rather than as a technical exercise in military science. This approach is favored in Japan, as illustrated by a well-known fictitious episode illuminating the contrasting personalities of three historical heroes: Nobunaga was felled on the brink of unifying Japan by the mutiny of a tormented general in his own command; Toyotomi Hideyoshi (1536–98) promptly avenged his master and cunningly seized hegemony to attain Nobunaga's goal himself; and Ieyasu bided his time until he was able to reap the full benefit of both men's accomplishments and founded the Tokugawa shogunate, which was to rule Japan for two and a half centuries. When told of a little cuckoo *(hototogisu)* that would not sing, each is supposed to have composed a haiku.

NOBUNAGA:	*Nakazumba*	If it would not sing,
	Koroshite shimae	Kill it and be done with it—
	Hototogisu	The little cuckoo.
HIDEYOSHI:	*Nakazumba*	If it would not sing,
	Nakasete mishō	I can make it sing—
	Hototogisu	The little cuckoo.
IEYASU:	*Nakazumba*	If it would not sing,
	Nakumade matō	I will wait till it does—
	Hototogisu	The little cuckoo.

One additional point may warrant an explanation. If tough warriors such as Dairoku and Sakai Tadatsugu (1527–96) seem to describe the young Kotarō in affectionate, even somewhat sensuous, terms, it is in all likelihood intentional on Rohan's part. Through the ages, fiction, plays, and professional story-chanters *(kōdanshi, naniwabushi-gatari)* have conditioned Japanese imagination until it is now difficult to picture Nobunaga (tall, lean, intense, handsome) without the attendant image of Mori Rammaru (1565–82). Popular legend glamorized this striking young man to the point of conferring upon him the dubious distinction of being the single major cause for Nobunaga's untimely demise (cf. Seikichi's reference to them in "The Five-Storied Pagoda"). Rammaru was a son of Nobunaga's trusted commander who had died in 1570 defending a castle in his lord's behalf. The most famous of Nobunaga's many young samurai lovers, Rammaru is commonly believed to have been extremely intelligent, quick-witted, loyal, and competent. His legend is filled with episodes illustrating his ability in discharging his successive duties as page, messenger, magistrate, and ultimately lord of a sixty-thousand-*koku* fief.

Popular accounts have it that as a reward for some trifling service, Nobunaga promised Rammaru a fief in Ōmi Province, but the fief happened to belong at the time to Akechi Mitsuhide (1526–82). It was the last straw for General Akechi—ponderously prudent, intellectually oriented, and humorless—who had suffered much abuse and humiliation at the hand of the mercurial, intolerant Nobunaga. Trapped in a Kyoto temple by Akechi's insurgent troops, Nobunaga committed seppuku after claiming many enemy lives. Aside from the more serious political and personal circumstances behind Akechi's mutiny, vivid in the mind of Japanese public is the vision of Rammaru—the beautiful, graceful, valiant seventeen-year-old samurai holding off waves of attackers together with his two younger brothers, setting fire to the temple to safeguard Nobunaga's head from falling into enemy hands, and finally rushing into the blaze to die beside his beloved lord. In "The Bearded Samurai," Kotarō is presumably also about seventeen years of age, judging from the fact that he has an adult name assumed at the coming-of-age ceremony, usually held no later than a boy's seventeenth year. Like Rammaru, Kotarō is the heir of a valiant commander who died in his lord's service.

Homosexual attachments between warriors have been far from uncommon in Japanese history and fiction. Buddhism is generally believed to view woman as a defiling agent and an impediment to man's salvation. In an age and a society infused with fatalistic Buddhist pessimism, a samurai would be considered the more masculine and self-controlled for his love of men and for his emotional detachment from women. In most cases, homosexual love relationships did not preclude both parties from marrying and fathering children indispensable for the perpetuation of the family line. (According to most sources, Nobunaga sired twelve sons and eleven daughters by a number of consorts, though some of the daughters seem to have been adopted for political reasons.) Far from being effeminate or effete, moreover, younger men were expected to be no less endowed with masculine virtues than their mature partners. In practice, the relationship often resembled apprenticeship or a tutoring of boys in the facts of life and the ways of the samurai. Many a famous man who left his mark on history as a hero in war or a high-ranking administrator in peacetime gained his training, opportunity, and recognition through such personal contact with older men, usually high in social status.

A case in point is Takeda's famed general Kōsaka Masanobu (1527–78), who is mentioned in "The Bearded Samurai" as Dairoku's commander. He had been a boy lover of his lord, Takeda Shingen (1521–73), and their relationship is indisputably established by an extant letter in Shingen's own hand pledging his unchanging love and loyalty. Kōsaka was later assigned the formidable task of guarding Takeda's northern border against their archenemy, Uesugi Kenshin (1530–78). Successfully fulfilling that responsibility for many years, Kōsaka earned well-deserved acclaim as well as a seventy-five-thousand-*koku* fief. He is the author of the original sources for the *Kōyō Gunkan* (Military record of Kōshū), which is one of the most popular volumes among the canon of bushido, the way of the warrior, even today.

Although Rohan never makes an outright mention of homosexual attachment between Tadatsugu and Kotarō in his story, one cannot overlook the deliberation with which Rohan creates the impression that Tadatsugu lives alone with an old manservant, omitting the pertinent information that Tadatsugu was married to Ieyasu's aunt in real life. Dairoku, who also admires Kotarō's beauty, is presented as a bachelor who chuckles, "No sophisticated prince of the Heike clan, I wouldn't know what to do if I met the fairest of women on the night before my death." Rohan's additional subtle touch can be detected in his supplying Dairoku with a background that placed him under General Kōsaka's command in the northern region over the years.

Sexual connotation per se is irrelevant in "The Bearded Samurai," but a feeling akin to the emotion of love free from a mercenary or pragmatic motive—a universal, noble, selfless sense of wonder that affirms humanity and aesthetic sensitivity in man—is absolutely essential in this story. Without it, the enemies could never transcend or sublimate animosity and grudge. The scene between Kotarō and Dairoku deliberately echoes one of the most popular episodes in *The Tale of the Heike*, a thirteenth-century war narrative. In "The Death of Atsumori"* the Heike nobleman Atsumori (1169–84) engages in mortal combat with the older Genji warrior Kumagai Naozane (d. 1208). Finding himself overpowered, Atsumori offers up his head, but

---

*Found in Donald Keene, *Anthology of Japanese Literature*, New York: Grove Press, 1955, pp. 179–81.

Kumagai hesitates to kill a young man "about the age of his own son and with features of great beauty." An approaching swarm of his own comrades forces Kumagai to cut off Atsumori's head, rather than leaving the inevitable to a callous hand, before which Kumagai tearfully promises to have prayers said for the boy's rebirth into the Pure Land.

If the confrontation in "The Bearded Samurai" is reminiscent of this moving narrative classic, the religious and psychological implications of the fictional encounter between Kotarō and Dairoku are closer to the more profound and poetic Noh play *Atsumori*.* In this version, the former antagonists realize that "Once enemies, but now in truth may we be named Friends in Buddha's Law" and that they are but two souls bound by some mysterious karma to lead one another toward salvation. Association with the Atsumori legend is unmistakable in "The Bearded Samurai," moreover, not only in Dairoku's abrupt reference to the Heike prince but also in his reflection on the nature of friend and foe, which recalls a passage from *Atsumori:* "Put away from you a wicked friend; summon to your side a virtuous enemy."

---

*Keene, pp. 286–93.

Central Japan at the time of "The Bearded Samurai" (late sixteenth c.)

HISTORICAL NOTES
on "The Bearded Samurai"

TAKEDA KATSUYORI (1546–82), the defeated commander in "The Bearded Samurai," is a rather tragic figure, to whom history seems unduly unkind. The popular image of Katsuyori is that of an exceptionally handsome, tall, aristocratic young man favored most by his father, Takeda Shingen, because of his beautiful mother. Known in history only as the Lady from Suwa, she had been forced to become a secondary wife of Shingen, who was an elder brother of her own mother. Marriage between blood uncle and niece was not unusual or considered immoral in itself, but her circumstances were tragic: the fourteen-year-old beauty was taken by Shingen in 1544 after he had defeated her father, Suwa Yorishige, and murdered him at the treaty conference. Shingen's exceeding love for his niece-wife, widely rumored at the time to be an incarnation of the sacred white fox serving the god of Suwa Shrine, is usually cited as a primary reason why, of his seven sons (by his other wives as well), Katsuyori is the only one lacking the character *shin* in his name. Instead, *yori* in Katsuyori is taken from the name of his Suwa grandfather, indicating Shingen's attempt to reassure his favorite wife and the conquered people of Suwa that her family line continued through their son. This pale mysterious beauty died when Katsuyori was nine years old, but the boy grew into a fine warrior-general and vindicated his father's favoritism by winning a decisive victory at the battle of Mikata-ga-hara in December 1572, at which he led a daring cavalry charge into the Tokugawa wing, putting the combined Oda-Tokugawa forces to rout. On his way to storm through the Tokugawa domain of Mikawa with his eyes set on Kyoto, the capital, Shingen succumbed to chronic tuberculosis in April of the following year, leaving instructions that his death be kept secret for two years. While Nobunaga waited with bated breath, the Takeda reduced their military activities in secret mourning as well as in succession dispute. But only two months after Shingen's death was at last made public through a formal funeral service in April 1575, Tokugawa Ieyasu installed Okudaira Sadamasa, a former Takeda vassal who had recently defected to the Tokugawa, as the commander of the five-hundred-man Nagashino garrison, to Katsuyori's great chagrin.

Historical assessment of Katsuyori's true caliber becomes divided only after the battle of Nagashino, for there is no denying that Nobunaga had been so afraid of Katsuyori's cavalry that he erected triple fences girded by a forward ditch to keep mounted Takeda warriors at bay. Another undisputed fact is that during the eight-hour engagement, Takeda's able generals, such as Yamagata and Baba, died along with great many of their men. It is generally believed that the Takeda fell victim to Nobunaga's plan to hold them at a distance and fusillade them with three thousand guns from behind secure fortifications. This view is advanced by the *Kōyō Gunkan,* originally compiled by the Takeda general Kōsaka Masanobu, then augmented and edited by a number of Tokugawa military specialists in the early seventeenth century. From this twenty-volume record of the accomplishments of Shingen and Katsuyori, military and legal codes of Kōshū, and presumably eye-witness account of battles (more in the tradition of war tales than history), Rohan borrowed several episodes, including the opposing opinions exchanged at the war council and the farewell toast with the well water.

Nagashino Jissenki (The true account of the battle of Nagashino), written by a member of the Tokugawa clan, provides more insight. It indicates that contrary to common belief only one Takeda general was killed at the Oda fence line; the other commanders died elsewhere during the chaotic rout, which reduced the Takeda strength from fifteen thousand to three thousand. This source also makes two additional revelations that throw new light on Katsuyori's behavior: Nobunaga had ordered Sakuma Nobumori, one of his commanders, to promise a Takeda agent that he, Sakuma, would turn his unit against Nobunaga as soon as the Takeda charge reached the fences; and Katsuyori's hope that the matchlock muskets would be rendered virtually useless by the continuous precipitation of the rainy season was foiled by the abrupt clearing of the sky around eight o'clock on the morning of the battle. Rohan makes use of both points in "The Bearded Samurai."

Katsuyori's heroic end is also known. Not surprisingly, the *Kōyō Gunkan* condemns Atobe and Chōkan as insidious sycophants responsible for Katsuyori's downfall, but it is interesting to note that *Nobunagaki* (Chronicle of Nobunaga, 1622, by Ose Hōan) more sympathetically labels them loyal vassals who stayed with Katsuyori to the end to die beside him. In any case, disloyal, or pragmatic, vassals seem to have abounded within the clan in its twilight period: Katsuyori's cousin (married to his sister) defected to Ieyasu; another brother-in-law pledged his fealty to Nobunaga; and disheartened vassals deserted en masse. In the spring of 1576 (about the time that Dairoku escaped in the story), Katsuyori led a supply convoy to reinforce the defenses of Takatenjin Castle, taken from Ieyasu three years earlier. When Ieyasu mounted an assault on this castle in 1581, however, Katsuyori was no longer in a position to dispatch a relief force to prevent its recapture. Katsuyori was compelled to evacuate his own castle in Kōshū under an Oda-Tokugawa onslaught in 1582. With his sixteen-year-old heir and about fifty relatives and hereditary vassals, he made his last stand in Tano at the foot of Mt. Temmoku, erected fences, and fought off overwhelming enemy forces. After his wife and women attendants committed suicide, the thirty-seven-year-old Katsuyori killed six enemy warriors and died an honorable death by seppuku.

The credibility gap that developed between Katsuyori and his elders may be attributable to an oedipal son's desire to best his father, but it also illustrates his failure to comprehend the enormity of his father's shoes, much less fill them. Both before and after Katsuyori's fall, Ieyasu actively recruited Takeda vassals in an effort to consolidate the Tokugawa strength. The military reputation of the Kōshū legions was not Ieyasu's sole consideration, either. Takeda Shingen had been a uniquely versatile warlord who proved himself to be an excellent civil engineer, an inventive agriculturist, and a progressive mining engineer as well. To accomplish the ambitious feat of increasing the rice yield of his mountainous domain, he harnessed swift-running rivers with water-control projects, encouraged land reclamation, and undertook forestry. And nowhere was his technical genius more evident or more remarkable than in gold mining. It was not until Shingen's days that lode gold, as opposed to placer gold, was being mined in Japan, and it was under Shingen and his samurai engineers that a lead-catalyst method (the Kōshū method) of extracting gold began to be used, predating the importation of the same idea by Western missionaries later in the century. It was thus by no means a matter of coincidence or a mere whim that Ieyasu mounted earnest campaigns to recruit Takeda vassals—they were superior technical specialists as well as stalwart warriors. In contrast to Katsuyori's distrust of his father's counselors, Ieyasu's faith in the Kōshū technology was lavishly repaid by one former Takeda retainer alone: in Ieyasu's employ he discovered and developed the Sado gold mine, which was to continue producing until after World War II.

The battle of Nagashino suggests many a possibility for the "what ifs" of history. Would the unification of Japan initiated by Nobunaga, completed by Hideyoshi, and solidified by Ieyasu have been possible if Katsuyori had not been laboring under the awesome shadow of his late father, the burly, overpowering, invincible Shingen? If his elder generals had wholeheartedly accepted Katsuyori as the legitimate heir over his brothers and as an able leader in his own right? Or if the famous Takeda gold mines had not been drying up, depriving Katsuyori of much-needed funds for purchasing a massive supply of guns and ammunition? If Katsuyori had not declined Nobunaga's invitation to join forces with him on a campaign against Uesugi Kenshin in 1577?

The very existence of firearms in Japan at that time provides for interesting speculation. A scant thirty-two years earlier, in 1543, the first two guns had been purchased from Portuguese voyagers by a lord of Tanegashima Island, southwest of Kyūshū. The manufacture and use of the Tanegashima gun rapidly spread northeastward, and many warlords, including the Takeda, organized musketeer regiments to bolster their military capabilities. Nobunaga was the first to make full use of his firepower in combat, in the battle of Anekawa in 1570. But it was the battle of Nagashino that was Japan's first test of modern warfare tactics in which firearms and plebeian musketeer regiments proved more than a match for the traditional weapons and samurai cavalry in actual combat situations.

While "The Bearded Samurai" focuses on the valorous but tragic story of the Takeda clansmen, the defenders of Nagashino Castle have also been honored by an unusual tribute. The heroic stand of the besieged garrison has been memorialized at, of all the unlikely places, the Alamo in San Antonio, Texas, by a Japanese who was born in Okazaki, Mikawa Province (present-day Aichi Prefecture). Shiga Shigetaka (1863–1927), a nationalist publisher, political theorist, geographer, and statesman, on a trip to attend the U.S. International Conference in 1914, stopped at the Alamo and donated a monument engraved with a poem, which still stands today in the courtyard of the mission. A prose poem in his *Complete Works* explains how the comparable valor of the defenders of the Alamo (1836) and Nagashino (1575)—the young commanders (William Travis, twenty-six, and Okudaira Sadamasa, twenty-one), each confronting a hostile force twenty-seven times his own, and the intrepid messengers (James Bonham,

Torii Sune'emon), who reported back at the cost of their lives —had inspired him to erect the memorial. Shiga's poem summarizes the Battle of the Alamo, extols the universality of heroism Eastern and Western, and pays particular homage to the dauntless action of Colonel Bonham, who, returning from a mission, galloped his beautiful cream-colored steed through Santa Anna's horde to report back and then died beside his commander and life-long friend Colonel Travis. Shiga compares Bonham with Torii, who was captured on his way back and crucified in full view of Nagashino Castle. Before he was speared to death, Torii managed to shout his report across that the Oda-Tokugawa reinforcements were on their way, thereby uplifting the morale of the besieged garrison immeasurably. Shiga's Chinese poem, thirty-two lines of seven characters each, is fittingly carved on a large granite from Torii's grave site in Shiga's native province.

Durable public fascination with the legend of the invincible Shingen and the unexpected, tragic fall of the House of Takeda has inspired a number of monumental historical novels by contemporary writers, and equally dramatic movies. Available to the English-speaking audience, for example, is the 1980 film *Kagemusha* (The shadow warrior) by the internationally known director Kurosawa Akira. The film focuses on a fictional protagonist who is forced to impersonate Takeda Shingen during the two critical years of secret mourning after his untimely death. *Kagemusha* achieves a bloody yet poetic climax in the annihilation scene at Nagashino. Kurosawa departs from historical records in his interpretation (e.g., Shingen dies of a gunshot wound; Katsuyori's role is reduced to near nothing; the time element is compressed), but the desperate efforts of the loyal Takeda elders are well represented. If Kurosawa exercises poetic license in his narrative and plot, his characteristically meticulous research of historical costume and settings culminates in a spectacular visual feast and an authentic reminder of a vibrant era when traditional ways confronted and blended with Western imports.